LAND HO!

We reached the position where Thompson Island was supposed to be.

The sea was empty.

As far as the eye could see, the sea was a turmoil of blowing spindrift under a blanket of cloud.

"According to my calculations, we're sailing over the solid land of Thompson Island at this moment," I said.

The irony in my voice brought him to me. "It's another filthy Wetherby trick!" he screamed. "It's a trick, I tell you! You bastard! . . . He thrust the Schmeisser against my chest. . . .

GEOFFREY JENKINS
GRUE OF ICE

A BERKLEY MEDALLION BOOK
PUBLISHED BY
BERKLEY PUBLISHING CORPORATION

Author's Foreword

Thompson Island exists. Its position, however, in the storm-lashed Antarctic waters some fourteen hundred miles south of Africa's southernmost tip, is one of the great mysteries of the sea.

Thompson Island was discovered by Captain George Norris, master of the British sealer *Sprightly*, on December 13, 1825. Sixty-eight years later an American captain, Joseph J. Fuller, sighted it again. Many famous sailors and well-equipped expeditions have searched for Thompson Island since Norris, but none has ever located it, except for Captain Fuller's chance sighting.

Captain Norris not only made a chart of Thompson Island but sketched it from half a dozen different angles.

I have examined Norris's chart and sketches as well as the Franklin Institute's interview with Fuller in his old age.

A ship's graveyard, similar to the one I have described, was found in May 1916 by Shackleton in King Haakon's Sound, South Georgia, during his epic voyage in an open boat.

Since I wrote this book, Tristan da Cunha, until last year "the loneliest inhabited island in the world," 1730 miles southeast of Cape Town, was partially destroyed by a volcanic eruption and became headline news throughout the world. The action of *A Grue of Ice* takes place before Tristan rose out of one hundred and fifty years of obscurity.

Pretoria
1962

"I mind yet the cold grue of terror
I got from it. . . ."

—JOHN BUCHAN, *Prester John*

Contents

A GRUE OF ICE

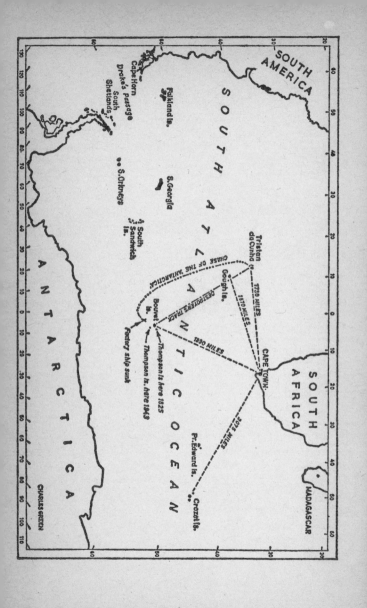

"Drake Passage!"

I shook my head. Sailhardy was wrong. The thin, sharp stiletto of wind did not even ruffle the surface of the sea, it was so slight. It was there though. Sailhardy unlashed the mainsail's crude fastening. His hands were as rough as the knotted wood of the whaleboat's ribs. The boom carrying the sail slatted untidily. Way dropped off the deep, thirty-foot craft. She settled into her own reflection, yellow to yellow, blue to blue, white to white. The islanders' garish use of paint did nothing to conceal the sweet lines of the boat.

"South Shetlands," I countered.

Sailhardy didn't seem to hear me. He crooked a knee into the starboard forward rowlock. His action was unstudied, but there was a pointer's tenseness in it. I found another lead sinker for my special net among the long oars on the gratings. I knotted it lazily to a hundred-fathom line coiled on the bottom-boards. Sailhardy's taut caution seemed out of place. Fishermen are, I suppose, fishermen the world over, and my enjoyment was as keen sending down my special nylon net to the depths of the ocean here on the fringes of the southern ice continent for tiny plankton as it would have been casting a fly six thousand miles away in Scotland.

15

Sailhardy's lean shoulders shrugged under the faded red-orange windbreaker. His was the inborn alertness which made a man survive the sea enemy, in these Antarctic waters more pitiless than anywhere else in the world. I was fishing, and it lulled me out of feeling that I was a man with a mission, let alone a scientist of the Royal Society of London.

"No, Bruce—" he began.

I grinned at him as I dropped the heavy lead sinker over the side. The use of my Christian name still came a little hard off his tongue. After all, a lower-deck man does not call his captain by his Christian name—not in the Royal Navy anyway. For two long, bitter years during the war Sailhardy had been my leading torpedoman aboard H.M.S. *Scott*. My job, as commander of His Majesty's South Shetlands Naval Force, based on Deception Island, five hundred miles south of the southernmost tip of South America, had been to guard the sea passage between the Pacific Ocean and the South Atlantic—the Drake Passage. It was the favourite route for German armed merchant raiders, U-boats, and Japanese submarines. They chose it because its fog-bound waters, continually lashed by gales, made it almost impossible to find a ship even if you were within five miles of it. I knew the Drake Passage only too well. The name sang in my mind like a gale through the fut-tock shrouds of an old clipper. It was perhaps fifteen years since I had last seen its wild waters from the bridge of my small destroyer, but its screaming hell-fiends of wind and ice still bit into my memory. Sailhardy's tenseness this quiet, sunny afternoon on the fringes of the wild ocean we had once guarded was a living memory too, of the inborn sea vigilance of a Tristan islander. Man against the sea: in these southern waters we both knew that the cards were stacked against the man.

I assumed my captain's voice. "Leading Torpedoman

Sailhardy—" I grinned at him again. His eyes were fixed on the horizon. "Relax," I said. "You look as if you were trying to see all the way to the South Pole."

"I wish I could," he said. "Then I'd know what sort of a gale is due to hit us."

I gestured towards the quiet scene. The big island lay some miles astern of the boat, and two smaller ones were visible above the horizon ahead.

"Nothing is going to hit us," I said. "Nothing at all."

Sailhardy glanced back at the big island, his home, as if to take strength from its sombre cliffs.

"The watch never goes below on Tristan da Cunha," he said with a curious intonation. "That is why we islanders have survived. There's a great storm behind this little wind."

I too turned and looked at the nearby island. A giant flock of Cape pigeons made a white socket of light against its towering throne of darkness; matching their whiteness, a crown of snow rimmed the island's seven-thousand-foot extinct volcano: Tristan da Cunha, the loneliest inhabited island in the world. It lies, its two tiny neighbours whose summits I could just see ahead, midway between Africa and South America on a line between Cape Town (1730 miles away) and Montevideo, and about two thousand miles from the nearest tip of the Antarctic ice continent. Before and immediately after Napoleon's time Tristan da Cunha was an important base for British and American sealing ships making for the hunting-grounds of the frozen South. Its first three permanent settlers, half a century before the Civil War, were, in fact, American sailors. During Napoleon's exile on St. Helena, fifteen-hundred miles to the northeast, the British stationed a garrison on Tristan, and the remains of that garrison, plus the Americans, formed the stock from which the island's present inhabitants have sprung. For nearly a century and a half the island remained cut off from the world, except for a rare visiting ship.

During the war I had brought to Tristan from Cape Town a force of Royal Navy and South African Air Force men to man a radio station. From Tristan I had taken my small task force two thousand miles to the south and had based it on Deception Island, a flooded volcanic crater on the edge of the ice continent. The two neighbours of Tristan were Nightingale and Inaccessible Islands. In every direction beyond them, for thousands of square miles, lay completely empty sea.

The Cape pigeons, in splendid white resilience, made for the haven of Tristan da Cunha. Sailhardy unhooked the triangle of foresail forward of the mast, as if to emphasize the danger he feared.

I could not take his forebodings seriously. It was all too peaceful. "I'm a scientist," I replied easily. "I've got a posh title to prove it—holder of the Royal Society's Travelling Studentship in Oceanography and Limnology. You do the sailing."

He caught my mood and grinned back. "I remember I was nearly sick with fright when you took me aboard H.M.S. *Scott* from Tristan during the war. Naval captains were God to me."

"Who ever told you to address me as professor-captain that day?"

"One of the midshipmen. He told me the captain had been a professor of science in peacetime before commanding the ship," he said, grinning at his own discomfiture. "So you had to be professor-captain."

"I wasn't a professor," I said. "I'd merely made special studies in oceanography. I was too young, anyway, to be a professor."

"You were twenty-seven then," he said. "That makes you forty-two now. Bruce—" He paused a moment and then went on. "You would have remained Captain Wetherby to me all my life—if it hadn't been for what you said that day you came back to Tristan right after the war. That's twelve years ago now. You had the world at your feet then. You'd had a brilliant wartime career, and a brilliant university career before that. I remember how you stepped off the freighter out in the roadstead. Mine was the first boat there. I didn't know you were coming. 'Captain Wetherby!' I said. I'll never forget your reply. 'No, Sailhardy. This is Bruce. Captain Wetherby went down with the raider. I've come back to the things I want—Sailhardy, Tristan, the Southern Ocean.' "

I smiled. "You forget—I said I wanted your boat too."

He gave a low laugh. "My boat," he said. "That is to ask everything from a Tristan islander. We are the poorest people in the world. A boat like this makes me one of the richest men on the island. A boat, you said: you would need a boat to try to find one of the greatest sea mysteries."

Sailhardy stowed the mainsail, and his eyes ran affectionately over the whaleboat, with its six long oars lashed to the bottom gratings. Just as the Viking longboats gave Greenland the kayak, the New Bedford whalers left the secret of their fast, seaworthy chasers to Tristan. And the islanders, born and bred to the sea, added to that knowledge, until today the Tristan whaleboat is as indigenous to the place as a Baldie to Leith or a Sixern to the Shetlands. There is almost no wood on Tristan, so the islanders make the boats of canvas. The wood for the ribs—as precious and as scarce as fine gold—comes from the stunted, wind-lashed apple trees that huddle close to walls alongside the stone houses, which are sunk half underground, like Hebridean crofters' cottages to escape the gales. I noticed that the forward portside strake of Sailhardy's boat was splintered; it would remain so, just because there was no timber to spare for repairs. The boats are daubed—one can hardly call it painted—in bright, garish colours of yellow, blue, and white. It is for a purely functional purpose, to waterproof the canvas, and the islanders

splash on whatever paint they can find, or beg from the occasional ship. The boats are the finest seagoing craft in the
world. I would go anywhere with a crew of ten Tristan
boatmen and a Tristan whaleboat. The boatmen have been
schooled the hard way by the great seas, and they have
learned to bring the whaleboats in to Tristan's rough
shingle beaches and seawashed cliffs in a way that, even to
my sailor's eye, is uncanny.

A hunk of kelp, as thick as a man's body and perhaps
twenty feet long, drifted past. We were about five miles
from Tristan, where the island is ringed by a huge barrier
of kelp. Inside that barrier the sea is tamed by the fronded
fetters to a grey sullenness. Sea mystery! At that moment I
wished that the drifting length of kelp was the pointer to
the mystery I had come thousands of miles to try to solve,
rather than the minute plankton my special net was seeking
hundreds of feet below the surface.

Sailhardy seemed to read my thoughts. "Any luck?" he
asked.

I shook my head.

The Albatross' Foot! It had a selling title, one of the
learned gentlemen of the Royal Society had said, and he
was right. That strange, almost mesmeric name was woven
into the fabric of my war years, with Sailhardy, with
Tristan da Cunha. Little had I thought, the day Sailhardy
had come aboard my destroyer in the Tristan anchorage,
that the Albatross' Foot was to become the star I would
follow actively down-horizon for many years.

Science had never heard of the Albatross' Foot! Nor had
I, despite my advanced researches into oceanography
before the war. It was, Sailhardy had told me, a fact of life
to the Tristan islanders, thought not a predicatable and understood fact, like the turn of the seasons. It was, they
maintained, a gigantic warm current that swept down at
long and irregular intervals between Africa and South
America, bearing countless billions of the microscopic sea

creatures called plankton, which are the food of everything in the Southern Ocean, from the smallest fish to the whale. The islanders called it the Albatross' Foot, so Sailhardy had said, because it resembled, in macrocosm, the warm double vein in an albatross' foot with which the great bird hatches its eggs. The only warm thing in an albatross' nest in sub-zero temperatures is that life-giving warm vein.

"Drake Passage," repeated Sailhardy. "There's a gale coming, and it's from the Drake Passage. I smell it. It's not coming from the South Shetlands at all." His voice, with its strange, fascinating accent, had a curious clarity of modulation, as if he had learned the trick of talking against a storm without having to raise his voice. The flat calm was broken only by an occasional cat's-paw of wind.

Tristan's long isolation from the world has left the islanders a curious heritage of speech: even today it is a strange mixture of English West Country speech shot through with the twang of long-dead New England whalermen, drawn out and enduring as the West Wind Drift.

"Does it matter?" I asked.

He looked at me sternly. "Bruce," he said, "you've been away from the Southern Ocean too long. You've forgotten. You came back to Tristan that once after the war—you stayed a whole year until the next ship—but for the rest of the time you've been in Cape Town and London."

I laughed. "A man must live, Sailhardy, even an oceanographer. I came back to Tristan after the war and spent every penny of my wartime gratuity trying to find the Abatross' Foot. You know. How many days of that year did we spend at sea together, you and I, in this very boat?"

He came over to the stern and unshipped the high, clumsy tiller, as if to reiterate his warning of an impending storm.

"I want proof," I said. "I want plankton. I want eighty-eight million plankton."

He pulled the battered, Navy-style cap back from the

red-brown Balaclava cap beneath and looked speculatively at me. "Eighty-eight million?"

I grinned at him. "My special net will hold exactly one quart of seawater, and in that one quart of seawater, there must be a concentration of eighty-eight million of the little so-and-so's in order to prove the Albatross' Foot. When—and if—we ever do find them, you shall see what a little beauty a plankton really is. Under the microscope it's octagonal, with a magnificent six-starred centre. The middle is round, and is all fluted and grained like machined silver wire."

"You'd better hurry and get that net up," he said. He reached out and took the hard collar of my buttoned-up anorak jacket and rubbed it against the cloth by my throat. "Listen!" he said. "Listen. If the cloth were dry, you'd hear it squeak. That would mean your storm is from the South Shetlands. But it doesn't. It's wet. It means it's from the Drake Passage."

I could see in his face that he was willing the storm. He looked to his right, to the southwest first, and then to his left, to the southeast. Then he swung round and gazed at Tristan itself, dominated by the old snow-capped volcano and slightly masked by cloud, like a miniature version of the famous Table Mountain "tablecloth" at Cape Town.

"Masthead," he said, so softly that I had to strain to hear his words, "Tristan da Cunha, the masthead of the world!"

I ran my eyes over the lean figure. He was, I knew, my own age, but wind, sea, and ice had weathered his face to an age anywhere between forty and sixty.

"And a masthead must have a lookout," I joked. "That is why I took you with me during the war. What did I know of the Southern Ocean then? I wanted a man with all the sea lore of this ocean at his fingertips. I was as scared as hell of losing my ships before I even got a sight of a raider. I found my man—Sailhardy."

"I nearly let you down the very first time we entered Deception harbour," he said quietly. "Do you remember Neptune's Bellows?"

"I still get the heebie-jeebies when I think of it." I grinned. "Thank God I brought you up on the bridge."

"Neptune's Bellows is just about right, the way the wind rips through the gap," said Sailhardy.

"It caught old H.M.S. *Scott*'s bows," I filled in. "Dear Heaven! The way her bows whipped in towards those rocks!"

I could still see the way Sailhardy had taken hold of the situation as the flagship teetered on the edge of destruction in the narrow gap that leads into the deeper anchorage —the flooded volcanic crater—beyond.

"It was that afternoon," I said slowly, "that you told me about the Albatross' Foot": an afternoon very early in the war, and I was remembering the strange and eager feeling of those first months of duty, when Sailhardy so quickly became the invaluable helper and friend.

Deception harbour had been full of bergy bits of ice. They had come in crabwise through Neptune's Bellows and started to freeze together in the inner anchorage. It seemed quite clear to me what would happen: my small force would be frozen solid in the harbour and remain bottled up there for the next six months, unable to move, while the U-boats and raiders sneaked past in the Drake Passage. Destroyers and frigates were not sturdy ships like whale catchers; the ice would damage them severely, and there were no installations or dockyards to repair them. I had climbed the cliff by the entrance and had been appalled at the gigantic phalanx of solid ice moving through the strait between Deception and the mainland. Some of it was turning aside from the main body into Deception harbour. If enough did, it would mean death to my whole task force.

Sailhardy had stood with me gazing at the fantastic sight. "The Albatross' Foot!" he had exclaimed softly. "The

warm current was sweeping past Tristan as we left the
other day. It will be here in a day or two. It will cut that ice
up like a hot knife through butter."

It did. I watched in amazement while Sailhardy's strange
story of the warm, life-bringing current came true. The
great moving battalions of ice, and even the landfast ice on
the mainland, wilted before the attack of the Albatross'
Foot. In a world where everything was frozen, the Albatross' Foot was the only warm thing. I blessed the day I
had brought the islander with me. My squadron was saved.
During the next two years Sailhardy told me many things
about the strange current of Tristan da Cunha—completely
fascinating to an oceanographer like myself. But it was
war, and we had work—grim work—to do and there was
no time or opportunity to carry out even preliminary
studies. But from then on Sailhardy had enjoyed a privi-
leged position on the bridge of H.M.S. *Scott.*

"I don't think Jimmy the One ever got used to my being
on the bridge," said Sailhardy, smiling, as if reading my
thoughts.

"Regular Royal Navy," I said. "The form, old
boy—everything according to tradition. Even the admiral
at the Cape never got used to the idea that I a mere volunteer sailor, had been given a strategic command. I was in
the same category as you—not a hundred per cent—a
weekend sailor, an upstart. An islander and a Cambridge
scientist—it was just too much for some of the old school
of regulars to stomach."

"Yes," exclaimed Sailhardy hotly, "their goddamned
prejudice! Jimmy the One asked me once, what does *your*
captain—you were always *my* captain—know of running a
ship the regular way?"

I hadn't heard this one. "And what did you say?" I
asked.

"I said," replied Sailhardy vehemently, "the Wetherbys
have explored and been in these waters for a century or
more. He's a Wetherby and a sailor first, and a scientist at

Cambridge second. The Wetherbys' goddamned ships were the first to discover the Antarctic mainland, and a Wetherby ship anchored in Deception harbour itself while Napoleon was alive."

"What did Jimmy the One say to that?"

Sailhardy gave his low laugh. "He said, 'If you ever use the expression "Goddamned" on my bridge again I'll put you on a charge.' "

Sailhardy was sitting on the rough thwart. He seemed to have forgotten his fears about a storm. The whaleboat rolled easily in the slight swell.

"At least the admiral made a hell of a fuss about your being purely a Volunteer Reserve man when he dished out the D.S.O. after you sank the German raider."

Sailhardy's words dissolved my holiday feeling. Maybe it was the memory of the *Meteor*'s deadly 5.9-inch salvoes bracketing my small ship as I went in with torpedoes. My guns were useless against the raider's. They had neither the range nor the calibre to match hers.

"Sailhardy," I said incisively. "As you know, I've been back on Tristan for only a couple of days. We've scarcely seen each other until now, what with my having to make social calls to almost every home on the island and the weather station men into the bargain." I looked hard at him. "I believe there is another Albatross' Foot."

"You believe what?" he asked incredulously.

"Listen," I said. "During the war you and I went over every shred of evidence, every accompanying phenomenon, from whales to weather, about the Albatross' Foot—the Tristan one."

"What do you mean—the Tristan one?" he asked. "The Albatross' Foot belongs to Tristan. It *is* Tristan."

"We sank the German raider near Bouvet Island," I replied. "From Tristan that is about two thousand miles."

Bouvet! If ever Sailhardy's wartime words to my first lieutenant about the Wetherbys held true, it was in regard to Bouvet Island. Thirteen hundred and twenty miles south of Cape Town towards the South Pole, and slightly to the east of the Greenwich meridian, lies an island. It is about five miles long and slightly over four across. It is the only point of land between Cape Town and the ice continent; and as Tristan is the loneliest inhabited island in the world, Bouvet is the loneliest uninhabited island. Men have succeeded in landing fewer than half a dozen times on Bouvet. It lies deeper in the heart of the Roaring Forties than ordinary ships ever go; even the daring clipper captains of the past had seldom ventured into such high, gale-lashed, ice-strewn latitudes. A Wetherby ship had been there before Napoleon died on St. Helena. I had seen Bouvet once, from the deck of a fighting ship in action; the waters of Bouvet had brought me glory in sinking the *Meteor*, one of the war's deadliest armed raiders.

"Bouvet," I said slowly to Sailhardy. "We'd cleared H.M.S. *Scott* for action. I was on the bridge of course. You couldn't see what I could. The *Meteor* was getting our range—quick. She was good, that raider. Kohler's gunnery officer was in a class by himself. From the bridge we officer was in a class by himself. From the bridge we could just see Bouvet in sight behind the raider. Every eye was on her. I took one last look round before opening fire. We'd dodged round a big icefield to the south. We all heard the *Meteor*'s guns open up. But it wasn't guns, Sailhardy."

Sailhardy stared. "What are you saying, Bruce?"

"It was the thunder of ice breaking up," I replied, "not guns. Everyone aboard H.M.S. *Scott* was so intent on the raider that they did not notice the time lag of the sound. I did, and knew it could not have been the *Meteor*'s guns. I also saw."

"You saw *what*, Bruce?"

"I saw a great spurt of fragments as the ice started to break up," I said. "Like the day it broke up in Deception harbour—the day you told me about the Albatross' Foot."

"Then why—"

I shrugged. "Who would believe a story like that? Strain of going into action, they'd say. Putting my hobby-horse to the front. I couldn't prove it, any more than I can prove the presence of the Albatross' Foot round Tristan. I couldn't even suggest it scientifically—that is, not until a year ago."

"What do you mean?"

"You know my story," I said briefly. "When the war was done I brought H.M.S. *Scott* back to Tristan to take home the radio-station men. I was demobbed. I did everything to get back to Tristan. The first freighter back was two years later—1948. I was aboard. *You* know. I spent that year with you searching for the Albatross' Foot. I spent every penny I had. You know the result—nil. I went back to the Scott Polar Research Institute at Cambridge. Three years ago they sent me to South Africa to act as liaison officer to the expeditions going south. A shore job, but at least there was no land between me and the Antarctic."

"Except Bouvet," said Sailhardy, grinning.

"Except Bouvet," I replied. "I used to listen endlessly to the radio talk of the whalers down south, but I heard nothing of any use to me. I decided I was wasting time and went back to London."

"How did you ever get backing from the Royal Society?"

"It was difficult enough to persuade them," I said. "It took a hell of a lot of talk. This scholarship runs for one year, and it's not worth much—only a thousand pounds. I've already lost two and a half months getting to Tristan. I was just plain lucky that the South Africans were sending out a relief ship to the radio station on Tristan."

"But Bouvet," Sailhardy demanded.

I shrugged. "But Bouvet!" I echoed. "They wouldn't hear of it. No ships go there. It would have meant a special charter, a special expedition. Neither the Royal Society nor I could raise tens of thousands of pounds for anything on that scale. No, Sailhardy, even if I prove the Tristan prong of the Albatross' Foot, I can't ever hope to prove the Bouvet one."

"You could try to collect reports from the catchers far south," he said rather helplessly. "But you've already tried that."

"You can imagine the reaction of tough catcher captains, can't you?" I said. "It isn't practical. My theory is simple: two great warm currents strike down towards Bouvet, one from the Atlantic side and the other from the Indian Ocean side of Africa and link up in the neighbourhood of Bouvet. The Atlantic one is ours here at Tristan. That's the theory, anyway. The combined warm currents then break open the pack ice that forms in winter between Bouvet and the Antarctic mainland. It not only breaks it up—it clears the sea for four hundred and fifty miles. It is, in fact, the whole mechanism that holds the Antarctic ice at bay. It is as important to South America, South Africa, and Australia as the Gulf Stream is to the United States. It's the most exciting thing that happens in the world's oceans, and the most dramatic. It is completely unknown." I tugged at the line to my net. "A hell of a lot depends on this one little net. Otherwise, it is likely to remain completely unknown."

I started to haul in the deep-level net. It came up. Something kicked feebly. It must have been a fish because it came out of the sea. It had a peculiar flat head and a protruding beak. The etiolated tail looked as if it had been put through a mangle. The underlying colour was lead, but near the surface the skin was a phosphorescent, shocking pink. The eyes . . . !

My exclamation brought Sailhardy over. The fish's eyes pointed in one direction only—upwards. It was horrible. It gased as if in supplication. It was about eighteen inches long. I held it at arm's length, and I saw that the eyes were fixed to look permanently upwards.

Sailhardy stopped me from throwing it overboard. He

took it and held it affectionately. The upturned, dying eyes winced in the sun.

"This is it, Bruce," he said quietly.

The thing writhed in his grip.

"This is an abyssal fish," he went on. "It comes from the deeps. He looked up—to see his food above him. He lives only on plankton."

"Plankton!" I exclaimed. "There isn't a sign of plankton!"

He went as taut as a jib in a blow. His eyes were on something near the kelp barrier of Tristan.

"Longfin!" he said with satisfaction. "Longfin! And bluefin!"

There was nothing in sight except Tristan, which seemed hazier. Clouds were starting to lock round the old volcano.

"What is it, man?" I exclaimed.

"Tunny," he replied. "Tunny."

There was a momentary flash from the surface of the sea near the kelp barrier.

"That was the forward fin of a tunny," he said crisply. "His aft dorsal fin stays erect, but the forward one he can fold and unfold at will. He does so when he wants to make a quick turn. He shoots it upright for a moment and swings round hard on it. The tunny wouldn't be doing it unless they were feeding—and feeding hard. That means—"

"The Albatross' Foot," I said. "My God, Sailhardy!"

"Here it comes," he said excitedly. "Look, Bruce, look at the seals! They're grabbing the tunny!"

It was more dramatic than I had ever imagined it to be. As the warm current swept round the southern point of Tristan, the sea boiled with the commotion of seals fighting longfin.

Sailhardy looked wistfully at the staccato glints. "If we had some Japanese longlines we'd be able to bring them up from as deep as seventy fathoms," he siad.

"I still want eighty-eight million plankton in my net," I joked.

"You won't have to wait long," he replied. "Maybe half an hour. There's no hurry. It will go on like this for weeks."

"Weeks?"

"When I was twelve," he said, "we nearly all died of starvation on Tristan. You know how it is—without fish we couldn't live. The kelp got some sort of disease and the crawfish disappeared."

The islanders rely on the inshore crawfish and deep-water bluefish as a perennial source of food. These, with seabirds' eggs and mollymawk chicks, are their main diet. I could imagine the week-by-week cutting of their starvation rations.

"We stuck it for a year," Sailhardy went on. "Then it came—the Albatross' Foot. I was so weak I could scarcely pull an oar. We hauled in some of the biggest bluefin that day I have ever seen—some of them up to two hundred and fifty pounds."

We were standing with our backs to the west, watching the current and its creatures sweep towards us.

It hit us then. Sailhardy's guard was down. The Southern Ocean waits for that in a man. Thank God Sailhardy had untied the mainsail halyard from the boat's ribs. The force of the wind seemed to pick up the light craft and toss it bodily sideways against the unyielding sea. I started to shout a warning. Sailhardy never heard. I swung to face it—a searing, breath-robbing mask of spindrift, salt, and foam choked me. Something scaly hit me in the face. It could have been a dead bird or fish. I spat out its briny clamminess. Tristan vanished. I could not see Sailhardy. The wind reached inside my windbreaker. I fought against being lifted. I tried to fall down, but the wind held me upright, like a man falling free in space. I hooked one foot under the tiller. The boat seemed to lift with me. I was torn loose. As I went over the side a noose and bowline slid over my chest. I found myself dragged against the canvas side of the boat.

I couldn't see Sailhardy, but knew he was crouched away from the wind under the bulwarks. I grabbed the gunwale. Sailhardy's arm reached over and held me. A jerk, and the bowline was a steel band round my chest. Then I was gasping on the gratings.

In the brief time it had taken him to get me aboard, his ocean-bred survival instincts were at work. The same titanic challenge of the storm had been thrown at the men of New England when they had broken open the ice continent in their clumsy, stinking New Bedford sealers a century and a half ago. On their way they had rested at Tristan—and sired sea-chasteners like Sailhardy.

Sailhardy fought the wild object which I identified as the mainsail. I saw the sweat break out on his forehead as he held the bucking thing. He half knelt, his arm about it. The animated fabric jumped and thrust to break his iron hold. I lay and retched salt water. The splintered strake worked along the cracks. I saw what was frustrating Sailhardy and tilting our lives in the balance: one of the mainsail halyards, which ran through holes bored through the mast, had snarled up, and the islander could not get at it. I edged along the gratings and got my fingers to it. It whipped free. In a moment Sailhardy had the sail captive and lashed a bight of rope round it. The boat lay over on its port side. The sea poured in.

Sailhardy gestured to me to bale. I snatched up a homemade pottery bowl which had contained our meal— the cooked mollymawk chicks floated pathetically in the rising water. I baled frantically.

Then, as if stunned by its own disbursement of force, the gale cut off.

"We're right behind the line of Inaccessible Island, and it's making a kind of huge slipstream," said Sailhardy. The normal modulation of his speech was doubly startling in the quiet. "In a moment we'll catch it again! Get the water out of her, for the sake of all that's holy!"

Although it was still light where we were, it was dark

half a mile away. We soared sickeningly and fell into the
troughs of the swell.

Sailhardy looked grave. "We must run for Nightingale
Island," he said. "Inaccessible is right in the teeth of the
storm, and we've been blown too far to hope to regain
Tristan."

"What if we miss Nightingale?" I said. The light was
brindled by blowing spume ahead.

"If we keep afloat we could be blown for a thousand
miles before the gale eases," he replied. "There's five
gallons of water, and a few mollymawk chicks to eat." He
looked sombre. "If I miss the beach at Nightingale I'm
going to spill her over and drown us both. It's better that
way."

From my knees as I baled I looked up into the lean face.
I knew he meant it.

"Reef that foresail right down," he said tersely. "We
may be lucky and get another lull. That's the way they
come from the Drake Passage."

The rag of sail slatted in the trough of each wave and
parachuted at the crest. The slipstream ended. The gale hit
us again like a piston. How Sailhardy steered in that wild
vociferation of untrammelled force I do not know. The
boat arced towards the sky in wild genuflexions. I held on
to the mast and tried to manage the fragment of sail that
kept her upright. I knew then why sailors speak with a special note in their voices about a Tristan whaleboat. She was
superb. Even in my fear I felt some of Sailhardy's exhilaration at the storm's challenge.

Under his hands the boat wheeled up to the top of each
comber and then, in the welter at the top, Sailhardy held
her as she shied and started to break away. The descent
was terrifying.

Sailhardy threw an arm forward, pointing. There, a
sinister tower ringing death from the tocsin which clanged
round its black cliffs, was Nightingale Island. White gouts
burst from its cliffs like signal guns as the water climbed in

awe-provoking slow motion up the black granite. Behind a barrier of kelp and sea bamboo was the beach. The boat swung heavenwards. Sailhardy wrenched one arm from the tiller and threw it across his eyes. Something black hit him. The boat, out of control, started a toboggan run down the wave. Sailhardy regained control. I had been crawling to his assistance but stopped short. The bird was shiny black, with fiery, bloodshot eyes. It looked like something conjured up by a sick mind to match the contortion of nature about us. I gazed unbelievingly. There was something wrong. It had no wings.

Sailhardy was shouting and grinning. I saw that one of his teeth had been knocked out.

"Island cock!" he yelled. "Luck! It's as old as the dodo! The wind blew it clean off the island! Lucky! Lucky!"

Lucky! We would need every bit of luck, I thought grimly, looking around. The bird's oversize talons gripped the gratings. The flightless rail, the bird that can't fly and lives in burrows in the ground. It's in the same category as The New Zealand kiwi. But I had no interest in ornithological curiosities at that moment.

Sailhardy began his run in for the beach. At the base of a thousand-foot cliff I could see the off-white streak of broken shingle that passes by the name of beach in these waters. He shouted, and I shifted the rag of sail. The whaleboat slewed to port. There was more drift on her now. Sailhardy fought to keep her head up into the gale. Water poured over the side. I baled. The pitch-black bird moved his grip and glared unwinkingly at me with drunken eyes.

Sailhardy shouted something and indicated the sail. The wind blew his words away, but I knew what he meant. He intended to go about! I flicked the sail free. The whaleboat began her next sickening plunge.

Then is was quiet.

On every hand was the evidence of the gale's dissoluteness. From the low level of the boat the sea was a

terrifying sight. Suds and spume lay six inches deep on the
jerking surface of the water. Nightingale Island
soared, appeared, and disappeared as the waves obstructed
our view.

It was quiet.

I heard an aircraft engine overhead.

The engine coughed. The sound in these remote waters, was as incongruous as the presence of the hovering helicopter. Tristan is too isolated from the world to have seen many aircraft; the South African Air Force men I took to the island during the war were not fliers but radio personnel.

"Helicopter!" I exclaimed. "Where the hell it comes from, though, I wouldn't know."

Sailhardy's strong hands were on the tiller. He guided the boat through the next crest before speaking. "The main body of the storm isn't here yet," he said. "If it was, that helicopter would be blown from here to Bouvet."

The black machine, its fat belly emphasized by red paint, came closer. The colours gave it away: black and red, seen easiest against ice. She was intended to operate over ice.

"It's a whale-spotter," I said.

Sailhardy jerked his head upwards. "I'd say it was fairly calm still at five thousand feet. Won't be for long, though."

"That's a damn brave pilot," I said. "I wouldn't care to fly in this lot even if it is clearer further up."

The helicopter manoeuvred. It was evident the pilot had not yet seen our whaleboat.

"He's searching," I said, puzzled. "It can't be for
35

whales. No factory-ship skipper would fly off an aircraft in weather like this."

Sailhardy was anxious. "Any moment the storm will hit us. Then I don't give a fig for our chances or the helicopter's."

The machine's movement became decisive. It started to drop towards the whaleboat. The pilot had spotted us.

"It could not be searching for us," I pointed out. "There were no ships at Tristan when we left the anchorage this morning."

Sailhardy reached out and scratched the head of the strange bird. "Whatever that aircraft is about, this chick certainly has brought us luck." He smiled.

"We haven't been rescued yet," I said. "Look at the sea. It's one thing to have a helicopter overhead, and another to pull you up from a swell like this."

He nodded. "We're rising and falling forty feet at a time," he said. "I reckon it can't be done."

As if to refute him, the machine came down with a rush directly over our heads. Its rotors drowned speech. From a winch on its side a rope snaked down. The pilot's judgment was superb. The rope was about three feet above the boat but slightly to one side. Before I had time to grab it we nose-dived into the trough. The helicopter waited. We shot upwards with the next surge of sea. My heart was in my mouth. I thought the sea would touch the Westland. I saw the pilot behind the perspex. There was a rapid movement of the controls. The machine edged out of reach.

The pilot waited this moment. So did Sailhardy. The whaleboat rose. The line snaked again. It hit one of the thwarts with a thump. I grabbed, missed, and something rushed past me. A flutter was all I was aware of. Sailhardy burst out laughing. Up our lifeline was clambering, foot over foot, the island cock. With remarkable speed it reached the helicopter window and dived in.

The Westland was snatched away by a gust of wind. It missed us by about fifty yards on the next run.

Sailhardy watched the southwest with growing concern. "It's hopeless," he shouted as the machine roared overhead again.

He was wrong. The pilot was really good. The line clattered aboard. I snatched it, but Sailhardy knocked my hand away. The boat yawed wildly.

"What the hell—" I began.

"It'll tear you in half if you even manage to get it around you," he replied. "The jerk as it lifts will be too much. Before you can get aboard you'll be dead."

"It's our only chance," I retorted heatedly. "We can't make the beach."

The machine came right down low this time, without making any attempt to drop a line. A man with a megaphone shouted at us. "Don't you want to be rescued?"

I left it to Sailhardy. His gale-cheating modulation would be audible. "Too risky," he yelled. "Cut a man in half."

The helicopter rose steeply as if in disgust. At the top of a wave Sailhardy took a sweeping glance at the southwest. He pointed the boat's nose at Nightingale.

"It's coming up quickly," he said. "The beach is our only chance. Get that sail up—quick!"

As the whaleboat gathered way, the helicopter dropped right down over us. The window opened again. "Get that mast down!" shouted the voice. It sounded slightly foreign. "Cooperate! We're taking the whole boat for a buggy-ride."

I knocked out the wooden wedge holding the mast and thrust it under the thwart. To me anything seemed better than the break for the beach. Sailhardy shrugged. This time a second rope dropped from the rear cabin window, in addition to the one from the winch. I saw what was intended. The two ropes would have to be secured within seconds as the craft of the air and the craft of the sea came together—if their respective pilots could achieve that hair's-breadth synchronization. Sailhardy's lean brown

hands on the tiller seemed to move almost in advance of his
eyes, which searched for an easier patch, a less broken
wave top.

We rose. The helicopter hovered at an angle to our drift.
At the very top of the crest, Sailhardy's hands tugged at the
worn tiller ropes and laid the boat beam-on. She hung uncertainly, and he held her there. She did not take the next
plunge, which would have torn us from the rescuers. The
pilot's reaction was equally swift. He dropped to within fifteen feet. One rope fell aft and the other forward of the
mast. I whipped mine round the metal skid of the foresail
with a running knot. I couldn't see what Sailhardy was
about, but if he did not succeed, the whaleboat would be
upended at the next lift by the very rope I had secured, and
both of us would be emptied into the water. The bow
started to lift. Sailhardy's reaction time was incredible. In
the few brief seconds the rope had lain within his reach he
had slipped it round the odd tiller plank which projects
athwartships on all Tristan whaleboats.

The wave dropped away. There was no sickening plunge
as before. The boat was airborne.

The pilot lifted the helicopter gently. The weight of the
suspended whale boat seemed to steady it, like a bee carrying a pebble to ballast him in the wind. I felt the stern
being pulled level with the bow. The pilot was working his
winches with the same nicety of judgment he had shown in
the rescue. The boat was draw towards the red aluminum
belly. Within a couple of feet the winches stopped and a
window opened. We climbed through.

A hand steadied me through the entrance. The interior
was hung with maroon quilting, dark as the storm in the
southwest.

"Welcome aboard, Herr Kapitän," said the man.

I should have remembered the cocksureness, and the
slight sneer of the Germanic gutturals. His hair was blond
and overlong. The steadying grip too—that wasn't learned

anywhere except in bringing a man over the side—the side of a ship, not an aircraft.

"Thank you," I said. "It was a magnificent piece of rescue work."

He helped Sailhardy aboard, shrugged and nodded forward to the cockpit. "Not me to thank," he said. "Up there."

I parted the quilting and stood behind the pilot's seat. The pilot did not look round. The island cock was perched on the compass mounting, gripping it with its oversize talons.

I saw a pair of eyes in the rearview mirror above the bird's perch.

They were a woman's eyes.

Women simply don't exist in the Southern Ocean. There are, it is true, women's names in Antarctica—Marie Byrd Land, Edith Ronne Land, Sabrina Coast. The women thus commemorated had not been there, however. They were at home.

I could not credit what I saw. I stepped forward, the thanks dying on my lips in surprise. I looked down at her, the face framed by the black leather helmet and its intercom wires. The eyes were the strangest and the most beautiful I had ever seen. They were the colour of the sea, I thought. Later, I knew they were not. Like the South African flower which has no colour in itself but takes its turquoise from the refraction of white light within its own heart, so hers reflected what she was seeing—the sea and the angry storm. The pupils were, like the central spot of that same strange flower, almost green-black, by virtue of some other intriguing juxtaposition of fabric and light.

"Please take that bird off the compass," she said. "I'll be flying on instruments alone in a moment."

The modulation in Sailhardy's voice was an acquired control. I felt the same about hers. Why, I could not guess.

I gripped a metal stay with one hand and prised the bird

off the compass. She looked past me, weighing the storm.

I was at a complete loss. "This bird is terribly lucky—" I started to say.

"There is no such thing," she replied. "Judgment is everything."

"To pick us up like that—your judgment was spot-on," I said.

Her eyes looked at the sea, and through them the sea looked back at me. There was no warmth in them. "So was your boatman's," she replied.

"Sailhardy and I are most grateful—"

"Sailhardy!" she said. "What a name! You can practically smell tar in the rigging."

Sailhardy balanced himself with his sailor's grace in the small cabin. She turned to him. "You know these waters well?"

"I do, ma'am," he replied.

"What are our chances against that lot?"

The islander shrugged. "It depends—on you, ma'am."

"Carl!" she called. He came through to the cockpit. "What's it like back there in the anchorage? What does the factory ship say?"

"Starting to roll. Like a drunken fiddler's bitch."

"That's what I thought," she said. She jerked her head towards me. "Captain Wetherby. Carl Pirow, radio operator. Oh, and Sailhardy—boatman."

He staccato, offhand manner grated on me.

"We're now all known to one another—except one," I said.

"Helen Upton," she said, as if it were no more important than the piece of metal she held in her hand. "Whale-spotter." She craned forward. "What is that over there —about two hundred and seventy degrees? Inaccessible Island?"

"Yes, ma'am," replied Sailhardy.

"Thank you, Sailhardy," she said. She looked at him for

the first time. "Sailhardy what? Obviously the Royal Navy wants formal introductions."

"That's all, ma'am," he replied. "Just Sailhardy."

"You must have a surname," she said.

"Sailhardy—no more," replied the islander.

"It's enough I suppose." She shrugged.

His eyes shifted, embarrassed, away from hers to the horizon. He stiffened. "Ship!" he exclaimed. He screwed up his eyes. "A small one. Maybe a catcher."

"Your eyes are as good as your boatmanship," she said.

That's praise indeed from Helen Upton, I thought. She was as impersonal as the instruments around her.

"It must be one of them making for the rendezvous," said Pirow.

"See if you can get her on the blower, Carl," she said. "Ask where the others are."

To me the horizon was blank. "I don't see a thing." I said.

She pulled my arm and pointed. Her heavy woolen sweater did not smell bitter of sheep grease, like a man's, but there was that curious, shut-off mustiness that all garments acquire in the South. The setting sun dyed the onrushing banks of cloud. Against them, Inaccessible Island took on an even more sinister air. Its flat, black silhouette seemed to cower away from the coming onslaught. By contrast, Nightingale's cliffs were splashed with great patches of early summer pelargoniums, incongruously bright in the last light. I saw no ship. Then I caught what might have been the flash of a tunny's dorsal fin—or a catcher.

"It could be," I said dubiously.

"Come, come, Captain Wetherby," she said. "Are you as skeptical about your oceanic discoveries?"

Captain Wetherby! Herr Kapitän! Oceanic discoveries! She knew who I was and she must have an idea of what I was doing off Tristan.

"I'm an expert on waterfleas," I said. My sarcasm

bounced off her impersonal air, but left me vaguely uneasy
about how much she knew.

"Is that oceanography or limnology!" she asked.

What was a whale-spotter doing out in weather like this
searching for someone whose interest was as abstruse as
mine?

"Limnology," I replied, taken aback. "Waterfleas mean
water is getting old. You never find them in young water.
Oceanwise, too, there are water fleas. It means seas are
old."

She started to shrug it off. As her left shoulder lifted and
she moved slightly in her seat, a flicker of pain passed
across her face. Her voice was toneless. "The Southern
Ocean is the place for you then. It's old already. The
Americans say it's a hundred million years old."

Rain drummed on the perspex like a Spanish dancer's
heels. Her hands on the controls seemed to have the same
economy of motion as Sailhardy's on the tiller ropes.
"Carl," she said quickly, "get aft and lash that whaleboat
securely. You too, Captain Wetherby. Winch it right up so
it's as high as it will go." She turned to Sailhardy. "How
deep is that boat of yours? I don't want it hanging below
the undercart as I come in to land."

"Four feet and some—maybe five," he replied.

"Might make it," she said, as if it didn't really matter.
"If it comes to the worst I'll dump it."

"No, ma'am!" Sailhardy burst out. "Not my boat!"

She put on the instrument lights and ran her eyes over
the panel carefully. She flicked a sharp glance at him. She
had heard the protest in his voice. "Right, then; I'll try to
land with that damn great thing hampering me. There'll be
a heaving deck, and you've heard that the factory ship is
rolling heavily. It won't be child's play."

I hesitated before going to the winches. The whaleboat
seemed scarcely worth it, even if it was everything in the
way of riches that Sailhardy had.

"It's the captain's decision," I said to her. "If it's going to mean four people's lives, then jettison it."

The eyes seemed as uninviting as the cold sea. "*I* am the captain," she said curtly. "*My* decision has been made. I land with Sailhardy's boat lashed to the machine."

I started to reply. "Carl"—she overrode me—"get aft and lash the boat. This isn't a warship's bridge, Captain Wetherby, and I can't force you to help. It does lessen the risk, however, if you do."

"Thank you, ma'am," said Sailhardy softly. He would be her friend for life.

"Miss Upton," I said, "I have every faith in your ability after the way you rescued us—"

"Then get aft and do what I ask," she snapped. "Carl!" She turned away as if I had been so much supercargo. "When you have done, tell my father I have Wetherby—in one piece, uninjured. Ask him if I should try to find the other catchers and bring them in to the rendezvous."

"I don't know who your father is or what he wants with me," I said angrily. " 'Tell him I have Wetherby—' "

She banked sharply and cut my words short. "Ask him yourself," she said. "He sent me to find you, and find you I did. My job is done when I deliver you to him aboard the *Antarctica*."

Pirow said, as if it were remarkable not to know, "Sir Frederick Upton is the biggest whaling man in the business. You must have heard of him."

"I haven't," I replied. "And I can't imagine why he should want to send his daughter out in one hell of a storm to bring in someone who was doing nothing more than looking for plankton."

I almost missed her aside: "Waterfleas."

"Ma'am," said Sailhardy, "the storm will last for days. You must get back to your base now—as hard as you can."

She seemed disposed to listen to him. "Even if I located every catcher of the five, there's not much I could do to bring them to the anchorage," she said thoughtfully. "Tell my father, Carl, I'll be coming straight back. Ask him to have Captain Bjerko hold the factory ship as steady as he can in the anchorage."

I went aft with Pirow. The whaleboat was swinging from the two ropes and bumping against the fuselage. We drew the boat up as far as we could. It did not lie under the belly of the machine, as the winches were higher up than the level of the top of the windows, but parallel to the fuselage. I could see that the keel was now a bare six inches above the level of the landing wheels. I thought of the heaving deck of the factory ship anchored in Tristan's open road-stead and shuddered. It would need all Helen Upton's skill to land. As I saw it, she would have to come in keeping the starboard side, the side opposite the boat, lower than the port side so as not to smash the keel against the deck. At the same time she would have to hold the tail high and keep it so. I looped a length of rope round one of the rough thwarts and pulled the boat hard against the side of the machine. Pirow did the same. The boat's destiny had now become one with the helicopter—and ours.

Pirow went to the radio. I preferred to stay with him rather than go forward into the unfriendly cockpit. Whatever Sir Frederick Upton wanted, he had scarcely sent her on a social mission. I stood in the maroon-quilted cabin at a loss. Something was gnawing at my subconscious, as I listened with half an ear to Pirow talking to the catchers. What was it? "Repeat," said one of the catchers Pirow was calling. "Repeat." Again, "Repeat." His transmitting was excellent. If my mind had not been on the girl and the risk she was running, maybe I would have become aware of what my subconscious was trying to tell me. And why did the catcher keep asking him to repeat?

I parted the quilting into the cockpit. Helen Upton was talking to Sailhardy while she held the bucking machine with a light snaffle. My undefined uneasiness about Pirow's signalling prickled my curiosity about the girl also. What had made her become a whale-spotter in the first place? Even the Russian ships down south never used women

pilots. It is the hardest life, requiring a high degree of ob-
servation and skill, plus long hours of accurate searching.
She had risked her life, apparently at her father's instruc-
tion, to find Sailhardy and myself. Why? I reckoned a factory ship must cost five thousand pounds a day to run, and
to come to Tristan, far away from the whaling grounds,
meant that Sir Frederick must have burned money
—literally—in order to find me. Why? Hardheaded
whaling tycoons are not that interested in plankton.

"Keep well out as you come round the point before the
roadstead," Sailhardy was telling her. "A sudden gust
might throw us against the cliffs."

She altered course slightly and edged into the teeth of the
wind. The island cock was back on his perch, but no longer
masking the compass from her view. The van of the storm
swathed the volcanic peak of Tristan. The island's water
supply is born in the old crater, and, strangely, never
freezes even in the hardest weather. Under the machine's
belly I could see the great fields of kelp in the sea,
stretching out tentacles like a nightmare octopus in the
dying light. To the east, sea and sky melted into a glory
of turquoise; in the west, the great battalions of cloud
came racing up.

We pulled clear of the headland by Tristan's anchorage.
A waterfall made a steel scar down the cliffside.

"Starboard forty?" Helen Upton asked Sailhardy.

"Sixty," he said. "Every bit of sixty. The cliff will completely blank out the sun in a minute. Turn sixty degrees."

She smiled wryly, the first time I had seen any animation
on her face. I didn't need to be told: flying was her whole
life.

"Aye," replied Sailhardy. "Aye, ma'am."

The sun went as we wheeled round Herald Point into
Falmouth Bay, the anchorage. Helen Upton clicked on the
machine's spotlight and swung a broad circle round the
Ridge. As if in reply, floodlights splashed the factory ship's
deck. She was big—every bit of twenty-five thousand tons.

I could not imagine how we could land among the steel
wires that held up the double funnel aft and the cum-
bersome masts. The deck seemed a conglomeration of
valves and bollards, with almost no clear space. Pipes, as
thick as a man's thigh, criss-crossed the deck forward of
the bridge. Among them were huge steel boxes, sur-
mounted by matching butterfly nuts. I could not guess what
they were for.

"Carl," she said rapidly into the intercom, "tell Captain
Bjerko I can't see with all those lights—they're blinding
me. Say I'm coming in from the stern. When I'm fifty yards
away, put out the lights. I'll come in on the spot alone after
that."

Sailhardy's knuckles were tightly clenched round the
cabin stay. "Bring her into the lee of the ship, ma'am," he
urged.

She looked at him swiftly and nodded. She started a wide
circle past the bows. The *Antarctica* had steam up. The
two high stacks, port and starboard, belched smoke.
Higher even than these were two ventilators. We lost height
as we came into the vessel's lee. Then everything went
black. The stacks were putting up a smokescreen equal to a
destroyer's.

"Luff, ma'am," urged Sailhardy.

Helen Upton laughed. It sounded as if she had not done
so for a long time. "Sailor!" she exclaimed. "I can't luff an
aircraft." But her hands were already busy at the controls.
We followed the smoke downwind and then pulled clear.
She made a new approach to the factory ship. The machine
neared the stern. The slipway grating through which whales
are hauled was picked up by the bright floodlights. It
looked as ominous as Traitors' Gate at the Tower of London. I felt my breath draw in as we came in low.

The lights cut. The helicopter spotlight stabbed out. We
would never get through the rigging to the patch of clear
deck.

"Bring her head round a little, ma'am," said Sailhardy

softly. He shot a glance the way we had reached the anchorage. "There's a big gust coming."

Her hands obeyed him. The two were in complete ac-
cord. It was the master in one element responding to the
master in another, the sea and the air.

She pulled the stick back hard and whipped the throttle
wide. We scraped past one of the high ventilators, circling
again.

"Jesus!" whispered Pirow.

"Carl," called the girl in a level voice, "tell Captain
Bjerko to light the flensing platform only. I'll try there this
time."

Pirow's radio key chattered as we swept round again.
Again, too, the nerve-tearing approach from the stern. The
wind was stronger now. It must have been gusting fifty
knots or more. Traitors' Gate came up to meet us. The machine canted as Helen Upton lifted the port side, the side
with the boat lashed to it, high. The Tail too was high. I
heard Sailhardy's intake of breath. We slid crabwise round
the middle gantry like a wounded dragonfly. A peckle of
rain blurred the perspex. It was too late to pull away this
time. We were committed. The starboard wheel touched
the deck. The boat side and the tail remained high. She
gunned the rotor at the tail. It swung slowly, deliberately,
into the wind. She placed it delicately, so delicately I
scarcely felt the bump, on one of the big steel boxes. She
let the boat side of the machine cant gently to the deck,
blipping the throttle. We stood square on the rain-slicked
deck.

She sighed softly and rested her hands for a moment on
the now-dead controls. Men were already lashing the machine to the big bollards.

I licked my lips. "You have to miss only once," I said.

She sat there immobile, not speaking.

"I reckon she was rolling twenty degrees each way,"
Sailhardy said. "You were magnificent, ma'am."

The strange eyes seemed to be filled with the hard glare

of the floodlights. "Carl," she said, "take Captain Wetherby to my father. He wants him urgently. And Sailhardy."

We climbed on to the heaving deck. She made no attempt to rise as we left.

"Careful!" said Pirow. "A factory ship has more places
to break your neck than any other ship I know."

The powerful lights threw everything into taut relief.
Above my head a huge piece of curved, grooved iron
looked bigger than it really was. It had a hook with projections and was secured to the gantry by hawsers as thick as
my arm.

When we reached the bridge companionway I remembered my things in the boat. "There are some of my instruments and charts in the boat," I told Pirow. "I'll go back
for them. Tell Sir Frederick I'll be right along."

I swung myself up into the cockpit. I stopped short.
Helen Upton was clinging to the central cabin stay, half in
and half out of her seat. Her face was as white as the
floodlights. She was trying to pull herself to her feet. The
island cock stared at her.

I went forward. "Take it easy!" I said, lowering her into
the seat. "I'm not surprised. After that landing—"

Her eyes were full of pain. "Why did you have to come
back and see me?" she said, half-choking. "Why did you
have to see me?"

"That landing—" I began.

She motioned at me to be quiet. "It wasn't the landing,"
she got out, biting her lips. "It's me."

"I don't understand," I said.

She spoke so softly I could scarcely hear. "The winches.
I forgot. Usually I use one of them to haul me up after a
long spell of flying. It gets my hip, you see. There's a bullet
in it. I just limp a bit ordinarily. When the flying is tough it
gets me. Once I'm on my feet I'm all right. I always send
everyone away."

"Your father shouldn't allow you—"

"He doesn't know, and won't know, unless you tell

him," she replied. "He must not know. Never. Help me up, please."

She pulled off the flying helmet. The stark light against the storm-darkened night set off her hair, fair, short, and curly. Her forehead was dented from the pressure of the leather. I put an arm around her. She leaned heavily against me for the first steps along the deck and then walked slowly, with a slight limp, past the bridge to a large chartroom-cum-office. Behind the desk sat a man. A light was at his left shoulder, etching the features.

His face was made of metal.

Incredulity, mixed with revulsion, stopped me as I saw the grey mask. The effect was more startling when he rose and the pewter crinkled into a smile. I could see the laughter lines at the corners of his mouth and eyes. There seemed to be no division between the line of his strangely coloured forehead and his short, curly grey hair. He was short and stocky, with a sailor's eyes. The change from what I thought would be a deadpan into a warm, welcoming smile left me at a loss.

Helen kissed his cheek. "Well, Daddy, I found your man."

He took my hand and shook it cordially. "I've spent a lot of time and money on you, Bruce. I'm glad to have you safely aboard."

His immediate use of my Christian name did not offend me, as it would have done with almost anyone else.

"Your daughter did a magnificent piece of rescue work," I said. "I scarcely expected to see the inside of a warm ship's cabin tonight."

He glanced keenly at me. "From what I know, I don't think a night at sea in an open boat would hold much terror for you. Good girl, Helen. I knew you'd find him."

She did not seem to hear. The eyes, so filled with distress in the cockpit, were composed. They were even warm

51

through taking on the colour of the cabin's panelling. Her unspoken attitude was that split-second timing and consummate skill were all in the day's work. It was clear that Upton expected little less than that.

I fumbled for something to say. The mask disconcerted me.

He laughed. "It gets you down the first time, doesn't it? I never notice it any more. Mine is no beauty, but you should have seen the chap with the silver pan! My God! He shone like a balloon-sputnik!"

"I'm afraid I don't understand," I faltered. I looked to Helen for help. She was busy rubbing oil off the back of her left hand. She might as well have not been there, she was so remote from our conversation.

"Of course you don't," said Upton in his rapid-fire way. "You can have the medical term for it if you like—argyria. I got it from fooling around with rare metals in Sweden. What happens is that the metal actually passes into your system. The doctor chappie with the silver face had been using silver nitrate. He was so self-conscious. We were in the same sanatorium in Stockholm."

My eyes had accustomed themselves to the light. The cabin was as distinctive as the man. One whole wall was taken up by a map of Antarctica, and no ordinary map. It was in relief, and the land contours had been demarcated by intricately inlaid pieces of whalebone. The long spur of Graham Land, which juts out from the ice continent towards Cape Horn, was exquisitely fashioned.

Equally eye-catching were scale models of the ships that had opened up the South, mounted on the map. They had been carved by a master: replicas of clumsy eighteenth-century British men-o'-war; of tough British sealers, the originals of which had had oaken planks thick enough to withstand pack ice and round shot; of the finer-lined New Bedford whalers; of the first steamers, aided by sails; of the armoured icebreakers of today. They clustered mainly round where I had operated from during the war, for Graham Land was the first part of the continent proper to be found. Near my base at Deception was an old brig, and I could read her name—*Williams*. In her Captain William Smith had discovered the South Shetlands in 1819. It was Captain Smith who had raced to Chile to a British naval officer, Captain Shireff, who realized that the Drake Passage was the key to naval power between the Atlantic and Pacific. It had been true in Napoleon's time; it had been true in my lifetime too. I had guarded that passage for two years.

Near my old base, too, was a tiny American brig named *Hersilia*. James P. Sheffield had sailed from Connecticut to look for a dream—the legendary, fabulous islands called the Auroras. He had failed. But his young second mate, Nat Palmer, had made history by being the first man to put a foot ashore on the Antarctic mainland. A Britisher, Captain Bransfield, had the distinction—a few days only before Palmer—of being the first man to sight and chart the coast of the Antarctic mainland.

Clustered around the long peninsula, too, were other ships with strange names: *Vostok* and *Mirny*, Russian among the first ever in those waters; Captain Cook's immortal H.M.S. *Resolution*, which got nearer to the coast of West Antarctica than any ship since; *Astrolabe* and *Zelee*, French; H.M.S. *Erebus* and *Terror*, British; Shackelton's *Endurance*, a pitiful wreck crushed in the ice.

In the Weddell Sea, that great bite out of Antarctica which adjoins Graham Land, was British Captain James Weddell's little ship *Jane*. No ship has ever navigated in the Weddell Sea in the same longitude as far as Weddell did one hundred and forty years ago. Weddell had been amazed that there was no ice at all almost within sight of the ice continent. The intrepid captain had turned back in clear seas; all subsequent attempts to pierce the thousands of square miles of solid ice have failed. The map showing

Weddell's historic voyage—in clear seas which should have been ice—brought the reason home to me right then: the Albatross' Foot!

The storm made the factory ship lean at her anchors. Drake Passage! The *Golden Hind*, Sir Francis Drake's flagship, was on the map, fighting her way round Cape Horn. There was almost a physical resemblance between the man in front of me and the famous Elizabethan. I wondered if Drake had found his tiny cabin aboard the *Golden Hind* big enough for his spirit. This one wasn't, for Upton's.

"Sit down," he said. He couldn't seem to get the words out quickly enough. "There's not another map like that anywhere. Are you wet? Get him a drink, Helen. She hauled you up out of the boat?"

I could go along with Upton, I thought. I didn't know what he wanted me for, but even among the tough-charactered men the Antarctic throws up Upton stood out.

Helen went across to the drinks cabinet. "Sailhardy believes it was luck. They have a strange bird with them. It hasn't got any wings, and I'm told Nightingale Island is the only place in the world where they're found. The rescue was a matter of luck."

There was an odd self-rejection about her. I disagreed. "It wasn't luck—it was spot-on, skilled judgment. She rescued the whole boat. What is more, her landing with it lashed to the side out there on the flensing platform was masterly. Lucky for me, since all my instruments and charts are in the boat."

He looked at me keenly. "They're safe, these things of yours?"

"Yes," I replied. "Yes. They were stashed under the bow."

Helen stood with the drink in her hand, her eyes fixed on me. They were alive with distress. She was begging me not to say what happened.

"That bird is strange," she said in an even voice. "It

makes little appeal at first. It has no flight." She splashed more spirits into the glass without taking her eyes from me. "I don't expect it sings. Perhaps somewhere there is a message in its disdain and isolation."

I could not fathom her. "Ask Sailhardy," I said. "I'll go and fetch my things from the boat."

Upton shook his head. He pressed a button on his desk. A sailor came in. He spoke rapidly to the man in Norwegian. "Can't lose personal property," he said. In the same jerky way he clicked off the desk lamp and put on the general cabin lights. It was all Southern Ocean and luxury. A chunk of baleen held down the charts he had been studying; the central chandelier was made of four seal skulls skilfully matched and joined; his chair was sealskin stretched over dark timber.

Pirow came in with Sailhardy. Upton nodded perfunctorily at the islander. "When will the gunner-captain boys be here?" he asked Pirow.

Pirow grinned. "All of them in time for a drink. You can bet on that. They're about as tough a bunch as you could hope to meet in a month's sail round South Georgia."

Helen stood with the drink she was pouring me in her hand. Upton went across to the cabinet. A heavy gust of wind shook the factory ship. I felt uncomfortable. She just stood there with the drink.

"I'm glad we got in before *that* started," I said.

"I had a good pilot." She addressed herself to Sailhardy.

"Sailhardy?" asked Upton, his hand on a glass.

The islander did not seem to hear him. He was as far away as Helen. I think he half regretted not being out in the gale.

Upton repeated the invitation. Sailhardy shook his head. "I like a drink, but food is more important on Tristan. One is only tantalized by alcohol."

Upton shrugged. He took my drink from Helen. "Water in your brandy? I've just come from the Cape. Full cellar of your national drink."

"For the record, I'm not a South African," I said. "I've lived there for the past three years. I was born within sight of the English Channel. Last of a long line of Wetherbys—sailors, explorers, hopeless businessmen."

Helen pointed to a group of islands on the map near Graham Land and to a model ship. "The Wetherbys did more than any private firm in the history of the exploration of the Southern Continent. I would like to know what drove them to it." She jabbed a finger at the model. "The *Sprightly*!" She lingered over the name. "The first Wetherby's favourite ship."

It slipped out—harmlessly, I thought then. "There was another, and their names are always linked," I said. "The *Lively* and the *Sprightly*."

"Yes," she said, "the *Lively* and the *Sprightly*! You could find them at any place between the Drake Passage and—"

"Bouvet," I said.

Upton gave me a keen glance as he handed me the glass of fine brandy. He slapped together a double dry martini for Helen. Then he took a beautifully blown bottle from the cabinet. In everything he did Upton was the supreme showman. He shook out of a bottle a couple of pretzel-like sticks. Into a tiny coffee spoon he carefully scraped a stick until it was full, put the softish scrapings into a glass, and added ice water. He took a metal tankard and put it next to the glass, pouring in a stiff slug of brandy. He set it alight, blew out the spurt of blue flame, raised the decanter and sipped quickly first from the ice water, and then from the hot brandy.

"I've been around," I said, "but I've never seen a drink like that before."

Upton laughed. "I must do this at some place in the Antarctic where they'll find a name for it. The ingredients are scarcely usual—"

"Erebus and Terror," I interjected. "You know, the two

volcanic peaks in the Ross Sea—belching fire and smoke from the ice."

He roared with laughter. "God, Bruce, what a name for guarana and buccaneers' brandy! Erebus and Terror it shall be!"

Pirow sipped his schnapps reflectively. Sailhardy's thoughts were still outside in the storm.

It was the calm, self-possessed way Helen said it which made me wonder if she were not something more than a cog in the whirring personal machine which was Upton, overshadowed by him, integrated, whether she liked it or not, in his pursuits. "I don't think Daddy ever got over playing pirates," she said. "Flaming brandy—buccaneers' brandy they called it on the Spanish Main. Morgan drank it."

Daughter filling in the gaps, I thought. That wasn't the whole answer though. No daughter tortures herself with a bullet in her hip, nor develops such flying skill, just because Daddy says so. Yet her knowledge of the Southern Ocean matched his map: you don't pick up knowledge like hers about the Wetherbys in the local library.

"Is guarana also something from the Spanish Main?" I could not keep the irony out of my voice.

"Not quite, but near enough," he replied. He held up what looked like a strip of dried meat—biltong, as they call it in South Africa. "In Bolivia the guarana drink is called white water—this is dried dough made from a creeper that grows near the Amazon. It's about three times as strong as the strongest coffee. Wonderful stimulant. No hangover. Leaves the mind clear. None of the deadening effects of alcohol. Everything is brighter, better, bigger."

Brighter, better, bigger: that could sum up the man, I thought.

"Walter will want to bring the catchers in," said Pirow.

Who was Walter, anyway? I wondered. It was all very well to give this extroverted display for my benefit, but

what did Upton want with me? Where did catcher skippers
fit into the picture? Tristan was far from the whale hunting
grounds. I suddenly mistrusted the whole set-up.

Sailhardy turned from the gale porthole. He was
bristling with suspicion. "I've never known catchers to
meet at Tristan," he said.

Upton was on the defensive. "I'll rendezvous anywhere
in the Southern Ocean I damn well like!"

"The toughest skippers in South Georgia would come all
this way for peanuts," Sailhardy retorted.

"Pirow," said Upton sharply, "go and signal Walter. I
want a definite time of arrival. Quick, now."

The man's nervous tension permeated the room. What
was it all about? Why the urgency in a wind wild enough to
blow away an anemometer?

"Plankton," he said briefly. "Tell me about plankton,
Bruce."

He's been studying up on me, I thought. I didn't like it
and wasn't going to be steamrollered. "All creatures that in
the Southern Ocean do dwell, sing to Bruce Wetherby with
a cheerful voice," I came back.

Upton's face did not flush—it couldn't—but there was a
pinkish tinge to the pewter skin which made it look formidable. The eyes were unnaturally bright. Before he could
reply, however, the Norwegian sailor he had sent to the
boat for my charts and instruments came in and dumped
the oldskin bag containing them on the desk.

The interruption gave him time to control himself, and
he held his voice steady. "Plankton are like people in a
crowd. They mill around like hell—within strict limits. Yet
the general direction remains the same. Plankton might
sing to you, but might they also not point to something?"

The inference was excellent. I was to know later that
guarana widens the associations. It was unlikely that he
had had the time to hear from the islanders about the Albatross' Foot. And the Royal Society would certainly not
have told him.

"Look," I said, "the Royal Society gave me a scholarship to investigate what I think is an unknown, major ocean current with certain odd characteristics." I told him about the Albatross' Foot. "It has no significance either commercially or militarily."

Upton was as tense as a boxer coming out of his corner. "The Albatross' Foot! What a name! Did you find it?"

"Yes," said Sailhardy. "Captain Wetherby found it all right."

"Just the beginnings—I should qualify that," I said. "I was starting to get the proof I wanted when the storm came. Nevertheless I feel certain I found one prong."

"One prong?" he echoed. "What do you mean, one prong?"

I told him my theory of the two prongs of warm current joining near Bouvet. Helen took no part in the conversation. She was fiddling with something on the map.

He slapped his right fist into his left palm. "Plankton! Current! Put these facts together and, my God! see what they add up to!"

Sailhardy went back to his porthole. This sort of talk was beyond him. I wasn't sure whether it was not beyond me too.

"It has no significance," I began.

"Like to have a look at that other prong of the Albatross' Foot?" He was tripping over his words, he was so excited. "You can! Free ride in this ship! It's on the house. I'll take you to Bouvet!" He did not wait for me to reply. "Krill! My God! Krill!"

"Krill?" I wilted under his bulldozing speech. "That's whale's food."

"The staple diet of whales—krill!" he went on. "You tell me: a current appears. Plankton appear—billions upon billions of them. Food for the little shrimp-like things we call krill. Food for every living thing in the Southern Ocean."

"I've seen krill by the million fall out of a whale's guts

like China tea leaves when he was cut open," I managed to get in. "What this has to do with the Albatross' Foot, except in a general way, I wouldn't know."

"Krill live on them, don't they?" he raced on. "Things breed. Young must have food. The life-giving currents meet near Bouvet . . ."

Bouvet was at the heart of the Wetherby story. Discovered by a Frenchman, it was lost sight of, its position uncertain in the wild seas, for nearly a century. An American sealing captain, Benjamin Morrell, made the first of the half-dozen known landings on its wild shores. Then, in 1825, John Wetherby sent Captain Norris to locate Bouvet. What Norris found near Bouvet had become one of the sea's great mysteries. Sometimes, they said, old John Wetherby could be seen pacing the Thames by the Roaring Forties Wharf in a storm, calling Captain Norris to come back from the sea-dead to tell the world what he had seen near Bouvet.

Helen was watching me thoughtfully. "You look as if you had seen a ghost."

"Men have ghosts, and so have islands," I replied. "So have the Wetherbys."

I, the last of the Wetherbys, had been drawn inexorably to the waters of Bouvet. Off the island I had sunk the notorious German raider *Meteor*.

I liked Upton, but everything was moving too fast for me. "I don't follow what you are saying about krill and whales, Sir Frederick." I said. "Your offer about Bouvet is all I could wish for. Why did you come looking for me at Tristan? Why *me?* You haven't come all this way just for the pleasure of indulging my oceanic whims. Time means money to you. What do you want from me?"

"Even modern business pirates have their quixotic moments," he said, grinning.

"That's no answer, and you know it," I replied.

"I quote the Admiralty and the Royal Society," he went on. "Captain Wetherby is one of the most brilliant and experienced sailors the Antarctic has seen since Lars Christensen broke open the ice continent thirty years ago." He added crisply, "I want your knowledge of the Southern Ocean. I want your knowledge of its currents. I want your sailor's skill. I want Sailhardy's know-how."

"If you want seamanship you can buy it a-plenty among the whalers in South Georgia," I replied. "You've refuted that argument yourself. You've got whaling skippers on their way here now."

"Shut that door, Helen," he said. "Turn the key." His movements were jerkier still. "What do you know about the blue whale?"

"It's the most profitable kind to hunt. I suppose a single one must weigh a hundred and fifty tons and be every bit of a hundred feet long."

He said rapidly, "The blue whale has been killed off by the hundred thousand. You'd have expected that the most elementary fact about it would have been known by now: where does it breed? The Norwegians, first under Lars Christensen, have been searching for that for half a century. It's never been found."

"What has this to do with me?" I asked. "I'm not interested in whales, blue or otherwise."

He went on as if he had not heard me. "To any whaling concern the knowledge of the whereabouts of the breeding ground of the blue whale would be the biggest breakthrough since the harpoon gun." He faced me. "You told me—tonight."

I stared at him. "I have not even mentioned the blue whale, let alone its breeding ground."

His words tumbled over each other like a pressure ridge of ice building up. "South of Bouvet, where the two prongs of the Albatross' Foot join—that is where it is. You've put a million pounds in my pocket!"

"I still don't understand," I said rather helplessly.

"The Albatross' Foot!" He turned the name over. "Don't you see?—plankton means krill, and krill means food, food for whales. Vast concentrations of krill, scores of square miles of them—food for young whales, blue-whales!"

"You must know that you're oversimplifying, Sir Frederick," I said. "A season's catch of blue whales is limited by the International Whaling Association to about eighteen thousand. You couldn't hunt undersized whales even if you knew their breeding ground."

Upton strode angrily across toward the map, but turned on his heel and tore open a drawer before he got there. He threw a pile of papers on the desk. "Somewhere there," he said thickly, "is a copy of the Laws of Oleron." The wicked pink tinge across the pewter skin was the most ominous danger sign I have ever seen in a man.

"I have never heard of the Laws of Oleron," I said. Sailhardy looked confused.

"I don't give a damn that you haven't," he went on. "I quote: 'Through the inspiration of these ancient laws and the common brotherhood of mariners throughout the world, men are able safely to pass on their lawful occasions.' That was said eight centuries ago. Nowhere have more men died, or come to a violent end, than on the sea. Brotherhood—bah!"

"I simply do not know what you are talking about," I said.

A flicker of a smile passed across Helen's face, but her contolled voice showed nothing of it. "What my father has got there, Captain Wetherby, is a copy of the new Antarctic Treaty. He's trying to tell you he doesn't like it."

"There is only one unexplored continent left," he said. "That is Antarctica. It was discovered by individualists. It is as big as the United States and Europe together. It is the one continent left for man's free spirit to break open. What happens?" He banged the papers again. "Government committees sit ten thousand miles away and decide its future."

"It is not as bad as that," I interjected.

"Listen!" he said. "Antarctica has a population of about four hundred men—all of them governmental committee stooges with not a drop of red blood among them. They live in preheated, pre-fabricated, pre-lined huts and take the predetermined, sissy readings they're so bloody proud of!"

"What has this to do with the breeding ground of the blue whale?" I asked.

He brushed my question aside. "Because they haven't got the guts of ice algae, twelve of these ntaions have got together and signed this shameful thing called the Antarctic Treaty, banning all activity but scientific investigation for peaceful purposes and—God's death!—the possibility of opening up a tourist trade to the South Pole!" He tossed off his guarana drink at a gulp. "It's the negation of the human spirit, Bruce! Every one of those four hundred men scattered about Antarctica is part of a committee, a weather organization, or—listen! This is how they spend their time." He read out from random papers which he snatched up: " 'Directional sensitivity of neutron monitors'; 'short-term decreases in cosmic ray east-west asymmetry at high southern latitude'; 'glacio-geomorphological features—' " He threw them down in disgust on the floor.

I picked them up. They were some kind of report on a scientific meeting about the Antarctic, held in Buenos Aires.

Upton pulled himself together. He picked up a long ruler and went across to the map. Suddenly he grinned. I could not help warming to the man. "It's a funny thing to be in love with a continent. Anything one loves must be different. That's the way it is with me. Some bright lad in the U.S. Navy has worked out a formula to predict the number of icebergs you will find in the North Atlantic in the summer. There aren't any formulas in the Antarctic. You can put a halter and bridle on the Arctic, but not, thank God, on the Antarctic!"

I too went across to the map. I picked out Bouvet. The

cut of the jib of the two models given pride of place in the island's discovery were unmistakable to my sailor's eyes— the *Lively* and the *Sprightly*.

"You may well look," Upton said bitterly. "In this treaty the Norwegians have inserted a clause laying down a ban of two hundred miles on hunting whales round Bouvet." He snatched up a pair of dividers, placed one point on Bouvet, and sketched a circle. "See? The ice mainland opposite Bouvet is also Norwegian. It's about four hundred and fifty miles from the island. So, with a territorial limit of two hundred stretching towards Bouvet from the mainland, and also stretching from Bouvet towards the ice, it means that there's only fifty miles in which you can legally hunt a whale. Put simply, Norway has closed one-quarter of the entire ocean between Antarctica and South Africa to whaling. Why? Lars Christensen surmised, and I know now, that somewhere in that wild waste of waters is the breeding ground of the blue whale."

"Is a territorial limit of two hundred miles usual for this sort of thing?" I asked.

"There was damn near a war when Iceland imposed a mere twelve-mile territorial limit ban on ordinary fishing," he answered.

Upton made the whole thing sound plausible. He was going after the blue whale because I had pointed the way to the goal whalermen had dreamed of for centuries. And I wanted to go after that other prong of the Albatross' Foot.

I said slowly, "If the Albatross' Foot is within twelve miles of Bouvet, I want nothing to do with your operation. If it is outside the twelve-mile limit, which I consider fair for any territorial waters claim, then we'll pool ideas. Fair enough?"

He shook my hand. "That's the spirit of the *Sprightly*!" he exclaimed.

Helen turned to Sailhardy. "Are you coming, sailor?"

He did not look at her. "I shall go with Captain Wetherby."

The eyes became luminous for a moment. "That is a very neat distinction."

There was a knock at the door, and she unlocked it to Pirow.

"Walter signals he's just coming round the point into the anchorage," he said. "He'll be alongside any minute in the *Aurora*."

4 The Man with the Immaculate Hand

"It is a wild night outside this anchorage," said the big man in the streaming oilskins. Upton did not seem to mind when he shook the water from his sou'wester on to the cabin's fine carpet. "The waves come forty feet high tonight."

"That's nothing new to you, Walter," Upton replied jocularly. "Or to Captain Wetherby here." He introduced us. "Gunner-Captain Walter is the finest harpooner in the Southern Ocean."

I disliked Walter at sight. He looked the sort of sailor for a night like this: his great hand as he gripped mine was scaled over from the kick of the harpoon gun and matched his massive frame. He stank of whale and schnapps, with an overlay of weatherproofing. He was half-shaven—I was never to see him otherwise.

"So you find your man, eh, Sir Frederick?" he said.

There was a suggestiveness about the way he said it that left a sense of unease in my mind. Upton had told me about the blue whale; Walter was obviously the type to carry out such a project; yet what had been imponderables to them before they found me seemed now to fit neatly—too neatly—into the pattern.

"Where are the others?" asked Upton.

"I kept them close to the *Aurora* all the way from South Georgia," Walter replied. "In fact, within W/T range. You

know what these catcher skippers are like—they spot a
whale and go chasing after it, and before you know where
you are, you are chasing them. No, they'll all be in within
half an hour."

"Good," said Upton. "I want to brief them as soon as
they come in."

"Where is Pirow?" asked Walter.

Was I imagining it, or was there some innuendo in the
way the tough skipper said it? The question and the answer
were harmless enough in themselves.

"Where do you think?" said Upton. "As always, in the
radio room."

"That Pirow," said Walter thoughtfully. "He should
have married a radio set." He thrust his big jaw towards
Sailhardy. "Who is this, heh?"

"Sailhardy," I said. "A Tristan islander."

"Ah, hell," said the big Norwegian. "Tristan islander!
Shipwrecks and black women."

Sailhardy came across the cabin towards Walter. The
only outward sign of his anger was a curious flicking of the
little finger of his left hand into the palm of his hand. I
knew Sailhardy's strength.

Upton intervened. "Walter doesn't mean it for you—"

"Sonofabitch," said Sailhardy.

"Come, boys," went on Upton. "You both need a
drink."

"I told you, not for me," said Sailhardy, glowering.

"A Cape Horner for me"—Walter grinned—"a full
Cape Horner!"

Upton splashed half a glass of schnapps and tipped a
pint of stout into it.

Two more men in oilskins pushed open the cabin door.

"Reider Bull, catcher *Crozet*," said one.

"Klarius Hanssen, catcher *Kerguelen*," said the other.

Their economy of words as they identified themselves
and their ships was typical: to them, the ship and the skipper were synonymous. They eyed the luxurious cabin en-

voiusly. I knew what their own quarters were like: a metal box containing a hard bunk, continuously soaked through leaking bulkheads. It was better to be on the bridge.

They were naming their drinks when another arrived. "Lars Brunvoll, catcher *Chimay*," he introduced himself.

"I laughed when Walter told me the name of your ship," said Upton. "*Chimay*—iceberg! Don't you see enough ice, Brunvoll?" The skipper was at his ease immediately. "We're still missing one though."

"Mikklesen," said Walter. "Where is he, Brunvoll?"

"He was tying up as I came over," he replied.

The door opened and Mikklesen came in. He did not look, like the others, as if he had been lashed together with steel wire. He was of medium height with a thin, pinched nose and the clearest of blue eyes.

"I am Mikklesen of the *Falkland*," he said. "You are Sir Frederick Upton?"

He was the odd man out, just as the islands after which his catcher was named belong more to South America than to Antarctica.

At a sign from her father Helen left. The skippers sat uneasily on the fine furnishings. Their concession to the social gathering was to open their oilskins without taking them off. They were as tough as a narwhal's tusk. Upton did his trick with the flaming brandy and raised the metal tankard with its blue flame to them. "Skoal! To the finest whalermen in the Southern Ocean!"

Only Walter responded. The others stared self-consciously into their drinks.

During the next few minutes I admired Upton's handling of the skippers. They were out of their element. Upton wanted them for something. They knew it, and he knew that they knew. To have put a foot wrong would have sent them all on their way.

Upton blew out the flame and gulped down the hot spirit. They looked surprised. He grinned at them as he threw in another dollop of brandy. "Surely I don't have to show whalermen how to drink spirits?" he asked.

Obediently they upended their glasses.

He raised his tankard. "To the *blaahval*."

Here it comes, I thought with that toast to the blue whale.

"*Blaahval!*" echoed the Norwegians.

"Captains," Upton began, "Peter Walter has asked you to come and join me here at Tristan to talk business."

They eyed him silently. I could see they were not impressed—you don't get men to voyage two thousand miles in partal radio silence just to talk business, not ordinary business.

Mikklesen broke in. "Sir Frederick, before we go further, who is paying for our fuel to get here?"

"I am," Upton replied. "You will draw all food, fuel, and supplies—liquor if you like—from this ship. Anything you want."

They murmured approval.

Then Upton played it rough, the knockdown for rough men. He gestured at me. "The professor here has found it. He knows where the blue whale breeds."

Each turned and eyed me with a long, appraising look, as if searching an uncertain horizon. That, mixed with a kind of unbelieving wonder. I started to speak, but Upton went on, "You captains will hunt the blue whale with me in its very breeding ground."

Hanssen said thickly, "Where is it, Sir Frederick?"

Upton laughed and punched him on the shoulder. "You bastard, Hanssen!" He turned to the others. "He says to me, where is it? Just like that! The greatest mystery of all time for whalermen, and he says, where is it?"

He'd got his audience. The Norwegians roared with laughter.

Sailhardy whispered to me. "Bruce, let's get out of this set-up. It is all wrong."

Upton didn't miss his cue with us either. "Only the professor knows," he told them. "You see, he has been a captain in the Royal Navy. You know what they are. They never talk."

Mikklesen's eyes were so clear they were devoid of expression. "Captain Wetherby of H.M.S. *Scott?*" he asked.

"Yes."

"The man who sank the raider *Meteor?*"

"Yes."

"They still talk about it when men get together," he said. He came over and shook my hand. "I was close, east of Bouvet, in my *Falkland*. I heard the signals. They were clear, not in code—he was a clever one, that *Meteor*. The twisting and the turning! He yapped over the air like a mongrel in a fight. From your ship there was nothing—then silence. I knew you had got him then."

Upton was abstracted. I became a punch line in his act. "Captain Wetherby, Distinguished Service Order," he said. "A professor of the sea in peace time and a man of death in wartime."

It was so sententious that I nearly laughed in his face. The captains did not think so. Solemnly each shook me by the hand.

"Captain Wetherby knows," Upton went on, "and he has promised to take us there."

"What is it worth, Sir Frederick?" asked Hanssen.

"This ship will hold about two hundred and twenty thousand barrels of oil," he replied. "That's worth about three million pounds."

Mikklesen chipped in. "To you, yes, Sir Frederick. But not to the men who will do the work."

"There's a hundred thousand pounds net for each of you in this," Upton said. "Net. I'll pay all expenses and, as I said, provide all fuel, all equipment." He didn't wait. "Bull?"

Bull nodded quickly.

"Hanssen?"

"Aye."

"Brunvoll?"

"Yes."

"Mikklesen?"

The skipper of the *Falkland* hesitated for a moment. I thought he might be going to refuse. He did not look at Upton but at some point on the great map near Bouvet, as if it could help him to a decision. "I have never had so much money," he replied slowly.

"That's not an answer," joked Upton. "Yes?" He didn't wait but started to fill up the glasses, talking rapidly. "This calls for a celebration. We sail in the morning. Keep close to the factory ship. Pirow will pass my orders to you on the W/T."

Mikklesen waited until his glass was full. "It is not as easy as that, Sir Frederick," he said.

The other skippers stared at Mikklesen in surprise.

"We agree to go with you—if so, where? It might be anywhere between here and Australia—or beyond."

Upton frowned. "It is not as far as that. A couple of thousand miles. You have my assurance on that."

Mikklesen shook his head. "I sweated for twenty years to buy my own ship. There must be safeguards."

"The safeguards are a hundred thousand pounds in cash," snapped Upton.

"Is this a legal or an illegal expedition?" pressed the Viking-eyed man. "Will I lose my ship? Why ask us to rendezvous at Tristan? I have never heard of whalers gathering here before."

He said pointedly, "Why didn't you bring your nice big ship and meet us where we belong, in South Georgia?"

"I had to meet Captain Wetherby here—" Upton began.

"Listen," I interrupted, "forget Captain Wetherby. The war has been over a long time."

Mikklesen smiled. "No, Captain. Seas and wars do not forget their captains." He confronted Upton. "Have you a permit from the International Whaling Association?"

Upton was on the defensive. "I will explain more to you—"

"Do we fish where we should not?" Mikklesen pressed

on. "What country's waters, eh? Is this a second Onassis and the *Olympic Challenger*? Will we also be bombed and arrested?"

"There is a territorial limit of two hundred miles which has been laid down, but it is completely unreasonable, and no nation would really adhere to it if—" said Upton.

Mikklesen certainly was on the ball. "So we fish in my own country's territorial waters?" he asked with a thin smile. "We fish for the thing every Norwegian whalerman has dreamed of since he first heard the crash of a harpoon gun or since he flensed his first whale—the breeding ground of the blue whale?"

Upton tried again. "Technically, I say, we will be inside territorial waters. With the knowledge I have I cannot risk a maritime court action; it would give everything away."

"It is Bouvet, is it not, Sir Frederick? Not so, Captain Wetherby? Inside Norwegian territorial waters, off Bouvet?"

"It *is* Bouvet, blast you!" roared Upton. "But, by God, Mikklesen, you can search until you are as blue as a blue whale, but you won't find the breeding ground—not without Wetherby!"

Mikklesen's answer was quick. "That I know. Every season for thirty years I have sailed near Bouvet. I have never found it. I try every time."

Walter said, "We are fishermen, and two hundred miles for a territorial limit is damn stupid. Twelve miles maybe."

The other captains, except Mikklesen, grunted approval.

"We are hunters," went on Walter. "We hunt where the game is. You cannot draw lines across the ocean and say, keep out. Where would we be if the British did what Norway has done and kept us away from South Georgia and the South Shetlands?"

"We Norwegians first thought of the breeding ground," Mikklesen retorted angrily. "It belongs to Norway, even if two hundred miles is a stupid limit, and as a whalerman I agree that it is."

Upton saw his opening. "You are a hunter first, or a

patriot first, Captain Mikklesen. Will Norway offer you the
hundred and twenty thousand pounds I will?"

"A hundred and twenty thousand pounds?" echoed Mikklesen. "A moment ago it was a hundred thousand."

Upton did not sense his mistake with Mikklesen in bid-
ding up. I did, and Mikklesen's grudging agreement should
have warned Upton.

"That's the new price," Upton said, laughing. "So that
everybody feels quite happy."

"This secret belongs to Norway, not to one man or one
expedition," said Mikklesen doggedly.

"I thought more of your spirit of enterprise," said Upton. "Does that mean you are not joining us?"

"I'll come," he replied sullenly. "For a hundred and
twenty thousand poinds. Now I must get back aboard my
ship." He gave me a further long glance, as if to satisfy
himself he had really seen someone who had located a secret so precious to Norway, and went.

"Some of these boys like jam on it," said Upton. He
turned to me. "He'll feel different once he sees the sea red
with dead whales. They just cannot resist it, you know."

Mikklesen's departure lifted the air of tension over the
gathering. I had heard of the drinking prowess of South
Georgia whalemen, but, even so, the way they downed
their Cape Horners astonished me. But then they were also
drinking to dreams of their hundred and twenty thousand
pounds. Upton became one of them as the strong liquor
and his camaraderie loosed their tongues.

". . . Fanning Ridge," Walter was booming. "It's the best
landmark on South Georgia as you come up from the
southwest. Damn me, I've seen it from as far away as fifty
miles on a clear day."

"Nonsense," said Brunvoll. "Why come from the
southwest anyway?"

Walter let out an oath. "I wouldn't have been coming at
all if it hadn't been for the emergency huts the Americans
put up on Stonington Island."

"Stonington Island?" Hanssen echoed. "That's to hell down the Graham Land peninsula, way in Marguerite Bay!"

"Too true," Walter replied. "I was caught by one of those violent gusts which come down the glacier near Neny Island—"

"In other words," said Upton, "you thanked God and the Norwegians who first set up the emergency depots they call roverhullets throughout the Antarctic and its islands."

"It was the Scots who started the idea on Laurie Island, in the South Orkneys, sixty years ago," began Reider Bull.

I stood aside as the argument developed. Mikklesen's shrewd formulation of the illegality of the proposed expedition worried me. There could be no doubt that, in the terms of the Antarctic Treaty signed by twelve of the major powers with possessions and interests in Antarctica, including Britain, the United States, and Norway, we would be infringing Norwegian territorial waters. If we were caught, Upton might buy or talk his way out of trouble; but for me it would be different. I, a Royal Society researcher, would acquire a permanent black mark for throwing in my lot with an expedition whose one and only purpose was gain, Upton's gain. In fact, the whole business could lead to a small shooting war if Norway got tough. That is exactly what had happened when Onassis allegedly flouted the 200-mile offshore whaling limit declared by Peru, Ecuador, and Chile in 1954. His *Olympic Challenger* expedition, as Mikklesen had pointed out, had been bombed by the Peruvian Air Force and seized by the Peruvian Navy. That had created a major diplomatic incident, and the ships had been released only on payment of a million-pound indemnity by Lloyds.

The breeding ground of the blue whale was far more important to Norway than Onassis's mere infringement of whaling limits. That was where the parallel with the *Olympic Challenger* expedition and Upton's ended. Had the *Olympic Challenger* had on board an oceanographer like myself who could have nailed down a killer current the Peruvians call El Nino—a warm, less saline stream that blitzes the lifeflow of the Peru Current and kills fish, whales, and seabirds by the million off the coast of South America—the knowledge in itself would have been worth that million-pound indemnity many times over.

The Albatross' Foot represented a mighty challenge. What, I asked myself as the catcher skippers grew more noisy, if a similar challenge had been rejected by the man who, only since World War I, had revolutionized all ideas on the great Gulf Stream itself? He was laughed to scorn—but he proved his theory. And until ten years ago the United States was unaware that yet a second great Gulf Stream, known as the Cromwell Current, swept in to its shores, this time from the Pacific; again, it was one man's persistence, pitted against all contemporary scorn, that proved that a 250-mile wide column of water—equal to the flow of the Nile, Amazon, Mississippi, St. Lawrence, Yellow, and Congo Rivers together multiplied several thousand times—washed the Pacific coast of the United States.

Here, at my fingertips, lay the possibility of a discovery as great as, if not greater than, either of these. The whole of the world's whaling industry would be affected by knowledge of my current. That, I argued with myself, could bring conservation on a global scale of the disappearing schools of whales in the Southern Ocean, even if Upton killed off a few hundred in pinning down that knowledge for me.

There was, too, a vital military aspect of the Albatross' Foot. In H.M.S. *Scott* I had sunk a U-boat deep in the Southern Ocean towards the ice. She had surfaced before she sank, and I had recovered his log. For submarines, knowledge of water temperature and salinity is vital. I had been surprised at the data the log had showed of the area where I now knew the Albatross' Foot must be: it was a picture of current and countercurrent, of rapid temperature changes in the boundary layer between surface water and the main body of the sea itself, which we oceanographers call the "thermoc-line." A study of the waters round Bouvet would yield new and invaluable operational information for atomic submarines guarding the vital sea route round the Cape of Good Hope.

How else but through Upton would I ever get near Bouvet? It had been difficult enough to persuade scientists at the Royal Society to let me investigate the Tristan prong of the Albatross' Foot; I knew that no government or scientific organization would spend tens of thousands of pounds on an expedition to the wild waters of Bouvet merely to test an unsubstantiated theory. The answer was: Upton's expedition must not be located. To me that meant only one thing—I must take command. Sailhardy and I knew every trick of the Southern Ocean. We had learned the hard way.

I grinned a little wryly to myself now that the decision had been formulated: I was deliberately seeking out the worst seas in the world, among whose fogs I would hide the factory ship and catchers from whatever ships Norway might have there, while I sought within my "circular area of probability" (as the missile men say of the target at Cape Canaveral) the missing prong of the Albatross' Foot.

Sailhardy moved away from the porthole when Upton tried again to press a drink on him and came over to me, frowning deeply. "Bruce," he said, "we can get to Tristan even in this gale. Let's get out—now."

I submerged my own misgivings. "Why? This is a once-in-a-lifetime opportunity for me to get to Bouvet, as you know."

"Look," replied the islander, "we've been shanghaied—politely, but nonetheless shanghaied. Upton has sailed all the way from Cape Town to Tristan in order to tell you that your plankton discoveries will help him discover the breeding ground of the blue whale. Fair enough—they probably will."

"Then what are you objecting to?" I asked.

"His methods, his timing, everything," he replied. "He could have written you a letter asking you to go to see him in England, or flown you there from Cape Town, for that matter. True, the letter might have taken six months to reach you, but six months are not important for something which has been searched for half a century. It must have cost five thousand pounds a day to bring this ship to Tristan. When he gets here, he sends his daughter off into one hell of a storm to find you. It all points to one thing: you must be valuable—very valuable indeed—to him."

"He told us, he could net a straight three million pounds."

"It's a big expedition, isn't it?"

"Yes."

"If he finds this breeding ground, you'd expect this factory ship to be mighty busy, wouldn't you?"

"Yes."

"Pirow and I walked through the crew's quarters when we landed, to put his gear in his cabin," he said slowly. "There are only enough men to cope with a moderate catch. I smelled a rat at once, so I asked the chief flenser about biomycin. Biomycin is the latest American way of preserving a whale—you know, normally the meat and fat of a whale are quite useless about eighteen hours after the kill unless preserved with biomycin. You can then keep them up to forty hours. You'd expect them to be cutting up whales on an assembly-line basis if Upton found the breeding ground. Yet there's no biomycin aboard, and almost skeleton flensing crews to cut them up."

"Upton may be a bit old-fashioned in his methods," I said.

"What have you got in that bag of yours?" Sailhardy demanded, indicating the oilskin bag the sailor had brought from the whaleboat.

"Charts, sea temperature reading—that sort of thing."

"*What* charts?"

"Admiralty charts of Tristan, Gough, the South

Shetlands—you can buy them anywhere. Oh, and an old chart and log that came to me when Wetherby's folded up. It's about 1825. It's probably the first of the waters round Bouvet—"

"Bouvet!" exclaimed Sailhardy.

The cabin door flew open. Pirow stood there, a radio message in his hand. It was the disciplined attitude of the man, his deference to Upton, his superior, and his taut bearing, which made me recognize him in a flash.

The Man with the Immaculate Hand!

I looked in wonder across the noisy room at the man who had lured so many British and Allied ships and men to their deaths during World War II. Carl Pirow, radio operator of the German raider *Meteor*, was a very different proposition now from the oil-drenched wretch that had been brought aboard H.M.S. *Scott* after the *Meteor* had gone down. I considered Pirow the most dangerous single man the war at sea had thrown up against the Royal Navy because of his uncanny ability to imitate any type of ship's radio transmission. When I had started my long search for the *Meteor* I had discovered that every ship, whether merchantman or warship, had its own idiosyncracies in transmitting. There were as many ways of sending as there were radio operators. I looked across at his hands now—yes, they were still beautifully manicured as the wartime legend recounted. It was said that Captain Kohler of the *Meteor* had first named him the Man with the Immaculate Hand; the German Navy had passed it on to their propaganda radio; the Royal Navy had perpetuated it as we hunted, month after month, in the Southern Ocean while the *Meteor* struck again and again.

A chill went through me, even in the warm, drink-laden atmosphere of the factory ship's cabin, as I remember the standard distress signal I had heard so many times from the ships placed under my charge in the wastes of the Southern Ocean, a signal, often blurred and incomplete as the raider's shells smashed home.

First, the frightened *QQQ—I am being attacked;* invariably followed by *RRR—I am being shelled by a warship.*

I jerked myself back into the present and crossed the room to Pirow. I looked at him steadily. "Is that a message from Seekriegsleitung, that it's so urgent?"

For a moment his glance faltered as I dropped into the jargon of the operational staff of the German Naval High Command; then he laughed. "I wondered how long it would be before you recognized me, Herr Kapitän." There was a spurt of anger behind the pale eyes which made the calm poise of the master technician-faker more sinister. "It was no thanks to that stupid clot of a radio operator of yours that you came in with the torpedoes. The last thing the Herr Kapitän zur See Kohler said to me was, 'I wonder if the British torpedoes will run true?' Ours always gave trouble."

"Bruce!" said Upton peremptorily. He drew me aside. "Here!" He thrust the signal into my hand. He wasn't drunk. The caffeine in his strange tipple offset the effects of the alcohol. The pink flush of anger was there though.

I read the signal, written in Pirow's neat, post-office handwriting:

Urgent repeat urgent stop Mikklesen skipper whale-catcher 724/004 Falkland to Norwegian destroyer Thorshammer via Tristan da Cunha meteorological station stop British Sir Frederick Upton has discovered breeding ground blue whale stop inside Norwegian territorial waters vicinity Bouvet Island stop Upton has no permits stop expedition factory ship and four Norwegian catchers starting ex Tristan dawn tomorrow stop suggest appropriate action stop

Under it was the reply:

Thorshammer to Mikklesen stop message acknowledged stop heading all possible speed for Tristan stop await my orders there stop

Upton jerked his head at the group of captains. "Walter!"

Walter read it slowly. "The bastard! The bloody, two faced bastard—"

"Shut up!" snapped Upton in a low voice. "Keep those boys drinking. Carl, come to the radio office. We've got plenty of time, and the Southern Ocean is a big place."

Pirow gave his half-smile, half-sneer. "Except that the *Thorshammer* is about twenty miles away—just the other side of Nightingale Island."

"How do you know?" rapped out Upton.

"I got a D/F bearing on her," said the Man with the Immaculate Hand. "She'll be here in an hour."

The *Thorshammer*'s message threw my doubts into sharp relief. Either I would go now with Upton or get ashore with no hope of ever seeing Bouvet. The presence of the Man with the Immaculate Hand had shaken me. What was a brilliant, if perverted, radio operator like Pirow doing with an expedition like this? You don't need radio to hunt whales, and wireless traffic in the Antarctic, as I knew from my long vigil at Cape Town listening to it, consisted mainly of weather reports and catchers' reports, all of it deadly dull. Pirow was there for some sinister purpose— that I knew. Was it his master-talent in deception which Upton wanted, or some knowledge from his days aboard the *Meteor*? In either event, the blue whale story was simply a cover, but a cover for what? On the surface one could not fault Upton's story, except that it was a little too slick. Even the lack of biomycin on board was not decisive—whalermen are naturally conservative and slow to adopt new ideas—but why did Upton want me so urgently? What knowledge, or part knowledge, did I share with Pirow, assuming that the blue whale story was a fabrication or a blind? Despite the risk, I was doubly sure now that I must assume command and go. The knowledge of what Upton, Pirow, and Walter were really about might prove my justification if the Norwegians caught me.

I turned to Upton. "We can't talk here. Let's get to Pirow's office." Upton started to demur when Sailhardy came too, but I waved his objection aside. We skirted the big bridge to get to the radio office. I was struck by the radio set. It was a powerful instrument, and the tuning dials were twice the size of any I had seen. Upton, Pirow, Sailhardy, and myself crowded into the small space.

"Sir Frederick," I said, "I now have a condition for coming to Bouvet. I must have sole and complete command of this ship, and the catchers must operate under my orders."

Upton shot a quick glance at Pirow. "I'll be damned! Why this sudden assumption of responsibility?"

"You can make up your mind, and it will have to be quick," I said. "The *Thorshammer* can't be here in an hour with this sea running. She can't make more than fifteen knots. I *know*. The *Thorshammer* is one of the new British Whitby class that was sold to Norway. She's big—every bit of two thousand tons. Even so, I feel sorry for anyone in her tonight. It'll be coming green right up to the bridge. Western Approaches stuff. But she'll catch you before you ever see Bouvet."

"Unless you are in command," he said. He didn't wait. He picked up Pirow's telephone. "Bridge!" he said. "Captain Bjerko! From now on Captain Wetherby will take over command of this ship. You will act on his orders and give him the fullest co-operation." He turned to me. "Satisfied?" I nodded. "Get on with it, Carl! Do something about it!"

Pirow looked at me with that half-smile. "I have your permission, Herr Kapitän?" I nodded again, and he sat down at his transmitting key.

The thoughtful pause with the hand held high was pure

Rubinstein. It was not a gesture to the three of us who stood round him at the key. It was the thought-mustering prelude of the artist. He was projecting himself into his medium. The left hand came down by the side of the key with the thumb and first finger splayed, the third and fourth slightly crooked. The right hand felt delicately for the key, live now as he put on the transmitting switch. He paused and looked up at me. "It was a South African who sent Mikklesen's message," he said. "He sent *breeding grond* instead of *breeding ground.* He was an Afrikaner—he spelled 'ground' as it is spelled in Afrikaans. One must, therefore, send like an Afrikaner; deliberattely, thoroughly, one must search out in his make-up the essential puritan, and one must manifest it in one's sending."

He depressed the key. I read the Morse as he sent. Carl Pirow as such was no more. This was the Man with the Immaculate Hand, and these were the hands of a superb, corrupt artist.

Mikklesen to Thorshammer via Tristan meteorological station stop Upton and catchers up-anchoring stop

The old thrill of the chase welled up inside me, despite my foreboding.

"The course, Herr Kapitän?" Pirow said urgently. "Quickly, Herr Kapitän! The course! I must not break or they will guess!"

Deception course! The layout of Tristan da Cunha and the anchorage rose to my mind's eye. The *Thorshammer* was approaching from the southwest. I must blanket her radar behind the cliffs which towered along the line of Hottentot Gulch at the back of the settlement—blanket her to give my fleet a flying start, and then double back. I would keep the catchers with the factory ship inside the kelp line round by Jew's Point and Blacksand Beach—that would put the island and its peak between the *Thorshammer* and us until I could run the factory ship straight at her in the storm. I would break out from the southern tip of the island just as she started to come by Anchorstock Point on the other side towards the roadstead—her captain would never think of using his radar to scan the south when he believed his quarry to be north and east. In this weather I could slip past him within half a mile.

"Three hundred degrees," I said.

Pirow tapped out the figures. "You and I would have made a great team, Herr Kapitän."

"Finish that the way Mikklesen might," I added.

Am awaiting your further orders stop anchored in nine fathoms off Julia Reef stop Julia Point bearing 174 degrees stop

Upton was visibly excited. "Walter must know, but not the others," he said.

"They're risking their necks, just the same as Walter—" I began.

"They won't, if they know there's a warship only twenty miles away. I *need* those skippers. They'll simply evaporate if they hear about the *Thorshammer*."

All my doubts came rushing in. Upton's concealment of the danger underlined the importance of his mission.

"Very well," I said slowly, "but they won't be very thrilled at up-anchoring in a blow like this."

"Thrilled or not thrilled, they'll do just what I tell them. Any special briefing for them, Bruce?"

"I'll leave the explaining to you—as much as you care to explain," I said. "I want them to keep in my lee, about a quarter of a mile apart on the port quarter of the *Antarctica*. We'll sneak past the *Thorshammer* not very far from where Helen rescued Sailhardy and me. If I know anything about the radar scanner of the *Thorshammer* class, he won't want to swing it more than is necessary in this wind. There must be no sudden opening up of the catchers' engines. They'll give a sudden spurt of flame in the darkness if they do. The convoy will work up speed gradually—nine knots at first, then eleven for twenty minutes, and then up to the maximum we can make into the gale."

Pirow's receiver started to chatter.

Thorshammer to Mikklesen stop keep me informed stop Heavy weather makes interception difficult stop will use searchlights and starshells stop keep clear of Upton's fleet stop

"Will he, hell," I growled. Maybe the Southern Ocean brings out the essential man, the eternal hunter, for all the ennui, the frustration of the long intervening years of study and research fell away. I had a ship under me; I was at sea on a night as wild as the Creation.

Upton must have managed the skippers, and from the bridge I saw the half-drunken, truculent men make their way by dinghy to their ships, and in less than half the time it would take the *Thorshammer* to intercept us, my small fleet was at sea.

The gale hit us with a vicious left hook as we swung clear of Stonyhill Point, the southern extremity of the island, and we took the full force of the storm after the shelter of Tristan's lee. The Kent clearview screen in front of the big bridge telegraph seemed to check for a moment in its quick orbit. The only light was the main engine revolution indicator—out of sight of whatever searching eyes there might be on the *Thorshammer*. The squadron was blacked out on my orders, to the mystification of the skippers.

I was not used to such luxury on a ship's bridge. The nine large windows exposed one to the eyes of the night, and every time the fancy clock which struck the time by ship's bells gave its melodious chime, I jumped. I went over to the telegraph on the port wing of the bridge and rang for more revolutions: the Ray's patent revolution indicator quickened its tempo.

We made for the *Thorshammer*. I spoke to the lookout

through the telephone by the starboard doorway. "See anything, lookout?"

The coarse voice came back. "Nothing, sir. Niks. Niks at all."

I double-checked on the bridge to see that everything was in order. "I'm glad I'm not on a destroyer's bridge tonight," I said to Upton. "Raw steel; raw sub-zero."

"What if the *Thorshammer* spots us?" asked Upton.

"She won't," I replied.

"No," said Pirow, who glanced at his sleeked hair in the reflection of the small light. "She won't. Not with Captain Wetherby in command."

The bridge phone rang. "Lookout, sir. *Aurora* coming in very close."

"Tell her to sheer off," I told Pirow. "Make quite sure the signalling lamp doesn't point the *Thorshammer*'s way." He smiled thinly at my precaution, redundant to someone like himself. The *Antarctica* yawed and trembled under a violent squall. Sailhardy, whom I had ordered to the small brass wheel, held her beautifully. The Chernikeef log chuckled to itself. We waited, silent, tense.

They say the eye sees best ten degrees off centre. Mine caught the telltale flicker of light away to starboard.

It wasn't a ship.

"Port twenty!" I ordered.

Sailhardy spun the wheel. It seemed ages before the *Antarctica* started to come round.

"Get my night glasses from the cabin—quick!" I told the Norwegian quartermaster whose place Sailhardy had taken. Upton handed me the bridge binoculars. I took one look at the name. "Standard British glasses are useless at night," I said. "I wonder how many ships were sunk during the war through not seeing a raider because of poor glasses?"

The man returned and handed me my own.

Pirow smiled at Upton. "Raider's glasses! Zeiss. Sevenfold magnification. It took months to perfect a single pair of binoculars for one of our raider captains. The Herr Kapitän Wetherby has all the answers."

The night drew in under their power, but I could not trace the momentary light which had alerted me. I opened one of the bridge windows. "We are in raiders' waters," I said. "The *Meteor* used to rendezvous with the *Neptune* off Tristan. U-boats too. I almost surprised one. His oil-hoses were still in the water." Gale-impelled rain deluged through the opening.

"Ice!" said Sailhardy. "Ice! I smell it. Ice, Bruce, very close."

"I smell it too," said Helen. I had not heard her come to the bridge.

The gale held an undefinable smell. There is nothing like it anywhere else'; not in Arctic ice, even. In the Southern Ocean the smell of it passes into men's clothing; the lookout in the swaying barrel on a catcher's mast knows that faintly wet, indescribable smell as his deadliest enemy and the companion of his labours.

We did not have long to wait. The night was torn by a splendour of white light. The incandescent burst was man-made. The *Thorshammer* had also seen what I had glimpsed. She had promised to use starshells.

The great iceberg appeared in sudden brilliance, and in only two dimensions. It must have been two or three miles long and a thousand feet high. From the bridge it was strange and beautiful under the slowly descending para-chute of the starshell. Towards its left-hand extremity, as if superimposed forward of the main body of the tabular berg, was a gigantic anvil, soaring nearly its entire height; it seemed disembodied from the rest. Disembodied in colour too: anchored for half a mile in a solid platform over which the sea spouted, it was deep green; where the blade of the anvil flared it was yellow, almost amber at the summit. The island of ice embayed itself near the right-hand cliff, and I could see in the ephemeral light a tiny lake of blue water, dominated by fluted, grooved cliffs on either side. The

weather face of the stupendous berg was hard and clear;
the lee was blurred by a tumble of disintegrating spicules of
ice, feathering their way on the gale.

"My God!" exclaimed Upton. Then he remembered the
Thorshammer. "She'll see us! Turn away! Turn away!"

"No," I retorted. "She's on the other side of the berg. It
will block out anything this side."

"She can't miss us with her radar," Upton said.

Pirow disagreed. "That berg is breeding enough radar
angels to fox anyone."

"Radar angels?" he asked.

"The ice, especially when it is disintegrating, produces
all sorts of unaccountable echoes on a radar," he said. "We
call them angels."

The starshell was doused. Darkness clamped down.

Helen was still next to me. "It is the sort of thing one
remembers all one's life. I didn't know icebergs came so far
north."

"It was probably ten times that size off Cape Horn," I
said.

From the starboard wing of the bridge I stared astern. Of
the *Thorshammer* there was no sign, not even a funnel
glow to pick her up in the blackness. I came back and shut
the window.

"Signal the catchers with the Aldis," I told Pirow.
"Steer"—I checked in my mind—"steer one hundred
degrees. Eight knots."

Sailhardy spun the wheel. My order had told him everything.

"Steady as she goes."

"Aye, aye, sir."

The *Antarctica* plunged southwards.

"One hundred degrees," said Helen. "Destination?"

I looked deep into her eyes. "Bouvet Island."

5 The Island That Never Was

For three days the *Antarctica* and the four catchers fought their way to the south through the storm. Now, on the fourth morning, the wind had dropped, but there was a tremendous swell running from the southwest. The heart of the gale had passed to the north and east and was on its way to spread snow on the distant high plateaux of the South African mainland. I was on the bridge, and Sailhardy at the wheel. A growler stood out on the starboard bow. The four catchers formed a ragged rearguard to the factory ship. Nearest was Walter's *Aurora*. She seemed to ride better than the others. She stuck her bow, blunt and aggressive like a boxer's nose, into the swell. A tarpaulin masked the deadly purpose of the harpoon gun forward. She sank down on our port beam, as if kneeling to the plunging factory ship, and took it green up to the cluster of winches below the bridge. All I could see was her masthead above the rollers. I watched the whip of the long flexible mast, which looked like an outsize fishing rod because of its cables to the harpoon. Water poured off her deck in triangular streams as she rose, channelled by the three-cornered bollards anchoring the whaling cables.

The sea had changed from the clear blue of Tristan's waters to a dirty, threatening grey. The fleet was now well to the south of shipping routes and striking across the

path of the Roaring Forties. The heavy top-hamper of the
factory ship, the four massive gantries, the big bollards by
the rails, and the heavy steel cables supporting the masts
were drenched in spray. A wandering albatross, whose
wingspan I guessed to be twelve feet, tipped the wind ef-
fortlessly from under his wings and hung above the stern
like a white boomerang. His presence copyrighted the
South. Of the other three catchers, the *Chimay* lay out to
starboard; the *Crozet* and the *Kerguelen,* farther away,
gave me on the bridge no more than an occasional glimpse
of the thick winch wires and lashing blocks which reached
almost to the height of their crow's nests while they
steamed beam-on to the seas.

"Someone built that ship good," remarked Sailhardy.

"Smith's Dock Company, Middlesbrough," I said absently. "They build the best."

My mind was not on the *Aurora*'s seaworthiness, although professionally I admired the way the rounded bows
of the catcher came up and their flare fought the sea. One
moment her cruiser stern plunged so deep I wondered if it
would ever come up again; the next, she shook her whole
fifteen-foot depth free in an explosion of spray. The wicked
handles of the harpoon gun stuck out of the weathered
tarpaulin like death in handcuffs.

I was worried: after the departure from Tristan and the
fleet's successful evasion of the *Thorshammer,* Upton had
taken over command from me, despite his assurances
before we had left the anchorage, with Bjerko playing
stooge to him. He had immediately altered the course to
one that was causing me the gravest concern. Upton had also been asking questions about the charts I had mentioned
at our first meeting. At first his probings had been
guarded; now they were more open and persistent.

The exhilaration of dodging the destroyer had given way
in my mind to gnawing fears about my complicity in Upton's schemes. Nor had those doubts been lessened by
Pirow's smooth radio deception of the Norwegian warship
and Upton's refusal to tell the other skippers except Walter

that the *Thorshammer* was not on our trail. We were now striking the fringe of the wild seas where I would have to seek the other prong of the Albatross' Foot, and the sight of the great seas rolling up from the ice continent also dampened the first flush of enthusiasm. It seemed an almost impossible task to try to find anything in an ocean as savage as this.

My apprehension had not been helped by Sailhardy. Two days out from Tristan he had told me that the flensing crews spent their time playing cards 'tween decks, and that no attempt was being made to get the factory ship ship-shape for the impending record catch. He maintained, so strongly that I had brought it up from my cabin to study through the long hours of the watch at night, that Upton's interest in me centred on the old chart in my oilskin case. My own suspicions revolved round some part knowledge Pirow and I might share from our wartime operations, and I thought Upton was aiming to dovetail the two interrelated pieces of knowledge held separately by Pirow and myself once we got to Bouvet. Helen too remained a mystery to me. On the few occasions she had appeared on the bridge she had been even more distant and withdrawn than before. Her questions to me regarding weather were, I felt, consciously professional, and I had noticed a decided uneasiness in her as the fleet neared colder waters.

Now, this morning, as I stood on the bridge shortly after sunrise, my doubts crystalized. I had gone below during the night to my cabin and, although I could not pin down anything specific, I felt my cabin had been searched. I had the old chart on the bridge. The oilskin bag, which served as a chart case, was almost as I had left it—but not quite. It was one of those indefinable things, an awareness more than a fact that it was not as I had left it.

I pulled the folded square of parchment from the inner pocket of my thick reefer jacket. It crackled as I unfolded it, to study it once again, to try to fathom Upton's objective.

"For God's sake, Bruce!" Sailhardy exclaimed. "Put

that damn thing away! What if Upton or Pirow comes
here?"

"You're seeing shadows, Sailhardy," I said. "This old
thing simply can't mean what you think it might. Neither
Upton nor Pirow will come to the bridge as early as this."

"Take the wheel a moment," he said. While I did, he
locked the bridge doors leading to Upton's cabin and the
radio office.

"We've been over this a score of times in the past three
days," I said. "I'm damned if I can see what an old—and
inaccurate—map of Bouvet Island in 1825 has to do with
a so-called whaling expedition in 1961."

The old parchment was intersected by wavy lines, with a
shape like a Chinese maple leaf in the centre. Both margins
were marked with tiny crosses. From the right-hand top
corner, meandering irregularly towards the maple-leaf
shape in the middle, was a line. Below the line and opposite
one of the quaint marginal crosses which said "54 degrees
South," were three dots, and a little farther down another
dot, which was labelled "rock." Its novelty had long since
been lost upon me, since I had had it ever since the end of
the war and had studied it many times.

It was the log and track chart of the Wetherby sealer
Sprightly, which had rediscovered Bouvet Island in 1825.
Her master, Captain George Norris, had not only charted
the island, but had also sketched it.

"That's not all, and you know it," retorted Sailhardy.
"And I think Upton guesses that too."

"You mean Thompson Island?" I said derisively.

"Yes," replied Sailhardy. "I mean just that—Thompson
Island."

My thoughts went back to the day upon empty day I had
trailed up and down the great staircase at the headquarters
of the Royal Geographical Society next to the Albert Hall
in London; the days upon days spent sitting outside
someone's office at the Admiralty, waiting to be fobbed
off and sent to yet another office. The stale smell of the

Greenland kayak on the Geographical Society staircase was synonymous in my mind with the endless questioning, my endless frustration, among the disbelieving experts. They did not want to believe, any more than the Admiralty wanted to believe, what I had seen.

I wondered if my innermost reason for accepting Upton's offer to go to Bouvet had been less of a desire on my part to nail down the Albatross' Foot and more an attempt to vindicate myself. The Royal Geographical Society and the Admiralty had both said, leave it alone, leave it alone.

When Captain Norris rediscovered Bouvet Island—it had been lost for nearly a century since the Frenchman Bouvet had first sighted—he had also found something Bouvet had not: an island fifteen leagues, or forty-five miles, north-northeast of Bouvet. Captain Norris had positioned it. His own original log lay open in front of me.

Thompson Island had never been found again—officially.

Captain Norris's discovery provoked the liveliest controversy for over a century and a quarter. Nations lavished millions on ships specially equipped to find Thompson Island. Ahead of the field were the Norwegians, who specifically explored the seas round Bouvet in the late 1920s under the great Lars Christensen. The Bristish RRS *Discovery* searched: Thompson was not found. German, American, and French expeditions had also failed. For years there had been no further searches.

Sailhardy took his eyes from the compass in front of him. It was fully a minute before he spoke. "You are the only living man to have seen Thompson Island."

"Yes," I said. "But there's no need to dramatize it like that. I know I saw an island as we went into action against the *Meteor*. It was near Bouvet. No one will believe I sighted land. I was told the same thing as Captain Norris when Thompson could not be found again: either I had seen a big iceberg and mistaken it for land or else it was simply water-sky."

"Yellowish reflected light over a big shelf of rice," murmured Sailhardy. "An Antarctic man like yourself doesn't make that sort of mistake."

"No," I said. "If I were one of the catcher skippers, I would have liked to use a very rude phrase to the armchair critics who rejected what I had to say. Curious—they said almost the same to Captain Norris. The Admiralty said he'd seen a large iceberg, and the streaks which he described on the cliffs were simply barnacles."

Sailhardy looked at me reproachfully. "You know the history of Thompson Island minutely, you know how many great sailors have searched for Thompson Island and failed, and yet you deliberately play it down in relation to Upton. It ranks with the island where Sir Francis Drake sheltered the *Golden Hind* off Cape Horn, which has never been seen again, as one of the greatest of sea mysteries."

"The vital phrase is, *in relation to Upton*," I replied. "He is neither a sailor nor an explorer."

"No," replied Sailhardy. "He's got a flashy act as a modern-day buccaneer. And he's after Thompson Island."

I shook my head. "If he'd wanted to discover Thompson Island he would not have gone about it in this hole-and-corner way," I said. "A man in his position could telephone a London newspaper and say he was endowing a special expedition to search for the great ocean mystery, Thompson Island, etcetera, etcetera. There would be no lack of takers. You don't have to string a fleet of catchers along with you, anyway, to look for an island. One ship would do."

"Keep that chart out of the way, that's all I ask," said the islander.

"What possible value could Thompson Island have to Upton?" I went on. "I have seen it. It's simply the tip of an undersea mountain range jutting out into the worst seas in the world. There's nowhere like it anywhere. Gales, snow, ice, gigantic seas, day in, day out, year in, year out."

"He wants that log," said Sailhardy.

"Take a look, I assure you there's nothing."

He looked at me strangely. "You are the only living man to have seen Thompson Island. There are only three others in history. One of them was Captain Norris."

I smiled at his earnestness. "One of the three was Francis Allen, an American sealer who started a line of islanders on Tristan—and you are of that line."

Thompson Island belonged to the Wetherbys, I told myself. It was the old John Wetherby's because his favourite captain had discovered it for him—and lost it to the world; it was mine, the last of the Wetherbys, because I had found it again after four generations, or very nearly, since it had slipped away into the ice and fog with the same spectrelike elusiveness as it had done with Norris. Sailhardy was in it too, and I could almost recall by heart the deposition made to the Franklin Institute by the man with whom Sailhardy's great-grandfather had sailed:

Captain Joseph Fuller, of New London, now (1904) lighthousekeeper at Stonington, served in the United States Navy during the Civil War and afterwards repeatedly went sealing and sea elephant hunting in the Antarctic. In 1893, in the *Francis Allen*, he saw Bouvet Island, and he saw Thompson Island bearing about northeast from Bouvet, but he could not land on either on account of the ice, wind, and fog.

Joseph Fuller named his ship *Francis Allen* after his friend and mate Francis Allen.

Sailhardy went tense. His keen ears had heard someone coming. He jerked his head at the wheel. "Take it!" he muttered. "Give me that damn thing!" Before I could object, he folded the log of the *Sprightly* and thrust it inside his windbreaker. With equal swiftness he unlocked the doors.

He was just in time. Upton came through. He looked
curiously at me. "Are you the quartermaster as well as the
captain, Bruce?"

I shrugged. "We may need two men at the wheel the way
we're going."

Something was eating him. He was morose, preoccupied.
"What the hell do you mean?"

"This fleet is putting its nose into trouble—big trouble,"
I replied.

Sailhardy took the wheel again.

"If you mean you're afraid of one little fisheries protection destroyer—" he began.

"I'm afraid of the biggest destroyer there is—ice," I
retorted. "I must know where the *Thorshammer* is and
what course she is steering. Our course is dead wrong. I
want to get to the north."

Upton's face went pink. "You'll stay on this course and
keep out of the way of the *Thorshammer*. Pirow's last D/F
bearing on her showed we were steering diverging courses.
We should soon be out of range of her seaplane."

"Pirow's bearing was two days ago," I said. "Anything
could have happened since."

Upton picked up the bridge phone. "Carl! Bridge! At
once. Bring Bjerko with you." He came back to me. "So
you're frightened of a little weather—the great Captain
Wetherby?" he sneered.

"Yes, I am," I replied, "when I am steering directly into
the heart of the atmospheric machine which provides the
energy for the storms of the Roaring Forties."

"Nonsense!" snapped Upton. "Walter agrees with
me—it will be stormy, but you are well used to that."

"Listen," I said, "I originally set course, after we had
given the *Thorshammer* the slip at Tristan, to approach
Bouvet from the north. Pirow got is D/F bearings on the
Thorshammer. I wanted to stay just beyond radar range,
but you put her on this course in order to approach Bouvet
from the south and west. I say it is suicide."

"The *Thorshammer* has a seaplane," said Upton. "Don't forget that."

"I'd like to see anyone take off in the kind of storm we've had," I replied. "The *Thorshammer*'s only got an old HE 114 for searching—Pirow heard that over the air. Its radius is not much more than a hundred and fifty miles anyway."

Pirow and the ungainly Captain Bjerko came to the bridge. "Carl," said Upton, "have you got a bearing on the *Thorshammer*?"

Pirow shook his head. "This part of the world is hell for radio. Thirty years ago Lars Christensen found that Bouvet was a radio 'dead spot,' as we call it. I can't get any good signals from the *Thorshammer*."

Upton was edgy. "You mean you can't get enough of her sending for a D/F bearing?"

Pirow's lip curled. "I can get a bearing if a ship sends eleven letters. I proved it to the German Decryption Service."

"So you don't know what course the *Thorshammer* is steering?"

"No."

I tried to cash in on Upton's nervous uncertainty. "Even this big factory ship isn't good enough to stand up to what we're heading for."

"I have been in the Southern Ocean many times," said Bjerko. "This ship is good."

"You've never steered this course or tried to make Bouvet from the south and west," I replied. "Bouvet is the heart of a fantastic, dynamic weather machine which tosses off more energy into the sea and wind than an atomic explosion. I could explain it all in terms of what is euphemistically called the millibar anomalies of the Westerlies, but what it boils down to is that Bouvet acts as a kind of high-voltage booster station to weather which already has two thousand miles of punch behind it. It is a wild hell of driving water, fog, ice, and icebergs, all racing at a hundred knots to God knows where. I repeat, it is suicide to approach Bouvet the way we are doing, particularly in early November."

"Early November?" echoed Bjerko. "That is the best time in Antarctica. It is the start of the summer. The ice melts—poof, it is gone."

"Walter says the same," added Upton.

"And I say simply this," I went on. "This ship will be nipped in the ice and sunk if we approach Bouvet the way we are doing now."

"My dear fellow, when the sea is starting to warm up—?" began Upton.

I cut him short. "On the edge of the continental pack ice the sea temperature is always just above freezing point at this time. It stays so—until Bouvet. Just south of Bouvet, it goes down."

Upton shrugged. "I'm not interested in a lecture on sea temperatures. I want to know about the *Thorshammer*."

I ignored him. "Into that freezing or near-freezing sea, I believe, cuts the other prong of the Albatross' Foot. I have only seen the results, not the cause. It is, with the Southern Lights, the most spectacular of many wonderful sights in the Southern Ocean. In late October and early November you get an explosive warming in the stratosphere shortly after the sun appears over the South Pole. This, coupled with the inrush of the Albatross' Foot, produces a fantastic fallout of energy and weather. That is what I am warning you about."

"These are a sick man's fears," said Bjerko.

"There's a giant glacier in the sea where we are going," I said. "The pack ice disintegrates northwards towards Bouvet from the Antarctic mainland. Yet the tip of this vast tongue of ice—it is four hundred miles from the mainland—remains untouched. It has a life of its own. It draws its life from the atmospheric machine I'm talking about round Bouvet. The Albatross' Foot and the glacier conspire. There is a grand battle between warm and cold.

Bouvet lies in no-man's land. No-sailor's-sea, I would call it. In a sea of slush and bergy bits, suddenly it freezes like a vice. Bouvet makes its own particular brand of pack ice. Within hours, before you can escape, the sea is frozen solid. I warn you, if you take this ship the way we are going now, the ice will close and tear her guts out. She'll be nipped along the waterline and be crushed to death."

"Wait," said Upton. He was back in a minute. The document he handed me sent a tremor of apprehension through me. Harmless in itself—my weather knowledge and Kohler's would probably add up to the same thing—it proved beyond doubt that my fears and Sailhardy's about the true purpose of Upton's expedition were well founded.

I read it aloud so that Sailhardy, too, would see its significance. " 'Kapitän zur See Kohler—Oberkommando der Marine.' " I took my eyes from the heading and watched Pirow as I translated for the islander. "Captain Kohler to High Command, Germany Navy. Top Secret. Raider *Meteor*'s climatological report on Bouvet Island area."

In other words, Upton had delved deep—as deep as a top secret document—in order to get information about Bouvet, or was it about Thompson Island? Had Kohler the sea-wolf not gone down under my fire, Upton might have had no use for Bruce Wetherby.

"All men have their price," Upton said jauntily. "Even for top secrets." Was Pirow's price the knowledge of Upton's objective? I asked myself.

I glanced at the opening sentences in order to compose my thoughts. "Situation with a westerly movement. Visibility poor in early summer. Fog and cloud frequency increases . . ."

I did not need Kohler to tell me about Bouvet's weather, secret and vital though it was to U-boats and raiders. The way we were headed meant certain disaster, but to reveal the fleet's positon to the *Thorshammer* would mean ignominy for me.

That is why I did not see the underlying motive of Pirow's suggestion.

"Why does not the Herr Kapitän take the helicopter and see for himself where the *Thorshammer* is steering? It's hopeless for me to try to get a bearing on her."

It seemed at the time as if this might provide a way out of my dilemma, or information on which to base my future course of action.

"Yes," I said. If I knew that, I might still avoid Bouvet's death-dealing ice. "You'll come?" I asked Pirow.

He shook his head. "I'll go on trying for a bearing: one might be lucky. I can be of more use aboard this ship."

My ready acceptance of the suggestion seemed to restore Upton's geniality. He tried to be conciliatory, but what he said only added to my suspicions.

"It will put you at your ease about Bouvet," he said. "Once you know the *Thorshammer*'s course, you will feel happier. "I'll tell you what, Bruce—if we take a bit of a pasting we'll lie up for a day or two at Bouvet. There's the one landing place in the southwest. Norris sounded out the Bollevika anchorage, and it's still the best."

Norris sounded out the Bollevika anchorage! If Upton knew about Norris and Bouvet, then he must know about Thompson. I could not help feeling it was an oblique bid: in other words, show me Norris's chart. Both Upton and Pirow seemed a shade disappointed when I replied. "Will you ask Helen to fly off as soon as possible then? I want Sailhardy to come with me."

Within a quarter of an hour the helicopter had risen from the flensing platform of the factory ship into the rear-guard fragments of cloud that rushed to the north and east to join the main body of the storm. The bucking of the ships far below was evidence of the wild weather which had left the swell behind. I was in the co-pilot's seat. Sailhardy stood. Helen swung the machine in a broad circle round the fleet. It was a superb horizon. Its iridescence was mirrored in her eyes, like Thai silk.

The strange bird from Nightingale clung to the compass platform.

"That lucky bird of yours won't budge from my cockpit," she said. "I've named her Suzie Wong."

I could not make her out. "She's like an African state—she's grown up to modern ways too quickly," I said. My quip sent her right back into herself.

"The pressure is one-oh-two-oh millibars," she said, stabbing at the wet-and-dry bulb thermometer, the rubber tube of which disappeared into the slipstream outside. "Is that normal in the wake of a migrating anti-cyclonic cell, Captain Wetherby?"

I glanced into the withdrawn face, whose high, fine cheekbones were emphasized by the leather helmet. Engine oil had insinuated itself in the tiny crack of her knuckles. They were fine hands, I told myself, almost in justification of her neglect of them, and they lay easily, confidently, on the controls. She was wearing a fleece-lined leather flying jacket and a pair of crumpled woolen slacks, thrust into salt-stained moccasin half-boots.

"It is normal," I replied absently. "Why call her Suzie Wong?"

I thought she wasn't going to reply, she took so long. "She's a bit out of the ordinary—something like the circumstances, something like— What course, please?"

I spread the big chart awkwardly. I pointed. "Is that where you think the *Thorshammer* will be, Sailhardy?" I had circled an area to the north-northwest.

"Maybe half a degree farther north," replied the islander. "The *Thorshammer* is ice-wise, Bruce. She'll get more benefit from the warmer water by keeping a shade farther north. She'll also get clearer visibility. She wants to find us, remember."

I ringed a new circle.

"Fine," Sailhardy said.

"Three hundred degrees," I told Helen.

As she brought the machine round and steadied on course, I looked back.

"South," she said, without looking at me. "You always look south, don't you?"

The question took me aback. After her resort to abstruse weather jargon I had been quite willing to treat her as a pair of competent hands only; now she was slipping a curious psychological punch under my guard.

"This particular day the south has more meaning for me than usual," I said. I told her about Bouvet's weather, the glacier in the sea, and the danger. She listened in silence. I told her how the sea would freeze.

She asked one question only. "Does that mean that we all could be stranded on the ice?"

"Yes."

She turned swiftly to me. A quick burst of terror—unalloyed terror—illuminated the strange eyes for a moment. Then she leaned forward and touched the island cock. "Then I'll go for your lucky bird, Captain Wetherby." Her voice was husky with tension.

I pulled a packet from my pocket. "Cigarette?"

"I don't smoke." She swallowed hard.

Sailhardy pointed forwards. "Whale."

She could not hide the relief in her voice to be among her professional pursuits. A tiny obelisk graced the sea to mark perhaps another whale grave in trackless waters.

"Blue whale," she corrected him.

"All whale spouts look alike to me," I replied.

"They are not alike," she said, getting a grip on her voice. "The blue whale is the easiest to spot—plume of condensation grows as its spout rises. A finback's is tall and narrow. The sperm whale gives himself away every time—he shoots it out at an oblique angle. Would you like a picture of it?" she asked.

She didn't wait for me to reply, but hurried on. Her eyes became animated, and for the first time since meeting her I felt aware of a personality behind the accomplished flier. "I've got a camera—two, in fact. I begged them from the Japanese who were down at Ongul Island last season. There's a Fairchild K17C for the vertical and a Williamson F24 for the oblique." She started to dip towards the whale's spout.

My words came automatically, and I regretted them as I spoke. "Keep course. Steady as she goes."

The eys snuffed out like a lamp. "Steering three hundred degrees," she repeated tonelessly.

We flew on steadily for the next two hours. Helen remained silent, completely withdrawn. Sailhardy and I exchanged technicalities, and when he went through to check the extra fuel we had loaded in the drums aft, I fiddled with the radio. It was, however, as Pirow had said. All I could get was some jumble from the American base at McMurdo Sound. After another twenty minutes' flying we were on the fringe of the area where I thought I would find the *Thorshammer*. We had overtaken part of the storm clouds, and I became anxious as I peered through the perspex, now clear, now obscured. Sailhardy turned his head this way and that, searching. If the destroyer was to be seen, he would spot her.

"This is going to be very tricky," I said. "If we stay at this height, the odds are we'll miss the *Thorshammer*. If we duck under the cloud cover, we lose our height advantage—and our ability to see her before she sees us."

"The orange and black will make this machine stand out like a sore thumb," said Sailhardy.

"What both of you have overlooked is the *Thorshammer*'s radar," remarked Helen.

"No," I said. "I've thought of nothing else since she left Tristan. I'm not particulary worried, however: she has not set about trailing us as I would have done. She's been quite open about it—by that I mean she hasn't kept radio silence like our fleet. She is not to know we have an expert like Pirow aboard. If it weren't for the radio dead spot there'd

have been no need to make this flight. We may find pretty
soon that we're close enough to get a D/F bearing on her.
Moreover, she probably does not know we have a helicopter. The *Thorshammer* left Tristan in too much of a hurry
to discuss things with Mikklesen even if he saw the
Westland aboard. In fact, we don't even know that the
Thorshammer anchored at the island."

"She'll still be using her radar—she'd be crazy if she
didn't," replied Helen.

"Very soon I'm going to ask you to take us right down to
sea level, and I'm going to try to get a D/F bearing on the
Thorshammer," I replied. "Radar will pick up nothing at
zero feet, as you well know, so we won't be detected. We're
almost at the area where I think we'll find her. She certainly won't be expecting us to come looking for her."

"Burce!" exclaimed Sailhardy. "A ship! Bearing green
three-oh!"

"Get her down!" I rapped out. "Get her down to sea
level quick!"

I saw nothing, and by the time I had tried to focus on the
spot Sailhardy indicated, the machine was dropping like a
lift.

"I saw nothing," said Helen.

I knew Sailhardy's eyesight. "How far was she, do you
reckon?"

"I could see forty miles on a day like this," he replied. "I
caught the flash."

"Steer thirty degrees," I told Helen. "I'm going to try to
get a bearing on her."

The sea came up to meet the helicopter. We skimmed
the wavetops. At that minimum height the huge swells were
no longer ironed out, as they had been a few minutes
before. Helen's eyes took on their colour, a pale turquoise,
flecked with deep ginger.

It was hopeless trying to locate the destroyer by radio.
Perhaps Pirow could have made some sense out of the
jumble which jarred my ears, but I could not even identify

the *Thorshammer*. After five minutes I gave it up and went up forward to the pilot's seat. Sailhardy was craning to see. I reckoned, however, that our height now was no more than that of an average crow's-nest, and, although the day was clear below the broken cloud, the horizon was hazy with the aftermath of the storm, which would cut even Sailhardy's keen eyesight to about ten miles.

"I think there must be some sort of solar disturbance interfering with the radar as well as the Bouvet dead spot," I said. "That means the *Thorshammer*'s radar is pretty useless anyway."

"We'll be up on her in less than half an hour is we keep this course," said Helen. "Providing it *was* the *Thorshammer* Sailhardy saw."

"It was a ship," asserted the islander.

"I simply must know her course," I said. "There's only one way, under these conditions, and that is to observe her."

"Ice right ahead," said Sailhardy.

Helen nodded agreement. "Sea clutter. Nothing very big. But some quite sizable growlers."

Even from our low altitude I could see the long lines of broken pack ice strung out in the wake of the storm, marching in orderly columns as the gale thrust them along.

"Look," I said. "That's how we'll observe the *Thorshammer*."

"What do you mean?" Sailhardy asked.

The simplicity of the idea made me laugh. "We'll creep along in the helicopter until we're reasonably close," I replied. "Then we'll land on one of those big growlers—on the side away from the *Thorshammer*. We can sit and watch her pass."

Helen bit her lip. "It won't work, Captain Wetherby. As close as that, she can't fail to pick us up by radar."

I shook my head. "It doesn't need Pirow to tell me that even under favourable conditions it is very difficult to get a radar echo from an iceberg, particularly if it's weathered

smooth like these. The iceberg itself won't even show on
the screen, let alone us."

She looked at me, and I was astonished to see the
anguish in her eyes. "No. I'm sure the *Thorshammer*—"

Sailhardy looked surprised at her reaction. "It's nothing
to land on ice, ma'am, and after the way you rescued us—"

She turned so abruptly to the controls that for a moment
I thought the machine would hit the top of the next
swell. She was breathing quickly. "I'll land anywhere,
but—but—"

I could not understand her fear. Putting the helicopter
down on a stable platform like a small iceberg offered no
problems for a flier of her proved competence. I dismissed
the idea that somehow her reluctance might tie in with my
suspicions about her father. How privy was she to
whatever his schemes were? She had said nothing which
would have revealed that she knew anything either of
Pirow's background.

"If you're afraid—" I started.

The strange eyes were alive with inner pain. "I'm not
afraid of landing." She pulled herself together, but I could
see the perspiration along the line of the leather helmet.
She swallowed hard. "Which growler?"

I glanced at Sailhardy. He shrugged at her agitation.
"No yet, eh, Bruce?"

"Ten minutes more?" I asked him, and he nodded.

Helen pulled herself upright in her seat. She neither
spoke nor looked at us. Her face was drawn and white. She
was so tense that I wondered if I should not call the whole
thing off. Could she make a landing in the state of nerves in
which she obviously was? The stakes were too big to turn
back now.

The sea clutter thickened as we flew on. I admired
Helen's skill as she dodged between the growlers, keeping
the machine just above the waves. Some of the bigger
pieces of ice towered twenty or thirty feet above us as we
passed. I saw the one I wanted. It was tabular, but there

was a small plateau sloping slightly towards us, while the top was as straight as a ruler. The helicopter could land on the shelf, and Sailhardy and myself would plot the destroyer's course from the summit.

I pointed. "There!"

Helen flew straight on, almost as if she had not heard. We swept along towards the ice now looming close. The plateau was steeper than I had anticipated. The perspiration splashed from her forehead on to her leather flying jacket. She pulled the controls. We rose slightly and checked. Then, like a fly clinging to a wall, we hung on the little plateau.

"Magnificent!" I said.

Her face was alive with terror. Her eyes were riveted on the ice. Her hands were shaking almost out of control as she cut the throttles. The engine died.

"Ma'am!" exclaimed Sailhardy. "What is it, ma'am?"

I sensed, rather than felt, a new danger. The helicopter started to slide backwards towards the sea about twenty feet below. Helen sat transfixed.

"Get the engine going!" I shouted. She just sat, staring, I swung round to Sailhardy. "Quick! You grab one wheel, and I'll get the other. The two of us can hold her!"

We threw ourselves out of the cockpit and grabbed the undercarriage. The machine was lighter than I thought. Heels rammed against the ice, Sailhardy and I kept the machine on the plateau.

"Miss Upton!" I shouted. "For God's sake!"

"What the hell is she up to?" asked Sailhardy.

"She's scared stiff," I said. "At what, I wouldn't know. Can you hold this machine by yourself?"

I eased my grip tentaively, but the helicopter started to slew round. It would need both of us to keep it where it was.

"Miss Upton!" I yelled, propping the strut against my shoulder and half kneeling, half crouching, to see past the cabin door, swinging in the wind.

"Try using her Christian name," said Sailhardy, breathing heavily. "It may make her snap out of it."

"Helen!" I called. "Helen!"

I had forgotten for the moment that she could not get out of her seat quickly. In perhaps three minutes she appeared at the doorway. She looked round her like a sleepwalker. She scarcely seemed to notice us. Her eyes, full of agony, had taken on the green-blue hue of the ice.

"Helen!" I said sharply. "Pull yourself together! There's no danger."

She looked at me without speaking.

"Pull yourself together!" I repeated. "Sailhardy and I can hold the machine here quite easily. Get my glasses and go up to the summit. Take a compass and give me four or five bearings. The *Thorshammer* must be pretty close."

She went inside like an automaton and returned with my glasses dangling loosely from a strap at her wrist. She looked down at the ice. Her face was ghastly.

"Come on!" I said. "It's a bit cold, but there's nothing to worry about."

She stumbled awkwardly, hesitated, and threw herself down on the ice. She landed on her knees. She sagged forward and lay face downwards, convulsive sobs shaking her. She slid slowly towards me. I caught her against the wheel.

"Helen, what on earth—"

She lay with her head resting on the ice. "It isn't on earth, that's the whole trouble," she said brokenly. "You made me land on ice—on ice, do you hear!"

"Ice? What has ice got to do with it?"

She still did not lift her head. "I've got a bullet—a German bullet—in my hip. I told you."

"You said bullet," I replied. "But what a German bullet has to do with your crack-up when you see ice I wouldn't know."

"For three days I lay in a ditch with ice and snow, with a German bullet in my hip," she got out. "He died, but I lived. I wish to God I had too!"

"Listen," I said. "You're completely broken up, and it's

something to do with ice and a German bullet. It will keep. Meanwhile, get up there to the summit and get a couple of bearings!"

She sat up. She looked in turn at Sailhardy and me. "Everything in your world is straightforward, uncomplicated. If neither of you understands, I still have got to say it. Even my father doesn't know about the bullet—and never will. To him I am the brilliant flier, to be depended on under any circumstances. He didn't hesitate to send me off in the storm to find you. He knew I would find you. I did. I—"

"What is it about the ice?" I asked gently. Despite its agony, the face was, in its own way, without any make-up, rather beautiful. There was a touch of colour under the right cheekbone where it had rested on the ice.

"When the Germans invaded Norway my brother and I were there with my father. He was busy on his experiments with metals—the time when his face was affected," she said, getting a grip on her voice. "We set off in two parties. My brother and I were in one, and my father in the other, with some Norwegians who were taking us to Trondheim. The British ships were still there. Our party was intercepted by a Nazi ski patrol. It was getting dark. I remember racing down a long slope, the two of us. There was a burst of fire from an automatic pistol. We were both hit, I in the hip and he in the chest. It took two days for him to die. We huddled together in a ditch in the ice and snow as the life ran out of him. I was conscious only now and then. Five days later I woke in a Norwegian house. There was gangrene in my hip. The doctor fought for weeks to save me. When I was well enough they smuggled me out to England. The day before I arrived my mother was killed in an air raid."

A nerve twitched in her face. She sat up and looked at me. "I am terrified of the ice."

"Then what are you doing in the Antarctic? There is no need—"

She cut me short. "There is every need. Why do you

think I fly a helicopter in these surroundings when I could lead a pleasant, easy life in London? My father's schemes give me the outlet—the outlet I need to challenge the ice. It is something innate, physical as well as in my mind. I must master the ice. I am the only woman pilot in Antarctica. I've flown over ice, hovered over it, gradually got closer and closer, and each time it was a living hell, but a conquest. I was winning out—until now. I wasn't ready. I've never had the courage to land on it."

The incline of the ice shelf brought her against me.

With my free hand I picked up the binoculars and handed them to her. "Here's another chapter of that challenge."

For a moment I thought she would draw back. Then she rose on her haunches. "It did not escape me, the way you looked at my hands." She smiled faintly. "Other things have been in abeyance, you see, while I fought it out with my jailer." She looked about her, as if seeing things for the first time. "No wonder my father finds it easy to include me in his schemes!"

I nodded at the glasses. "Those could be the key to the door."

She tried to rise but could not. Then she leaned hard on my shoulder and got to her feet.

"Special glasses, aren't they, Bruce, for seeing in darkness?"

She started away from us, but Sailhardy called her back. "The compass, ma'am. You don't want to have to come back to fetch it. It will be tough enough going once to the top."

She stood looking down at us, braced against the ice in order to hold the machine.

"Thank you, Bruce, and thank you, Sailhardy," she said slowly. "There are more things than ice in the Southern Ocean."

Slowly, painfully, with a physical and mental torment we could only guess, she clawed her way to the summit of the growler. When her voice came back to give us the first bearing it was as colourless as plainsong. "*Thorshammer* bearing eight-oh degrees, eight miles."

At five minute intervals she gave us a fresh bearing. In half an hour she came back to the machine. He face was white, but for the first time since I had known her, the eyes were vital.

"I'll start the engine, and you can come aboard," she said. She laughed softly. "What a pilot! I'm glad you are the only witnesses."

She revved the engine, the rotors swung, and we climbed aboard while she held the machine gently against the little plateau. We gave the *Thorshammer* another clear quarter of an hour before threading our way back through the growlers at zero feet towards the fleet. Once we were certain that we were beyond range of her radio we picked up our altitude. Although Helen flew in silence the tension was gone, and several times she leaned forwards, and stroked Suzie Wong, still clinging to the compass platform, and said something which I could not distinguish above the roar of the rotors.

It was Sailhardy who spotted the catcher fleet first. As we pulled round in a wide approach circle to the factory ship he tensed and pointed. "Bruce! The *Aurora*! Look! Just aft the bridge!"

Twin muzzles pointed skywards.

"Walter was on the Russian convoys," he said.

I nodded grimly. "No wonder he survived. I'm going to have a closer look at what Mr. Bloody Walter has rigged up there. Can do?" I asked Helen.

She nodded. She brought the helicopter to hover twenty feet above the barrels of the anti-aircraft gun. It was the most sinister piece of improvised ack-ack armament I have ever seen. A heavy, slow-firing, water-cooled Spandau was mounted side by side with an air-cooled, rapid-firing Hotchkiss. From the base plate to the height of a man's chest was a heavy swivel mounting: screwed into it on a

hexagonal plate fore and aft were two narwhal tusks, forming a bow of about three feet in height at head level. The
two weapons swung on a cross-bar about an inch and a half
thick. Drums and belts of ammunition were already in
place. There was also a double harness, like a car safety
belt, for each gun. It was a killer weapon for use by two
men. The helmsman waved cheerfully, but there was no
sign of Walter.

Sailhardy and I looked at each other. There was no need
to say it. The Spandau-Hotchkiss confirmed everything
about Upton. And the chart was the key.

As if reading my thoughts, Sailhardy drew back out of
Helen's line of vision. He put his hand into his windbreaker
where he had concealed the chart and looked inquiringly at
me. I nodded. Upton must not find it on either of us if he
got tough. Sailhardy looked round tentatively. Behind
Helen's seat the interior quilting was loose from the skin of
the machine. It was the best we could do. There were only
a few minutes before we would be down. Sailhardy edged
behind me and tucked the folded square of parchment
behind the quilting.

We landed. Sailhardy and I went to my cabin. I was
scarcely surprised when I opened the door to find Upton,
Pirow, and Walter. The place had been ransacked. Walter
held a Luger in his hand.

The Luger was, I felt sure, Pirow's, although it was Walter who pointed it at my chest. Pirow was on his knees at my chart case. Upton's eyes were bright and hard, as if he had been on the guarana.

I talked quickly to distract Walter, so that Sailhardy could jump him. "So Norris sounded the Bollevika anchorage?" I sneered. "Breeding ground of the blue whale—bah! A blue whale's dorsal fin!"

I sensed when Sailhardy started to move. I threw myself sideways at Walter. The crash of the shot deafened me. I struck him a wicked blow in the kidneys. He gasped, but he was strong and cunning. He dodged to prevent my crowding him and fired again as Sailhardy grabbed at his hand. The bullet screamed off the steel wall. Walter ducked, picked up the heavy lead sinker I had used for my plankton net, and swung it with a sickening thump against the islander's chest. Sailhardy collapsed. While the big Norwegian turned to come at me with a running crouch, Luger in one hand and sinker in the other, I struck him with all my force under the right ear with my forearm. I heard the gun clatter, but at the same time my feet were whipped from under me. Pirow—the bastard! I thought. As I fell, Walter caught me a glancing blow across the left side of my face with the sinker. I lay on the floor, sick with the pain. Pirow grabbed the gun. I saw Walter's seaboot come up to

113

kick me unconscious, but I had no strength to roll clear.

Upton stopped him.

"Steady, Walter," he ordered. "We need him."

"I do not care for this British captain who fights foul like a South Georgia whalerman, nor for his bloody islander," he said thickly, rubbing his neck. "Let me finish both of them. We'll find the chart on one of them, for sure."

"Shut your bloody mouth!" snarled Upton.

"He seems to know anyway," said Pirow.

"Get up, Wetherby," snapped Upton. It was the first time he had not used my Christian name. "Go over him, Walter. And if he hasn't got it, then the islander."

Walter's paws tore at my clothes, while Pirow covered me with the Luger. When he had finished searching me, Walter turned the unconscious Sailhardy over roughly and searched him.

"It's not on them," he said. "It's here somewhere. It must be."

Upton grasped the lapels of my reefer jacket. There was a curious air of exhilaration and menace about him. Although the name had never been mentioned between us in relation to the chart, we both knew tacitly what the other had in mind. "Where is Captain Norris's chart? Where is it, man?"

I jerked my head at the chart case. "In there."

"It is not. I've been through everything," said Pirow. "He's lying."

"Of course he's lying," snapped Upton. "I would too, if I had anything as priceless as Captain Norris's original log and chart of Thompson Island."

"Thompson Island!" I exclaimed. "There you have it! Thompson Island!"

The formidable pink flush suffused the pewter. I was weak from Walter's blow, but even so I was surprised at Upton's outburst of near-maniacal strength. He shook me like a cat mauling a rat.

"Yes, blast all the Wetherbys and their secretive Captain

Norris!" he snarled. "Eight words for everything in my life—the log and track chart of the *Sprightly*! Norris, rot his soul! He faked up—or your precious John Wetherby faked up—a duplicate for the Admiralty's benefit. It's useless, as everybody knows. What I want is Norris's original. You've got it, and, by God, I mean to have it. At any price whatsoever, do you understand? Any price whatsoever!"

My mind raced to the chart. I knew every minute detail of it. There was nothing of any value to a man like Upton. He must have some other knowledge about Thompson Island, apart from the chart, but to which the chart was nevertheless complementary. I had to find out what it was.

"I'll take this ship apart rivet by rivet to find the chart," Upton went on savagely. I believed him. He rounded on me. "Will you take me to Thompson Island?"

I evaded a direct answer. "How should I know where Thompson is?"

"You've got Norris's chart, and that shows the true position of Thompson Island."

I saw the fallacy of what Upton was saying. What I—and I only—knew, was that Captain Norris's chart was priceless—up to a point. Beyond that point the centuries-old secret of the lost island was one man's only—mine. Kohler must have known too; Pirow obviously did not.

"Will you take me to Thompson, according to the chart?" Upton rasped. Even Walter stood back at Upton's anger.

"No."

"No?" he replied. "We'll see. Walter! The islander. You know what to do."

Walter's seaboot crunched into Sailhardy's face. Pirow stood grinning. Walter raised his boot to kick again. Norris's chart—without me—wasn't worth risking Sailhardy's life. It was obvious that Upton considered Sailhardy expendable.

"Stop!" I shouted. "Stop!"

"Where is it?" demanded Upton.

"Walter," I said softly, "never let me find you alone, particularly if I have a flensing knife in my hand. Remember that!"

The big skipper looked uneasy, but Upton seemed beside himself. I thought I still might find out what he knew that I did not about Thompson Island.

"I'll take you to where the chart says, providing you tell me what you are looking for on Thompson Island," I said. "We could make a deal." I knew in advance what his share would be from a bargain like that—square miles of open sea. He'd receive the same share if he trusted to the chart by himself, without me. I thought wryly to myself that I was somewhat in the same position as old John Wetherby after Norris's original discovery had started the world talking, except that in my case it was my life and Sailhardy's which were at stake. John Wetherby had faked a chart when the Admiralty had insisted; he had kept back his superior knowledge by virtue of Norris's original. Now in my mind—it was not written down—was the knowledge which superseded the information of the Norris chart. I could afford to let Upton have the original chart. He had obviously seen through the fake at the Admiralty.

"No deal," snapped Upton. "On lesser matters, maybe, but not on this. Think quickly! Walter has an educated boot, and what is one bloody Tristan islander more or less?"

I played for time. "Or one Bruce Wetherby more or less?"

Upton gave a brittle laugh. "In principle, yes. In practice, it is harder to get rid of a Royal Society man than an unknown islander."

Walter grinned. "All sorts of accidents happen on factory ships, with all the machinery and knives—strange things." He glanced at Sailhardy's battered face. "Who would know whether it was a boot or a falling tackle block which smashed in his face?"

"If it's a question of disposing of one body or two—" I began.

"Shut up!" Upton snarled. "Don't talk round it. It's the chart or—" He gestured at the unconscious form on the floor.

"It's in the helicopter cabin," I said. "It's tucked away behind the quilting near the pilot's seat."

"God help you if you're lying," he said. "Walter, get up to the machine—quick! Bring it here!"

Upton and Pirow both drew back to the doorway as Walter left. Pirow kept the Luger trained on me. I felt like a battered bull whale after a deep-sea duel.

"So the whole business of the blue whale was a bluff?" I asked slowly.

Upton had regained some of his composure. "Not entirely. Not entirely."

"Then why the hell drag along four catchers—you wanted five—to look for Thompson Island? It's beyond me."

What quality of doom did Thompson hold? John Wetherby had died mouthing the name; Norris and his famous *Sprightly* had gone to their deaths in the wastes round Thompson on their return voyage, following the first discovery—when and where, no one knew; Joseph Fuller, Sailhardy's American captain, had been drowned at his Stonington lighthouse; Francis Allen had been lost in the ice with the ship bearing his name. Now Thompson was driving to madness and murder a whaling tycoon.

"The blue whale story was ideal cover," he explained. "I had to have a string of ships—you remember Nelson's frigates before Trafalgar? The catchers were to serve the same purpose in scouring the waters round Bouvet for Thompson. They were to be my eyes. That was before I knew you had the chart."

"If Nelson had had a helicopter he would not have needed a string of frigates," I replied.

He grinned. "Touché. But I have read Kohler's weather

study of the Bouvet area. If it's not blowing a bloody gale, it's fog; and if it's not fog, it's total cloud; and if it's not total cloud, it's an impossible sea. An American Coastguard cutter flew a helicopter near Bouvet a couple of years ago. They damn near lost it after only half an hour in the air. I don't have to tell you about Bouvet's weather."

"If you didn't know I had Norris's chart, why bring me into it?"

"Not even I could wheedle out of the Admiralty your secret report on the sinking of the *Meteor*," he said. "I know, however, that you sighted land as you went into action. Once I knew you had the chart, that naturally became redundant. The two things are the same."

I looked away in order not to betray my reaction. Let him go on thinking they were the same! He'd never find Thompson Island his way. If he went on regarding Sailhardy and me as expendable, my knowledge might well buy our lives.

The door burst open. Walter and Helen tried to push through simultaneously. Walter held the folded chart triumphantly. His right hand was smeared with blood.

Helen gave a gasp as she saw Sailhardy on the floor. She looked in disbelief at Pirow and the gun and at me. Her face was flushed with anger.

"Daddy, what on earth—?" She indicated Walter, speaking rapidly. "What right has this lout to break into my cabin and tear down the fittings like a madman? It is my machine, and what I say goes. He grabbed the quilting and tore it to pieces. Bruce, Bruce! He killed Suzie Wong!"

"You bastard, Walter!" I said.

"Who the hell is Suzie Wong?" demanded Upton.

"My good-luck bird—this oaf killed her!" She repeated, "What right has he—"

"I wring the bloody thing's neck," said Walter. "It is unimportant. It flies at me when I look for the chart."

Upton did not seem to hear her. He stood mesmerized by the parchment Walter held in his hand. "Get out!" he told her roughly. "Get out! One miserable bird does not matter. Nor would a life—for this!" He took the chart from Walter. "Get out!" he said. "If you want to cool off and mourn your bloody bird, go and fly your precious helicopter in circles."

Helen stood back, stunned by his outburst. His megalomania sickened me. She backed to the door. "Yes, that is just what I will do," she said in quiet anger. "I don't know what you all are up to, but remember I have seen this little scene, even if no one else of the crew has."

She shut the door, but I do not think Upton even noticed. In less than a minute I heard the machine take off. Upton unfolded the chart. Then he stabbed his finger again and again at a little circle from which the wandering line of the *Sprightly*'s track radiated. "Thompson Island! Thompson Island!"

He turned on me. The fury was gone, and the eyes seemed even brighter. He could not control his hands. He pointed at the corner of the parchment, where there was a marginal note: November-December 1825. The log and track of the *Sprightly*!

"Thompson Island!" he whispered.

Pirow edged round, keeping the automatic trained on me. "There's Bouvet too. There are Norris's soundings of the Bollevika anchorage."

Upton could scarcely get the words out as he fumbled to decipher Norris's writing. "December the thirteenth, 1825, Log of the *Sprightly*:

"2 p.m. saw a small low Island bears W 6 miles
"3 rocks in a cluster bears NW.
"another rock NW nearly level with the water's edge.
"This island is in Latd 53.56 Long 5°30. this
"island we have named Thompson's Id bears NNE 15
"leagues from Bouvet Island. The three rocks we
"named The Chimnies SE 4 or 5 miles off Thompson's
"Id and another small rock 3 miles south of them."

Upton was silent for a long time. "So that is where Thompson Island is!" he exclaimed at last. "Fifteen leagues, or forty-five miles, north-northeast of Bouvet!"

For the next half hour Upton relapsed into long abstracted silences, as if he had forgotten the presence of the three of us altogether, broken now and again by a volley of words. It was then that I first seriously doubted the man's sanity. The only sounds were Sailhardy's unconscious moans. We dared not break in upon his silences.

Once he turned the parchment over and over. "God! Imagine that little ship *Sprightly* of Norris's at two o'clock in the afternoon coming out of the fog and being confronted with the island! Now it is mine!" He fell into a long silence, as if he were reliving Norris's great discovery.

Then he came over to me, eyes gleaming, and grabbed me by the shoulder, completely carried away by what was going on in his mind. "Tell me, man, does it look the way Norris says—small and low? How could it ever be confused with Bouvet, which is all cliffs and peaks? Did you see it like that? Tell me!"

"I saw it like that," I said. "I saw Thompson Island."

He looked thoughtfully at me. "The only man living," he said.

I remembered the ice, the dirty grey sky, the shroud of fog. Upton's next words added to my doubts about his mind.

His finger traced with almost reverential care the old sealer's track past Thompson Island and its rocky outcrops. "Heavenly blue," he said. "Heavenly blue."

The Tannoy loudspeaker above my bunk came alive with its disembodied crackle. "Bridge here! Bridge here! Sir Frederick Upton! Stand by for a repeat from radio office of an urgent message." Upton had been thorough. He'd told the bridge he would be in my cabin before leaving so that he would not be out of touch while he searched my things.

Something inside me cleared like a lift of fog when I

heard Helen's voice, for it told me she had had no part in her father's scheme for Thompson Island. She came over the loudspeaker clearly, which meant she must have been fairly close to the fleet, in view of the radio interference at any distance.

"H for Helen! Do you hear me? H for Helen! Helicopter NRWH calling factory ship Antarctica."

Upton wheeled on Pirow. "Get up to the radio office— jam her, swamp her, do any damn thing, but get her off the air— quick!"

I felt, somehow, that the formal overtones in her voice were for me—the way she might think Royal Navay formality ran under stress. But her excitement overrode everything. *"H for Helen! Position approx fifty-six degrees south, one degree west."*

Pirow stopped in his tracks, white-faced. "Plain language transmission! The *Thorshammer* can't miss it!"

"Dear God in heaven!" shouted Upton. "Stop her, Carl! Perhaps the radio interference is too bad for the *Thorshammer* to hear."

"No," snapped Pirow. "Never. Some temporary sunspot fade, but nothing like as bad as I made out to the Herr Kapitän to get him off the ship."

"Bouvet's a dead spot—" began Upton.

"Dead spot for equipment thirty years ago, but not now," Pirow replied.

Helen's voice cut in. *"I can't see the end of them! There are thousands and thousands of them! There are blue whales everywhere! I have found the breeding ground of the blue whale! Big, small, bulls, cows, calves! I've never seen anything like it!"*

"Blast the girl!" roared Upton. "Blast! Blast! Blast! Just at this moment of moments! Everyone between here and South Georgia must have heard our position!"

Pirow stood as if undecided, the Luger in his hand. Helen's bombshell had put them off their guard, but I missed my opportunity.

"Give me that gun!" went on Upton. "Get to your radio! Do something!" Pirow hurried off; Upton and Walter remained behind. "They'll be safe enough if we lock them in here for the moment," said Upton. "How long will it be before that bloody islander comes round?"

"An hour, maybe two." Walter shrugged. "What does it matter anyway?"

"Yes," echoed Upton, "what does it matter anyway? It's Wetherby who is the problem." He smiled without humour. "I thought I was up against something in the great Captain Wetherby of wartime fame. I didn't even get a run for my money. One kick in the face of his friend, and the whole show was over. Come, Walter!"

The door crashed to and I heard the lock turn. I knelt down and tried to do something about Sailhardy's face. It was a savage wound, and he would carry the scars to the end of his life. The way Upton talked, he did not intend either Sailhardy's life or mine to reach its natural span. I looked round the cabin: escape seemed hopeless. My cabin was situated at the end of the corridor. Beyond the solid steel bulkhead were the big compartments for processing the whales. The porthole was there, but, short of jumping into the sea, it offered no escape for me.

My own danger was not uppermost in my mind. I was thinking of Helen, and I hated Upton for his part in moulding her, fashioning her whole existence, to be the instrument of his dream, Thompson Island. It was typical of the man that he had not confided his secret to her; but the shock of her own escape long ago in Norway, the lack of a mother, had influenced her—not unwillingly, I told myself, but that was her part of the story, unknown to him—to be the brilliant but soulless automaton I had first met. I could not get out of my mind the transformation I had witnessed on the ice, and the vital, attractive personality I had seen as she had stood in this very cabin doorway.

Sailhardy stirred but did not regain consciousness. I tore off part of my sleeve and improvised a bandage. I waited.

After about half an hour I heard the roar of the helicopter's rotors overhead as Helen came in to land. In less than five minutes there was a knock at the cabin door. I did not reply.

"Bruce!" Helen called. "Bruce! Are you all right?"

"Yes," I called. "Helen! For God's sake, get me a gun or a knife and let me out of here!"

"My father seems beside himself," she called softly. "I gave him the slip for a moment." I heard the sound of her footsteps running back along the corridor.

I nearly jumped out of my skin as the Tannoy spoke. *"AXM. Canberral International Antarctic Weather Analysis Centre. WMO code Fm four-five on the OO GMT analysis . . ."*

I looked at the grilled space above the bulkhead in astonishment. Upton and Pirow must have forgotten to switch off the repeater from the radio shack.

Then I heard Upton's voice. "Nothing but bloody weather reports! That's all there ever is from the Antarctic!"

Pirow's voice, intent, came through. "I told you, let a ship send eleven letters, and I'll find her. The *Thorshammer* is silent."

"It does not surprise me," I heard Walter say. "Christ! After all we've done to keep our position dark."

Upton was rattled. His voice was harsh with anxiety. "Try and get the *Thorshammer*, Carl! Change frequency! Do any damn thing!"

"The Herr Kapitän Wetherby should be here," came Pirow's cool voice. "We'll try eighteen and twenty-four metres—raider's frequency."

There was a pause, then Upton's voice:. "What is it, Carl? Have you got her?"

"The *Thorshammer*," replied Pirow. "She's flown off her seaplane!"

I heard the crash of a telephone receiver being picked up. "Bjerko!" snapped Upton. "Alter course! Turn away, south and west! Full speed ahead!"

I felt the pulse of the factory ship start to quicken under the cabin floor.

"That won't help at all," said Pirow. "The seaplane will be using radar anyway. The *Thorshammer* took a hell of a risk flying it off in this sea."

"It just shows how important she considers us," said Walter. "There's nothing we can do now to avoid being caught."

"Don't throw in the bloody towel before you're even hit," said Upton curtly. "I'm not beaten by a long chalk. By all that's holy!" I heard him say slowly. "Wetherby has been of more use than he thinks. We'll keep our previous course. We'll hide away in the heart of his so-called atmospheric machine. If it's anything like he says, there'll be so much fog and ice that the *Thorshammer* will never find us. And in that weather she won't be able to use her seaplane."

My heart sank as I heard him pick up the telephone and order Bjerko to return to our former course. The ship had scarcely had time to settle on the south and west course. We were now racing towards our doom as fast as the screws could turn. By the vibration I could tell that the *Antarctica*'s engines were being pushed to the limit. In my mind's eye I saw that deceptively calm sea, damped by the ice as the crystals formed, and thickening to a viscous, porridge-like consistency; the loss of speed as a ship fought against the massive drag of the sea starting to freeze; the great bank of fog which was the invariable accompaniment of the freeze-up; and, finally, the rapid coagulation of water into jaws of ice which would clamp like a vice round the ship and crush her to death.

"Anything from the seaplane?" asked Upton.

"Yes," said Pirow grimly, "steering straight here. It can't miss. It'll be overhead in less than a couple of hours."

"Walter," came Upton's voice, "when do you think, at our present speed, we will be in Wetherby's danger area?"

"Maybe twelve hours—this time tomorrow," he replied.

"We could avoid the *Thorshammer*'s intercepting us herself today, and during darkness tonight we could dodge her," went on Upton. "By early tomorrow the weather will probably start to become pretty bad. With the *Thorshammer* minus the seaplane, we have a sporting chance."

"Minus the seaplane," echoed Pirow.

Upton's voice was brittle when he spoke after a pause, even allowing for the quality of the loudspeaker. "Your Spandau-Hotchkiss is a very fine weapon, Walter."

Pirow's voice held a thrill, whether of dismay or astonishment I could not tell. "You'll get Walter to shoot down a plane—a naval plane—in cold blood in peacetime?"

"No, not Walter." I could tell by the way Upton said it that he had just thought this up, and the novelty of the idea appealed to him. "Captain Wetherby will do the shooting."

I went closer to the loudspeaker grill to make sure I was not dreaming. It was a closed circuit affair between the cabin and the radio office, but the voices were as close as if they had been talking next door and I were listening through an open ventilator. The diabolic ingenuity of Upton's mind revealed itself as he went on.

"We now have the chart, and both Wetherby and the islander are only in the way," he said. "Sailhardy is easy to dispose of. Walter will rough him up a bit more, and he'll be found tomorrow morning, or the morning after, lying under one of the big tackles aft. Poor fellow, they'll say, the tackle came adrift in the gale and its whole two tons fell on him."

Walter interjected. "Someone else will have to do the job, especially since it will be at night. I can't shuffle backwards and forwards from the *Aurora* in a small boat with a tiny engine in these seas. It was bad enough today. If the weather becomes anything like Wetherby says, it will be impossible."

"It is not vital," said Upton. "I'll smash him up myself."

I wondered wryly if Pirow was thinking of the *Meteor*'s end when he spoke. "The Herr Kapitän Wetherby is the one to be afraid of. I want to see you force him to shoot down that plane."

"So do I," said Walter.

The voices receded, and I jumped up and jammed my ear against the loudspeaker. I heard only a word here and there: "Luger . . . take him across to the *Aurora* . . . clear them out of the way, of course, they're your crew, Walter . . . lash his wrists, one each side of the trigger . . ." Their voices sank into an incomprehensible mutter.

So I was to be tied to the Spandau-Hotchkiss and be made to take the blame for shooting down the seaplane. How? Then I saw: Since it was a double weapon, Walter would take one harness and I would be lashed into the other—it must have been the crew Upton had been referring to in clearing them out of the way. In the sort of seas we were encountering, the only members of the crew who would be about would be those strictly on duty, a handful of men who could easily be ordered out of the way. The gun itself was situated aft the wheelhouse, and the helmsman would not be able to see what was going on without leaving his post. I guessed Walter would come to take me across to the *Aurora*. He'd stick the Luger in his pocket and be at my back . . .

The voices became stronger. I could pick up Upton's words, faint at first and then stronger. ". . . other harness. Wetherby will be helpless. Shoot the bloody thing down and don't fluff it, do you hear, Walter?"

There was a surly mutter and then Pirow's voice was clear. "It is clever, Sir Frederick. So Wetherby takes all the blame if *Thorshammer* should catch us?"

I lost the end of Upton's sentence, but the beginning sent me cold. "The blame . . . and the bullet . . . through the head with the Luger . . . cut him loose . . ."

I could see it in my mind's eye: a burst from the

Spandau-Hotchkiss by Walter which would send the seaplane into the sea; a bullet for me and then a fake rescue attempt, Walter shouting to the helmsman to alter course to the crashed plane, knowing full well that the cold water would kill them in three minutes; and then Walter explaining how he had been obliged to shoot me to stop my madness with the gun. The pieces fitted together with diabolical cunning.

The voices became so faint I had to strain to hear. Then came a mirthless chuckle. "If you miss the seaplane, Walter, I'll come after you with a Luger myself."

I looked at the unconscious man on the floor. Sailhardy and I had been in some tight spots during the war, but this looked tougher than any of them: I could see only one way to save our lives, and that was to tell Upton the real secret of Thompson Island. The bargain would be purely one-sided, for Upton would certainly never tell me now what he was really after on Thompson Island. It would be a plain barter for our lives, with Upton raking in all the winnings.

The Tannoy repeated the crunch of footsteps, the slam of the radio office door. It remained alive but silent, except for the occasional splutter of Morse. Pirow must have been left alone on watch. An hour dragged by, and then another half. Sailhardy moaned and stirred from time to time but did not come round. A kick like Walter's would have killed anyone less tough than the islander. My only ally outside the cabin seemed to be Helen. Would she, though, having been so long under her father's sway, assist me, even if she wanted to? I strained every sense to hear her footsteps outside, but everything remained silent.

Another five minutes dragged by. The Tannoy broke into life. I heard a door open and almost simultaneously Upton's voice. "Yes, Carl, yes?"

I could not help admiring the brilliant, dispassionate professionalism of the Man with the Immaculate Hand. "Seaplane reporting ship contacts to the *Thorshammer*.

Five ship contacts on her radar."

"She's picked up the fleet," said Upton. "She's picked us up!"

Pirow's voice was impersonal. "No sighting reports, only radar contacts." He spoke slowly, an indication that he was reading back the seaplane's signals to the destroyer as it came in towards our fleet. *"Radar contact five ships two-zero-zero degrees. Surface wind forty-four knots."* There was a pause. Then he resumed. *"Preparing to orbit fleet as soon as I make visual sighting. Will run in and turn on target. Roger."* A tinge of irony crept into Pirow's voice. *"Thorshammer replies Roger. Signal fleet's position and course."*

I tensed as I heard Upton's words. "Walter," he said. "Fetch Wetherby and get over to the *Aurora.* You know what to do. You're sure you will be okay in the boat by yourself?"

"I'm okay," I heard Walter grunt. "Have someone start the engine while I collect Wetherby. I have one hand on the tiller and the other on the Luger, heh?"

"Good man," replied Upton.

I heard the heavy clump of Walter's seaboots as he left the radio office to come down to my cabin. The weakest link in Upton's plan for my disposal seemed to be the time I would be alone in the boat with Walter crossing to the *Aurora.* He would be fully on the alert, but he would not know I had overheard them. I told myself I must get out of the cabin as quickly as I could before Walter realized the Tannoy was switched on. I prayed that neither Upton nor Pirow would speak while Walter was in the cabin.

The door swung open. The Luger looked like a plaything in his massive fist. "Come!" he said. "I want no tricks from you, you Royal Navy bastard."

He started to move towards Sailhardy, but he backed as I walked quickly to the entrance. "You swine," I replied. "I think you've killed him."

"Good," he replied. "Then there is no need to look

closer." He shut the door. The Tannoy had kept silent.

I walked away from the cabin door and then stopped in the long corridor. I faced Walter.

"Up on deck," he snarled. "No tricks! I am an excitable man with a gun. We go to my ship now."

"Not until I have spoken to Sir Frederick Upton," I said.

"No!" he retorted.

I leaned against the steel wall. I knew their plan. They could not dispose of me down here. "If you're so keen to get me to your ship, hammer me unconscious like Sailhardy," I sneered. "Go ahead."

Walter looked nonplussed. "If it was me, I would shoot you here," he blustered. "Why must you see Sir Frederick?"

"Go and jump over the side," I said. "Either I see Sir Frederick or I stay here."

"Okay," he conceded after a pause. "We go to the companionway there, where there is a telephone. No speaking on deck. You can tell Sir Frederick what you want to say."

There was an emergency telephone by the companionway leading up to the main deck. I rang the bridge and asked for Sir Frederick Upton. His voice came back, vibrant, full of good humour. I cut short his bonhomie. "Listen, Upton," I said. "I've been thinking over this Thompson Island business."

Upton's voice went cold. "No whining, Wetherby. You played—damn badly, I might say—and lost. The chart is mine. It stays so."

"That chart is not nearly so valuable as you seem to think. I assure you you won't find Thompson Island in the position given on the chart. The key is missing. I alone know where Thompson Island is. I'll take you there in exchange for an unconditional safe conduct back to Cape Town for Sailhardy and myself, unharmed, and with the run of the ship."

Upton laughed so loudly I had to keep the phone away from my ear. "It is really incredible," he said. "A cock-

and-bull story—the chart wrong, you the only person who knows where Thompson is situated. Balderdash!"

"I'll go further," I said. "Let us take the fleet to where the chart says Thompson is. If it is there, you can turn me over to the *Thorshammer* and I'll take the rap for all this business. If not, then—"

Upton gave his answer, characteristically. The receiver was slammed down the other end.

Walter gestured with the Luger. "Up on deck! Quick! There is not much time. We go to the Aurora."

I had no option. I walked ahead of him. On the deck he kept close behind me, the Luger hidden out of sight in his jacket pocket. Once I caught a sideways glimpse of the half-shaven face: I could see that Walter was all set for his killing orgy, for he was grinning slightly and the face was alive with a kind of sadistic joy. He would not need any excuse to kill me.

The *Aurora's* boat hung in the davits, engine running. Walter motioned me ahead mockingly. "After you, Captain Wetherby." Two stolid Norwegian sailors were at the boat falls. There was nothing to do but obey. I climbed aboard, and the two sailors dropped the boat skillfully into the sea. Walter threw in the gear with one hand, keeping the other on the concealed Luger. As we gathered way he held the tiller and the Luger as I had overheard him tell Upton he would. The tiny craft bucked in the swell. To throw myself at Walter would have meant upsetting the boat and drowning both of us. The *Aurora* had lost way, and I saw the measure of Walter's seamanship as he brought the tiny boat alongside the low bulwarks of the catcher.

"Jump, Captain!" Walter grinned. "Jump for your life! I'll be right behind you!"

I jumped as we swung level with the bulwarks and came down heavily on the deck. Walter had judged it to a nicety. He did not even wait for the next wave. He too jumped, rope in hand, while two of his crew secured the boat. Despite his bulk he was on his feet as agilely as a cat.

He grinned again and stripped off his jacket, thrusting the Luger into his trousers' pocket. In the thick black woollen sweater his chest seemed more massive than before. He shouted something in Norwegian to the two men on deck, who disappeared below.

"You are a fighting man, Captain," he said, leering. "Now you see my own special ack-ack gun in action, heh? You even sit in one of its harness." He laughed again. I said nothing. His face went heavy with anger. "All right, you Royal Navy bastard! Get up there ahead of me!"

As I started to go up the bridge ladder Walter snarled something to the first mate, who also went below. Above decks the only person visible was the helmsman, and the lookout was in the crow's nest. Walter bellowed at him too. I glanced upwards at the lookout. I saw a tiny flash of silver in the sky, far out to port. Walter saw it too.

Walter half thrust me up the last few rungs on the steel ladder leading from the bridge to the gun platform. At the top, out of the helmsman's sight, he pulled out the Luger. The brutal face was tense. "Into the Hotchkiss harness—quick! We haven't much time!" He grabbed me by the neck of my jacket with his left hand and savagely rammed the harness down over my head and shoulders. Once I was in its strait-jacket grip, he came round and deftly threw a loop of rope round the trigger guard, but not about the swivel bar, leaving my arms at half stretch to the trigger, with my face hard up against the sight.

Walter pushed the Luger loosely into his wristband and slipped quickly into the harness of the Spandau. He swung the double weapon round, taking me with it. I could see the seaplane passing over the outermost ship of the fleet, the *Crozet*, still fully five miles away from the factory ship. The Hotchkiss's long metal sight was at full extension above the cooling ribs in the middle of the weapon. Walter's right eye was screwed up against the rubber-mounted sight at the rear of the Spandau, and I could see the line of his teeth as he kept his left eye firmly closed. Our faces

were only nine inches apart. His breath was foul with stale
schnapps. His right hand was on the trigger beneath the
long curve of the narwhal tusks.

The seaplane started to make a long dive towards the
factory ship. It came into my sights. Although I was expecting it, the heavy, 400-round-a-minute burst of the
Spandau took my breath away. Cordite fumes blew back.
The two weapons were beautifully synchronized, and as
Walter swung the Spandau to keep his sights on the
seaplane, so mine were held steady on it too.

I saw my chance.

If I too joined in the firing, using my left hand to pull the
Hotchkiss's trigger, I could not help having my right-wrist
hard up against the spent cartridge ejectment outlet. The
Hotchkiss fires 1400 rounds a minute. Thought and action
came simultaneously. I pulled the trigger, pushing my right
wrist against the outlet. The searing blast of white-hot gas
snapped the rope. I yelled with pain as it scorched my
wrist. At the same moment I threw my full weight against
the harness to drag the double weapon down. A double
stream of tracer-lighted lead arched through the sky, wide
of the seaplane. I cut my fire, jamming my left knee against
the centre metal support of the gun to win control from
Walter. The tracers flew wide of the plane in a golden orbit. Using all his strength, Walter swung the double weapon
back round against my hold, sighting on the aircraft. The
heavy bullets from the Spandau tore into its flimsy
fuselage. The machine fluttered down towards the *Aurora,*
yawed wildly, passed almost between the big gantries of the
factory ship, and fell into the sea beyond. The splash
looked like the combined spout of a family of blue whales.

My hands were already at Walter's throat as he fought to
get clear of his harness. I kicked his feet from under him as
he fumbled. I was still held in the strait-jacket grip of the
Hotchkiss harness. Walter fell, rolled, dragged himself on
one elbow, pulling the Luger from his waistband. He raised
the automatic to fire.

I swivelled the twin interlocked muzzles to their maximum depression, fixed on Walter. Stark terror leaped into his face. I fired. The spray of bullets ripped into the deck plating, turning everything into a blinding hell of red-hot ricochets and noise.

Walter was too close. Even at maximum depression, the guns, although firing straight at him, could not reach down far enough. The stream of bullets was passing over him, missing him by about fifteen inches. Six feet behind him the deck was shredded, but Walter was unharmed. He launched himself forward under the swath of death, grabbed the silent Spandau by the chain which runs from its water-cooler backwards, and swung the double weapon backwards so that the barrels pointed wildly skywards. I hung, off my feet, above the gun platform, looking at the *Antarctica*.

The helicopter was rising from the flensing platform. I shouted insanely, impotently, at Helen. Walter raised the Luger and fired. Terror struck through me at what I saw below me.

It was the sea. It had turned to honey, I knew what that meant.

I gasped for breath. I was drowning in the bland, jelly-like stuff which I had seen below me from the *Aurora*'s gun platform. Wavering between consciousness and unconsciousness, I snatched a lungful of air. The honey jelly had tried to drown my ship once, my soggy mind said, and now it was trying to drown me. I gulped down some more air. Its life-giving oxygen cleared my brain momentarily.

I saw that the pale, mercuric oxide yellow light was not honey jelly. Nor was I in the sea, as I imagined in my semiconscious state. The colour of the light was reflected from the ceiling. And it was the ceiling of my cabin aboard the *Antarctica*. I fought again for air. I remembered hanging from the Hotchkiss harness, and beneath me in the sea there seemed to be a substance floating everywhere, like silky jelly. Below the *Aurora*'s rail the sea had been covered with it, some of the individual slabs up to two feet square. Simultaneously came the recollection of Walter firing the Luger into my face.

The agony of the recollection and of what the honey jelly meant broke my semi-consciousness. I jerked myself upright in my bunk. The cabin swam round me, and as I put my hand to my head I felt the bandages.

"Take it easy, Bruce," said Helen.

I had not seen her in the pale, diffused light. I wondered

135

how long I had lain unconscious. Hearing her speak brought a new surge of recollection: Walter had fired the Luger and almost simultaneously I had felt the gouge of pain in my head from the bullet. I remembered falling out of the harness into the sea, the honey-jelly sea; and then the roar of the helicopter's rotors overhead, and the unutterable relief of feeling the machine's "horse-collar" rescue gear snatch me from the icy sea. I had been in the water less than a minute. For the second time Helen had showed her superb skill in saving my life. All the rest was blank.

"Helen!" I got out. "How long have I been here? What time is it?"

"It is hours since I picked you out of the sea," she said. "It's late afternoon."

"Late afternoon!" I echoed. I knew there could be almost no hope of saving the *Antarctica* now.

My eyes slewed to the gyro-repeater. I tried to get out of my bunk, but Helen held me back with a restraining hand. My head seemed to split with pain. I scarcely recognized my own voice. "Helen! Get on to the voice-pipe! For God's sake, tell Bjerko to alter course. We're steering right into it! It's death, I tell you!"

She looked at me with her strange eyes, which were full of shadows in the pale light. "There are a lot of things I want to hear—from you and you alone, Bruce—before I start worrying about our course."

"I can wait, but the course can't," I said. "I told you about the danger of being nipped in the ice. The honey jelly in the sea is the outrider of the pack ice, and that yellow light outside means we're running into the second advance guard—fog."

She shook her head. "If that is so, it is too late anyway. You're wounded, and I want to know why. I saw you being held up at pistol point, and I want to know why. I saw you fall from Walter's ack-ack weapon into the sea. Minutes before, I watched that same weapon shoot down a defenceless seaplane. After I had picked you up I tried to find the seaplane or its crew, but it had already sunk. Why are you wounded?"

I realized that the heavy Luger bullet must have shattered off the casing of the Spandau and that the fragments had knocked me senseless. Walter had missed me—but only just. The bandage had stopped the blood, so the wound could not be deep. I hauled myself over the side of the bunk and called the bridge on the voice-pipe. Helen made no attempt to stop me this time, but sat immobile, watching me.

"Bjerko!" I said. "Wetherby here. This course is suicide. We might still get clear on another. Steer"—I glanced at the gyro-repeater—"six-oh. Full speed ahead!"

There was a pause, and I heard Bjerko say something. When the Norwegian captain replied there was a note of sarcasm in his voice. "I thank you for your advice, Captain Wetherby, and so does Sir Frederick. Sir Frederick says you have had a nasty experience and you need rest. The ship is in good hands."

"Good hands!" I started to exclaim, but the instrument clicked off. "We're steering eight-five degrees," I said to Helen. "Bjerko says—" I trailed off at her shrug.

"I asked how you came to be wounded," she said levelly.

I stumbled to the bunk and half sat, half lay on it. I told her in detail about Norris's chart, the ransacking of my cabin, the fragments of the plot I had overheard on the Tannoy, and how my fears had been realized when Walter had lashed me to the Spandau-Hotchkiss and tried to kill me. She listened without saying a word. Her only outward sign of agitation showed when I mentioned her father's mysterious interest in Thompson Island and his instructions to Walter to get rid of me.

"When I landed in the helicopter with you unconscious, my father told me that Walter had been through to him on the W/T. Walter, my father said, told him that you had gone berserk at the sight of the ack-ack gun. It happens, my father says: a man like yourself has some dormant

killer instinct left over from the war. He sees a weapon like
the Spandau-Hotchkiss. All his wartime agonies come alive
again. He isn't really responsible. Yet he is a killer all the
same. Walter says it happened on the Russian convoys
too."

"And how does Walter account for this?" I said, finger-
ing the blood-stained bandage.

"He says you were hit by an exploding Spandau shell
splinter after you had turned the gun into the deck for some
unexplained reason," she replied. "Walter considers he was
lucky to have got away with his life."

"And what do you think?" I asked. I stared at her. There
was something different about her. I noticed then that she
was no longer wearing her leather flying kit, but a warm
dress of mulberry as deep as the colour we had seen
together in the sea. Her answer suddenly became of great
importance to me. Only hours ago the importance would
have lain in my having an ally. Now . . .

I could have watched the light change through her eyes
for hours had I not known that each darker shadow from
the outside brought the *Antarctica* one step nearer her end.
The pale yellow glow which seemed to heighten the fine
line of her cheekbones and illuminate the strange eyes
was—death.

"Something of the Southern Ocean has passed into my
father, into Walter, into you, into Sailhardy," she said
quietly, as if exercising all the control she had built up in
the past. "Kill or be killed. Now you give me your
reason—Thompson Island."

"That isn't an answer to my question," I said.

"No," she said. "The answer perhaps is that I am sitting
here—have been sitting here for hours—waiting for a man
everyone else considers a cold-blooded murderer to come
round. My father swore I wouldn't be allowed to.
But"—she smiled faintly—"here I am. I also know that
when I saw you fall off the gun into the sea something died
inside me."

"I might have lived three minutes in the cold," I said.

"I know that," she answered. "I also know that the person who couldn't muster courage to land on an ice floe died when you sent me up to watch the *Thorshammer*. That person could not have brought you up alive out of the sea."

"Do you believe I had some sort of blackout and shot down a defenceless seaplane?" I pressed.

Again she replied obliquely. "I gave the fleet's position away deliberately when I said I saw the blue whales."

"What!" I exclaimed. "You were in effect turning your father over to the Norwegian authorities? Deliberately?"

"Yes," she said.

"So you suspected, too, that something was behind all this! Guarana, buccaneer's brandy—these are the accoutrements of a ruthless killer."

I had underestimated the bond between her father and herself. She was on her feet in an instant. "How dare you! How dare you! I admire my father and I intend to protect him. I gave the fleet's position away to prevent him coming to further harm. If we're inside Norwegian territorial waters—so what? My father can afford a fine, even a stiff one. He hasn't killed a solitary whale. The *Thorshammer* can arrest us. My father may have gone a bit astray in his enthusiam to find the breeding ground of the blue whale—"

"So much so that he is prepared to shoot down a seaplane and kill two innocent lads in it?"

"Either Walter or you or both shot down the seaplane, not my father," she flashed back. "No wonder Pirow says 'Herr Kapitän!' "

"What do you know about Pirow?" I asked.

She looked surprised. "He's a first-class radio operator. That's all."

I told her about the Man with the Immaculate Hand.

She sat down, her eyes wide. "What are you trying to say, Bruce?"

"I've said it," I replied. "Thompson Island. What do you

know about Thompson Island? Why does your father want
so desperately to find Thompson Island?"

Her face was drawn in the odd light. "I'd never heard of
Thompson Island until you mentioned it."

"Your father is quite prepared to kill off Sailhardy and
myself now he has the chart," I said. "I have tried to tell
him the chart is useless by itself. I alone know where
Thompson Island is. It is not where the chart says."

She got up impulsively and held her hand across my
mouth. "Bruce, for God's sake, don't! Some unknown rock
sticking out into an ocean suddenly becomes a killer and
the thing that dominates all our lives! I'm frightened.
Something wicked and enormous is building up. Even the
sky is ghastly. Look, it's getting quite dark—"

"Your father is building up the evil," I said. "He has got
to be stopped."

"Perhaps that is why I gave our position away," she
replied thoughtfully. "I didn't know any of this you have
told me, but intuitively I felt my father—" A flicker of fear
passed through her eyes.

"Helen," I said gently, "don't you see? All this means
one thing and one thing only—your father must be pro-
tected, from himself."

She stood above me as I half lay on the bunk. She
reached out and took my hands in hers. They were
cold. "You're saying—you're saying—my father is mad?"

I talked round it. "When a leading interest becomes an
obsession, as it has with your father, it is only one stage
further to a state of monomania. I don't know enough
about what has led up to this expedition. Nor do I know
what your father's obsessional interest is. I do know,
however, that it centres on Thompson Island. However, no
one goes to the lengths he has just in order to rediscover an
island which admittedly is one of the sea's great mysteries.
I have tried to find out what your father is after. I failed. I
am only seeing effect, without the cause. And"—I grinned
wryly—"one of the effects was damn nearly my death."

"I feel so alone in this," she said. "I have only you to turn to."

"Try to think back," I said. "How did this expedition come to be fitted out? Did something sudden happen? Did your father say anything?"

"He was crazy about rare metals," Helen replied. "You see what happened to his face. He threw himself into that research with everything he had."

"That was twenty-odd years ago," I said.

"Wait," she said. "There was something, now you come to mention it. Both he and I have made trips to the Antarctic for about five years now. He was never like he is now though. He enjoyed the voyages and he was always full of interest, always asking everyone we met about unusual places and discoveries."

"Thompson Island?" I suggested.

"I never heard him mention it," she said. "I've often heard him speak about Bouvet. I—"

"What was the something?" I persisted.

"It wasn't here in the Antarctic at all," she said. "It was back in London, perhaps about eighteen months ago. I remember he came home one evening and I could see he was very excited. He said he had bought out an old sealing firm and he had found some interesting things amongst some old junk."

A thrill of disbelief passed through my mind. Two years previously the firm of Wetherby's had finally passed out of existence. It had been bought by a small company called Stewart's Whaling Company. Upton had not figured, as far as I knew.

"What was the name of the sealing firm?" I asked.

She shook her head. "I don't know. I wasn't really interested. All I remember is that he spent most of the evening examining some things that looked like bull's-eyes."

"Bull's-eyes?"

"You know, those black sweets with the white streaks in them."

"And then?"

"After that everything seemed to go with a rush. He was here, there, and everywhere, negotiating for ships, stores, maps, and so on. He practically organized this whole expedition himself. I presumed it was just another trip south."

She smiled. "You see, Bruce, I wasn't the same person then as I am—have become—now. My own reaction was that my challenge was to be met, and I geared myself both physically and mentally to meet it. Most of my time was spent flying, doing tricky landings, being in the air when the weather was at its worst. Until now I never thought of this expedition except as being strictly subjective, in relation to myself and my problems. My father gave me everything I wanted, encouraged me in every way."

"You never saw the bull's-eyes again?"

"No."

"He never said what they were?"

"No. He spent a good deal of time at the Admiralty and later he flew to Germany. He was there a couple of weeks."

"And Pirow?"

"He joined the ship the day before we sailed. I have had no reason to suspect him before you told me who he was. To me he was simply a first-class radio operator."

"Where is Sailhardy?" I asked. "Is he still alive?"

"He's in irons, locked in one of the cabins opposite. I patched him up as best I could."

"How does your father allow you to have keys to these cabins? Surely he might fear you would release us—or at least get possession of the keys?" I asked.

She shook her head. "I appointed myself nurse to both of you. My father shouted and swore but obviously thought you were both so far gone that you would not be a threat to anyone. It would be different if he knew I sent off the message about our position deliberately. He couldn't stop me nursing you without giving away his real intentions about you. I'm only the nurse in their eyes. You see"—she smiled faintly—"he still sees me as I was. How was Sailhardy hurt?"

I told her, and she shuddered. "Dear God! There has been enough violence already! What are we to do?"

"Your father has got to be restrained," I said. "That means I must get control of this ship. I shall—if you will help."

"What are you going to do?" she asked, wide-eyed. "You're not—not—planning to harm my father?"

"No," I replied. "I won't promise about Walter, however." I got down from the bunk. My legs felt a lot steadier. "I want a flensing knife and a hacksaw. You'll find plenty of both in the racks in there." I nodded to the bulkhead, beyond which lay the whale-processing compartments. "Are you sure there are no guards on the doors?"

"No—Bruce, we're stopping! The ship is stopping!"

The *Antarctica*'s heart beat slowed.

"Yes," I said. "This ship has made her number for the last time at Lloyds. She won't last long now."

"What are you saying?"

"The yellow stuff in the sea," I replied. "Honey jelly of the Southern Ocean. As I told you, it means that the ice is right on top of us."

"But this honey jelly—what is it, really?"

"It's millions upon millions of tiny little creatures called ostracods. They come from a thousand, maybe two thousand, fathoms deep."

"You mean to say they are living ceatures?" she asked incredulously.

"They're dead," I said. "That's why they're on the surface. It is also why I say the ice is here. Listen, last year when the liner *Corinthic* sailed nine hundred miles through a sea of honey-coloured stuff near Pitcairn Island, in the Pacific, the papers dressed it up as the number one sea mystery of the year."

"I still don't get the significance of it," she said.

"It doesn't matter a damn whether or not millions of

ostracods live or die," I explained. "What is signif-
icant—and especially to this ship at this moment—is
that they died suddenly. And they died because the cold
killed them. They were born when the Antarctic winter
came to an end. The spring brought warmth. Now the cold
has returned."

"And the return of the cold means—?"

"Ice," I said. "Ice. Bouvet's own pack ice."

"But the ice is five hundred miles away,' she protested.
"The dangerous ice is safe and sound now on the Antarctic
mainland for the summer, which is just starting."

"I told you what we were heading into," I replied. "This
is it. When I first saw the honey sea from the *Aurora*'s
gun, I reckoned the *Antarctica* was on the outer wing of a
gigantic crescent of ice. That is the way the Bouvet pack
forms. There are two huge wings, anything up to a hundred miles apart. The rapid freeze spreads from wing to
wing like a running fuse once it starts. When I realized
the way we were steering I yelled at Bjerko to turn sixty
degrees—in other words, due east—at full speed, to avoid
the freeze-up between the wings. We're finished."

"Are you sure?"

"I'm surer of this, Helen, than anything—except some
inner feelings at the moment," I replied.

She turned away.

"Take a look at the barometer," I added.

She got up and faced the glass in open disbelief. "It can't
fall twenty millibars in three hours. A pressure drop like
that would mean a storm to end the world!"

I smiled grimly. "I've seen it do better. Just south of
where we are it went down twenty-seven millibars in six
hours during the war. I saw it happen. The bottom is dropping out of the weather."

She paced up and down. "I'm frightened, Bruce—
frightened of what is happening to us, to the weather
—frightened of what is happening to my father. What
now?"

"The weather atom bomb is being primed," I said. "There's nothing to do but await the explosion. The simplest way to visualize it is as two extreme air masses about to join battle. We are now awaiting the onslaught."

"Bruce!" she exclaimed. "You—you of all people—just can't sit back fatalistically and await death. We're at a standstill, but there's no swell, no wind even."

"We have thrown ourselves into the heart of the machine that makes the worst weather in the world," I replied. "I once got clear of a similar situation in H.M.S. *Scott*, in these very waters. It took a destroyer and every bit of her thirty knots to get clear. This is literally the calm before the storm. And that storm will rage for a week or more across four thousand miles of empty ocean and smash anything that lies in its path."

"You can't just write off five ships like this!" she said.

Beyond the porthole it was growing darker. Five ships! I had been thinking in terms of one. "By heavens, Helen! Five ships! I know—I'll bring the catchers in line astern and keep an ice lead open, even if it starts to freeze round the *Antarctica*! The catchers are smaller, more mobile, with a shallower draught. It will be tricky, but it can be done!"

I saw in my mind's eye how I could take the *Antarctica* out stern first along a lead through the ice, which the catchers would patrol at their best speed possible to keep the thick sea from coagulating before I could get the factory ship clear.

"I'll want your help with the helicopter too," I told her. "Think you can manage in this sort of half fog?"

She smiled. "It's just this sort of situation I have been grooming myself for for years."

I looked for my seaboots. I grinned at her. "Who changed me? This is a new pair of polar socks."

A faint flush spread beneath the fine cheekbones. "Your seaboots are under the bunk. They weren't very wet. I dried your sweater. It's in that drawer, with your shirts."

I looked at her as I pulled the polo-necked, cold-cheating sweater over my head. "We have to be quick. I'll carry these boots so the others won't hear me coming. We must free Sailhardy first."

"Wait a moment while I get the hacksaw and the knife," she said.

I stood back from the entrance as she opened the door carefully and looked up and down the corridor. She disappeared, and was back within three minutes with the things I had asked for. It wasn't a hacksaw but a baleen saw for whale tusks, but it would do. Together we crossed the still corridor. The fog seemed everywhere. Even the lights seemed dimmer. Helen unlocked Sailhardy's door. The cabin was dark, and the switch gave a click as I turned it on. The electric-light bulb had been removed. I groped and found the islander.

"It's Bruce," I whispered.

There was a faint clink from his manacles.

"How are you, man?" I asked.

His reply was stilted, as if he had difficulty in articulating. "Okay, Bruce, boy. Are you free?"

"Yes," I told him and outlined my plan. First, I said, we would overpower Pirow in the radio shack and then break suddenly on to the bridge and seize Upton and Bjerko. I hadn't worked out how to get hold of Walter, and with her wicked weapon the *Aurora* would be a handful.

Helen said, "What about Walter though? He'll be on the bridge too."

"How did he get aboard?" I asked.

"While you were unconscious," she replied. "My father ordered me to fetch him."

"That is very good," said Sailhardy. The menace in his voice sent a shiver through me. "He's mine, Bruce, mine!"

"Are you strong enough to tackle him?" I asked anxiously. "I don't want anything more to happen—"

"Leave him to me, boy," came the voice in the darkness. "Now get these damned things off my wrists."

I felt for his wrists and started to saw.

"Why are we stopped, Bruce?" he asked.

"Honey sea," I said.

"My God!" he exclaimed. I heard the sharp intake of his breath. "Has the ice closed on her yet?"

"No," I said, sketching my plan to save the factory ship.

"Is there still any water-sky?" asked Sailhardy.

"I think so," I said. "I couldn't see too well from my porthole."

"Water-sky?" asked Helen. "What's that?"

"Big leaden patches in the fog where the sky should be," I said. "It means that below it there are open leads of water—unfrozen sea. It shows its reflection against the sky."

The saw cut through the centre section of the manacles. "We're wasting time," he said. "We still have a sporting chance of saving our skins."

"Leave Pirow to me," I said.

In the dim corridor outside, Sailhardy looked like an avenging fiend. There was a mask of dried blood over his face, and his teeth glinted raggedly. The steel was still round his wrists, and a piece of cut chain hung down from each.

"Come!" I said to Helen. "Keep well behind us, out of harm's way."

"Look after yourself, for God's sake!" she whispered.

In single file, myself leading, Sailhardy behind, and Helen in the rear, we went silently up the steel ladder towards Pirow's radio office. We dodged through Upton's empty cabin. Pirow's door was closed. Putting on my sea-boots, I held the long knife in my right hand and opened the door quickly with my left. Pirow wore his headphones, his back to us. I put the point of the knife against his neck.

I said softly in German, "The Man with the Immaculate Hand."

Sailhardy moved like a panther to Pirow's right. Perhaps it was his initial terror at the sight of the bloodied islander

which made him say so much. "Her Kapitän!" he
mouthed. "Herr Kapitän! I do not know, I swear it!
Heavenly blue, that is all I know. It is Sir Frederick's secret, not mine! I don't know—"

"Heavenly blue what, Pirow?"

I noted the quick flash of comprehension in his eyes.
When he saw the knife thrust wasn't coming then and
there, he started to fumble for words. The immaculate
hand edged over to the Morse key. I reversed the knife and
struck his knuckles with the handle. He rose to his feet,
white with pain.

"Come," I said. "You'll go up on the bridge first. I'll be
right behind you, and you'll catch the first bullet if your
friend Walter starts shooting."

Helen was white too as we threaded our way back
through Upton's cabin. I put Pirow in the lead up the short
ladder to the bridge. Sailhardy was almost alongside me.
His eagerness made me feel almost sorry for what was
coming to Walter. We emerged silently on to the bridge, my
knife point touching Pirow's back. Walter was standing
near the helm indicator trying to see out into the fog. Upton and Bjerko were close to the starboard wing. Both were
engrossed.

"Walter!" I called. With my left hand I held Pirow in
front of me as a shield.

The thick-set Norwegian swung round. Upton and
Bjerko stood rooted to the spot. Sailhardy's little finger
tapped against his palm with that idiosyncrasy of his which
preceded physical action. Walter cast one startled glance at
my knife. He whipped the Luger out but was still fumbling
with the safety catch when Sailhardy slid forward and
struck him with the sawn-off manacle. He screamed with
pain as the shackle bit into his wrist. I leaped forward and
snatched the automatic from where it had fallen on the
gratings. Knife and Luger in hand, I guarded the four men.

Before I could say anything there was a heavy bump forward by the bows. The indeterminate definition went from

the light. We were out of the fog. In place of the veil-like, watery obscurity of a moment before, the light was clear and hard. The razor-edged bank of fog lay immediately astern.

It was forward that we gazed, transfixed. The sun hung like a blood-filled grape. Underneath, the whole world was blue.

It would have been less terrifying if the *Antarctica* had rushed head on through the fog and destroyed herself against the massive ice cliff which rose before us. As it was, the bump of her bow against the ice held the menace of a long-drawn-out death. The sudden drop of the fog curtain astern heightened the awe-provoking spectacle that lay before our eyes. The fact that I had warned Upton against just this did not mitigate my own fear, the same fear as had once made me thrust the bridge telegraph of H.M.S. *Scott* to full speed ahead—anything, anything to escape, with all the thrust of her great turbines, from the same platelike crystals of ice, called by whalermen frazil crystals, which now hung half submerged in the sea everywhere; plates of ice that come together with uncanny speed and form the ice belt that is Bouvet's killer. The *Antarctica* seemed to have touched against the central The *Antarctica* seemed to have touched against the central buttress of the encircling semi-circle of pack ice. Nowhere was any white ice to be seen. To port, the cliff blocked out all view, but to starboard the field was low, perhaps only twenty feet above the level of the sea. A vast agglomeration of blue hummocks and pressure ridges stretched away into the distance as far as the eye could see. Within a hundred years of the ice edge was a huge, domed mound, smoothed and fashioned by the wind, and a series of lesser mounds stretched away behind. The ice was all shades and variations of blue—azure where the parody of a sun struck down, royal blue where the fluted, striated cliffs to port overhung the leaden-blue sea. At our backs lay the bank of strontium-yellow fog. The knife I held had turned aconite. The air off the blue icefield was as raw and sharp as the blade itself. I wanted to cough as it took me by the throat.

The human antagonisms that had been present a moment before were swamped by what the Southern Ocean had conjured up before our startled eyes. The blue light gave Pirow's shocked white face the pallor of a ghost. There seemed almost no need to guard Upton, Walter, and Pirow, they were so overcome by what they saw.

"This is it," I said to Upton. "I warned you, but you wouldn't listen."

His eyes were very bright, and the way he spoke made me surer of his mental state. I had a gun and a knife in my hands, but he addressed me with the same easy, inescapable charm as on our first meeting. "Bruce, boy," he said, "you wouldn't be here if I didn't think you the finest sailor in the Southern Ocean. I should have listened, but it's all yours now. Put those damned toys away. This is what matters for the moment." He jerked his head at the icefield. His smile in the pewter mask was grotesque, reflecting the blue.

The *Antarctica* was bumping gently against the ice cliff in the still sea. She was in no danger from the movement beyond the buckling of a few plates in her bows. Her danger lay in the millions of small spicules or thin plates of ice floating in the sea in the first stage of freezing; soon they would lock together and add to the cliffs, hillocks, and ridges before us, and in that process crush the big factory ship's steel plates. The offshore mass of bergy bits, growlers, sludge, and pancake ice was witness of how quickly the sea was freezing; the curious, upturned edges of the pancake ice were already kissing and coalescing into ever-growing acres of thin ice. For the moment there was a strange stillness, broken only by a faint tinkling as the ice rind splintered against the ship's sides. I remembered that deadly tinkle as I had shaken H.M.S. *Scott* clear: it had paralleled the distant sound of her engine-room telegraphs. The *Antarctica*'s bows could still cut through the ice plates, but in a couple of hours these would freeze iron-hard. I knew that the intensity of the cold which now gripped us was changing even the structure of the metal of the weapons I held; soon they would become as brittle as glass. So would the *Antarctica's* plates, making the task of the ice vice easier still.

By now, I thought, Upton must have read the annotation on the back of Captain Norris's log. Norris had been a sensitive man—his sketches showed that. What he had written to complement the laconic deck-log version of his discovery revealed his terror at seeing the same ice killer we were seeing now. Norris had known then it meant death, and who knows to what eventual ghastly end he and his gallant *Sprightly* had gone? I could recall by heart what Norris had written, the impress of fear as so vivid upon his words:

I saw Thompson Island on the mid-afternoon of December 13, 1825. There was fog, floating ice, and a Force 8 gale from the northwest. There was the island, long and low in the foreground, and a high peak more distantly. The crew of the *Sprightly* gazed awestruck at this unknown haven of refuge amidst seas which, by contrast with their wild tumult, made its ice-bound shores seemed like paradise. The giant glacier which capped Thompson Island like a nightmare caul continued into the sea as a solid tongue of steel-blue ice, linking a gigantic, unbroken icefield on the southern horizon. The grotesque nature of this single massive tongue, like that of a malice-filled and possessive viper from the unknown regions of the Pole, struck a cold grue of terror into my men, used, even as they were, to the hardships and evils of the wild Southern Ocean.

A cold grue of terror!

Norris had used the Scots' word in all its force, and the grue, the thrill of naked fear, which ran through me as I gazed at the blue icefield was as primordial as the birth of the killer pack.

"Yes," I said to Upton, "it's saving our skins which matters most." I spoke to Sailhardy. "Put them, Upton, Walter, and Bjerko, in irons in Upton's cabin. The same with Pirow, in his radio office. Chain him near his transmitting key. I may need him later."

Sailhardy came over to me to take the Luger. Simultaneously our ears were stunned by an immense thunder. It was the icefield. Every rivet in the ship trembled. A cluster of Skua gulls rose in white detonation from the foot of the blue cliff. The reverberation roared through the yellow fog. Helen buried her head in my thick sweater. Across the flat side of the icefield I saw a new mound ejaculate itself, rusty-rose, as some hidden pressure force threw up ice the size of St. Paul's Cathedral. Bouvet's conquistador with his sword of ice was coming at us. If the ship were nipped we could still get stores ashore on the ice pack, but we would not survive as Shackleton and others had done. Their ice had stayed solid. I knew that Bouvet's pack would, when the Albatross' Foot reached it, dissolve and leave us to drown. We would either die of exposure on the ice or of drowning when the life-giving warmth came. I had to save the *Antarctica,* I told myself. Before, the challenge itself would have been enough, but now . . . I looked down at the fair hair against my shoulder.

I found myself shouting, I was so deaf. "Pirow! Signal the catchers! Tell them to form up in line astern and come through there." I pointed at the plumes of vapour ghosting above the blue ice forming in the sea, the way the *Antarctica* had come. "Tell them to rush it, and to keep the lead open. Each one is to go full astern within three cables' length of this ship. I'll then go full astern and try to break out. Understood?"

"Yes, Herr Kapitän."

Sailhardy ushered the prisoners away. Walter was cursing under his breath and holding his injured wrist.

Helen drew herself away from me. "God! It looks hopeless!"

"There are still open leads of water," I said. "Look at the clouds there above the icefield—see the dark patches? That's water-sky, which means that somewhere, even amongst that lot, there is some sea which is not frozen solid—yet."

She shuddered. The frost-smoke or vapour plumes which the whalermen call "the Barber" could guide us to salvation yet. My first job was to get the head of the factory ship clear of the ice buttress and keep the sea reasonably ice free at the stern. Even if the ice closed, I thought rapidly, we might escape the fate of the factory ship if I brought the catchers in to surround her: with their shallow draught they might pop like peas in a pod out of the clutches of the ice without fatal damage, whereas the *Antarctica* would be trapped because of her greater depth. It was worth risking as a last resort. There were, however, more immediate things to do aboard the *Antarctica*. In the piercing cold, I must get the water drained from the deck mains and have a steam hose run through them, to clear the drain cocks, or else they would soon burst, leaving us without a water supply. I must also have the rudder strengthened with wire pendants to prevent its being unshipped as we crashed stern first through the ice. My mind raced on: I hoped that the *Antarctica* had been fitted out by someone ice-wise and that she had a propeller with removable blades, for we seemed almost certain to damage one of the blades on projecting pieces of ice in getting clear. Breaking propeller blades was, I knew from hard experience, the commonest damage when trying to extricate a ship in a situation like ours.

"Bruce," said Helen, "what do you intend to do with them, particularly my father? Are you going to hand them over to the *Thorshammer?*"

"That question will have to wait," I replied. "The ice is

the danger. Go and get yourself as warmly dressed as you
can. Pack something small. Let the valuables go, if you
have them. A pair of warm gloves might be more use in
the long run."

"You're going to abandon ship without even a fight?"
she asked.

"The fight is on," I said. "Quick now. Then come back
here."

Sailhardy returned to the bridge. He smiled grimly as he
looked about him. "She's sick, this ship—sick with the
cold."

"Get aft and trim her down well by the stern," I ordered. "Rig some steel wire pendants to the rudder-head
from both quarters. My God!" I indicated the echo-
sounding equipment. It showed fifteen fathoms, in the
middle of the Southern Ocean! This meant that the cold
was so intense that even the anti-freeze in the transmitter
and receiver tanks had started to freeze. The ice was clos-
ing in quicker than I thought.

Sailhardy let out a long whistle.

"Get steam through the mains," I snapped down the
bridge telephone to the main deck. Scarcely had I said it
when there was a scream of metal immediately below the
bridge. The winch through which the steam had to pass
gave a quarter-turn as the head of steam tried to burst
through. Then the heavy piping, already frozen inside,
ripped along its whole length, as if it had been opened by a
huge unseen can opener.

Helen came back to the bridge in a heavy coat of sea
leopard skin. She heard the scream of the metal, but
without speaking thrust my heavy gloves, reefer jacket,
cap, and duffel coat into my hands. Dragging them on, I
raced to the port wing of the bridge and looked at the sea.
It was viscous now as it froze.

"Sailhardy!" I said. "Get down on the main deck first
before you rig the tackles. Have them bring ice axes,

crowbars, boathooks, and poles up from below. You know the drill—get every man on the rails with the poles and try to keep her sides free of ice. Then get a boat and dynamite and blow the ice at intervals of twenty yards astern. We must keep it open!"

"Aye, aye, Bruce," he said tersely. "A moment later he was among the men. If any man could save the ship through my last-ditch drill, he could.

Helen was gazing astern. "The fog is rolling back, Bruce, but I don't see the catchers."

"It's ominous that it should roll back. It means the cold is spreading," I replied. I picked up the phone to Pirow. "Pirow! What the hell is happening to the catchers?"

His voice was cool, professional. "No reply to my signals, Herr Kapitän. They're talking among themselves on the W/T—"

Sailhardy's call from the main deck interrupted. "What size charges, Bruce?"

"Make them up into pieces of twenty pounds apiece," I told him. "Fuse 'em right up. Short." I returned to Pirow. "Pirow! I'm going full astern in a moment. I may go hell-bent into an iceberg. What's the score with the radar?"

"Too much sub-refraction," he replied levelly. "We'll be right on top of anything before I can locate it. The normal detection range means nothing in conditions like this."

Helen came with me to the starboard wing of the bridge. I wanted, if possible, to see what was happening between the main body of the ice and ourselves. As I leaned over I saw. I gripped her arm.

"Look!" I said. A long underwater spur had grown out from the cliffside towards the ship. It was perhaps ten feet long. Four others, like the teeth of a steam shovel, reached out at intervals farther aft.

"What is it, Bruce?"

"Those spurs," I replied. "I can't wait now. Any one of

them will rip off a blade of the screw. In this cold each blade is twice as brittle as normal. One touch, and it will splinter."

I raced back to the engine-room telephone.

"Chief engineer," said the voice.

"Chief," I said, "there's lots of trouble. There's sludge and brash ice everywhere. In ten minutes your condenser inlets are going to choke. Before that I want everything your engines can give me. Understand? Get a steam hose to the condensers so that there's hot water circulating round them. And for your own sake, see there's no condensation in the main steam pipes, or else you'll be blown to hell. In a moment I'll be going alternately full ahead and full astern to shake her free. If the inlets block with sludge I can't wait to stop. Can do?"

"Aye," said the Scots voice. "Can do. Is five minutes enough?"

"Just," I replied. "I'll ring down."

I called Sailhardy on deck. "Belay the dynamite," I said. "Get the tackles rigged if you can. I want you on the bridge in five minutes."

I turned to Helen, gazing white-faced about her. There was no sign of the catchers. In her sea leopard coat she looked like one of those dead things I had seen so often on the icy outcrops of Graham Land.

"Do you want me to fly off the helicopter—?" she started to say, when suddenly she coughed. I felt the sharp dagger of wind too. It came softly, furtively from the south. I felt its sinister touch by the slight condensation on the inside fold of my duffel coat. The wind was the last stage of the Bouvet pack: it would advance the ice edge more rapidly still towards the factory ship; it was also the precursor of the storm which I knew would follow the freeze-up.

"The wind," I said quickly. "I can't give the chief even his five minutes now," I rang Sailhardy and ordered him back to the bridge. The islander joined us. The shoulder of his coat was streaked with red rust where he had slung himself over the ship's quarter in a vain effort to rig the rudder-head tackles. A white streak of frozen spray was daubed alongside the red.

"The south wind, Bruce?"

There was almost no need for him to say it. He too had felt its message. I nodded to the port wing of the bridge and together we looked down at the sleazy sea. Catching some of the sun's attenuated light, it had turned to a pale, gelatinous, coagulating mass.

"Sailhardy!" exclaimed Helen, seeing the look on our faces. "You and Bruce together, you two—"

The long vowels were in his voice. "Ma'am," he said gently, "if this ship is a-dying, you can be sure of one thing: under Captain Bruce Wetherby she'll die the hard way." He pointed across to the dark blue cliff where the ice rind had become young ice, anything from a couple of inches to half a foot thick.

Helen took the lapels of my duffel coat in her hands. "At first, when I lay in that snow-filled ditch after the Germans had shot me, I prayed. I prayed to God. I prayed with every formal and informal prayer I knew. I ran out of prayers. After my brother died I just lay there, without hope, almost without thought. Now"—the strange eyes were luminous, and she shuddered as she looked at the ice-field—"now I want to live. Then I did not. If my prayers had names at this moment, they would be Bruce Wetherby and Sailhardy the islander."

I could find no words as I watched the light—blue, rusty-pink, and steel-rose—in her eyes. It was Sailhardy who spoke. "Aye, ma'am, praying words don't help you any here in the Southern Ocean. Prayer words don't break the ice like an icebreaker, and at this moment I'd give all the Jesu-lover-of-my-soul for a northwest wind and two degrees on the mercury."

A cold grue of terror! I relived Norris's fear as I saw the distant water-smoke start to throw up its dazed meridians into the dusty pink-blue light. The transparent membranes surrounding the brain's nerve centres contract and contort their spider's web as a blow approaches—that is how I felt as I watched and waited for the blow from the killer pack.

"Bruce—" Helen started to say, but I strode across to the bridge telegraph. "Sailhardy!" I said. "The wheel!"

"Full ahead!" I rang. "Port twenty," I told the islander as he took over from the Norwegian quartermaster. "If she responds at all."

I picked up the phone to Pirow. "Pirow! What are the catchers doing? Why aren't they coming to help us?"

"They're not answering my signals, Herr Kapitän," he replied.

"Send: *stand by to render immediate assistance. Factory ship in grave danger.*"

I heard the rapid tap of his key as he called up the catchers. He was back on the phone in a moment. "No reply, Herr Kapitän."

"What the hell are they playing at? They can't leave us like this! Have you got them on the radar?"

Again I admired the cool professional detachment of the Man with the Immaculate Hand. "Five radar contacts—ship contacts—bearing eight-oh degrees. Receding."

"They're deserting us?" I asked incredulously.

"Yes, Herr Kapitän."

"How far astern?"

"Four, five miles, maybe."

"Are they moving?"

"Yes, Herr Kapitän. Fast. Twelve knots, I would say."

That meant they were in clear water, beyond the deadly grip of the ice crescent.

"Shall I give a May Day call, Herr Kapitän? It means the *Thorshammer* will hear it too."

May Day—a ship's last desperate call for help.

"Yes," I said. As I put down the earpiece I heard the

start of the distress call: *May Day! May Day!*

The *Antarctica* started to shudder, but she scarcely moved. It was like handling a car with a slipping clutch. The screws thrashed. Sailhardly spun the spokes. His look of despair told me everything. I must try to shake her free astern.

I called the engine room. "Chief! Sorry about this. Full astern!"

There was a muffled oath. "Ever heard of torsional stresses in shafting, laddie?" But he'd already shouted my order. "The shaft—"

I slammed down the earpiece. Unexpectedly the great ship moved quickly astern. As she did so a growler seemed to pop up in her wake. Perhaps the thrust of the screws had dislodged it from the main body of the icefield.

"Starboard!" I helled. "Hard astarboard, Sailhardy!"

The isalnder couldn't make it. The sea was seven-tenths ice. It cloyed round the ship, killing her manoeuvrability. A sickening thump shook every rivet. The rudder-head must have taken the force of the blow as the *Antarctica* crashed into the growler. Under full power, she yawed wildly and tore, in a crazy semicircle, stern first at the cliff. At the same moment I saw a long weal of splinters as the hummocked wall of ice could stand no longer the pressure which had built up in the icefield behind. It broke off. The roar of the avalanche drowned my shouted commands to Sailhardy. The great raft of stuff, half a mile long and a quarter thick, towered and then, losing its balance untidily, toppled, and tossed the ice rind high into the air in a thousand fragments. The deadening power of the ice could not stop the huge wave which now rocketed towards the ship. I rang "full ahead" to try to miss the wall of ice coming at the stern.

It may have been an underwater ram from the cliff or simply another growler, but I felt the propeller go in a scream of tangled metal that rose above the thunder of the ice. As the blades stripped, I felt through the bridge plates the race of the engines and the shattering of the main shaft, already weakened by the cold. The explosion from the engine room followed almost simultaneously. I rushed to the starboard wing of the bridge with Helen. The plating was ripped, and through the hole, where he had been catapulted, was the mangled corpse of a greaser who a minute before had been a man. Through the ship's side pulsed sprays of boiling oil from the cylinder whose casing had burst.

Helen was not looking at the scene of destruction but along the main deck. "God!" she whispered. "Dear God! Look!"

Reeling along the deck came the oil-blind man. His arms were held wide. The nose, lips, and eyes had been filed away by the flaming oil, and the charred tongue bubbled against the roof of his sawn-off mouth. He fumbled blindly at the rail of the bridge companionway and then, as if the slightest touch sent another chill of agony through him, he turned and stumbled over the side; the curdling sea held back the splash. He sank only about ten feet under the surface, arms and legs wide.

The wave struck the doomed ship, pouring in through the engine-room gap. Gouts of white-hot oil pulsed once or twice. The fumes condensed whitely. The ship canted over ten degrees as she started to fill.

"Shall I try to get the pumps going, Bruce?" asked Sailhardy dazedly.

I did not recognize my own voice. "No need. She'll freeze solid now. She won't sink. The ice has got her. It will hold her up."

"What about the catchers?" Helen asked. I shook my head. I picked up the bridge microphone and switched on the loudspeaker system throughout the ship. "Prepare to abandon ship," I said. "All food stores are to be brought on deck immediately. We are in no immediate danger of sinking. Everything movable and of use will be loaded overside and stacked on the ice." I clicked off and rang through to Pirow. As he replied, I could hear the fateful *May Day, May Day* call going out.

"No reply from the catchers," he said briefly. "But they're in touch with the *Thorshammer*."

"I'll send Sailhardy to bring you here," I said. "What are they saying?"

"It is bad for us, Herr Kapitän," he replied. "Very bad for all of us."

Without waiting for him to tell me what was bad I ordered Sailhardy to bring the prisoners on to the bridge. If they were going to die, I certainly wasn't going to allow them to die down below in irons.

I went over to Helen and put my arm round her shoulders. We felt the ship settle a little farther. The light was going from the sick sun as it dropped out of sight behind the blue cliff, darker now. It was pertrifyingly cold. Tenuous fingers of ice reached out towards the doomed ship. A small growler, looking like a porpoise, in incongruous imitation of the tropics, lay immobile under the factory ship's blunt bow. The light brought with it, too, that strange inward colouration of the ship's bulwarks which I have never seen in any other sea: the factory ship's bluff forepeak had become a gangrenous green, which had spread to the tarpaulins covering the boats, splintered by the explosion in the engine room under them.

We stood, not saying anything. There was a sudden, flat scream as the forceps of ice prised loose the first of the factory ship's plates. A white kelp pigeon wheeled over the far end of the lifeline lead of water towards the fogbank. It seemed to add immeasurably to the distance and desolation of the scene. Another plate gave in agony. As if in echo, the strange, lonely cry of the kelp pigeon struck back dully from the sound-absorbing edges of the pancake ice.

The *Antarctica* was on her way to join Captain Norris and the *Sprightly*. Helen shuddered. The light went. The wind rose.

Next morning the *Antarctica* presented a sorry sight. All night the crew, under my orders and Sailhardy's unflagging direction, had brought up on deck every available case of food, every blanket, every item of warm clothing. I had got the emergency power plant working, since the main supply from the engine room had disappeared in the explosion. Now the deck was stacked with tons of supplies. Over everything, as I looked down from the bridge to the main deck shortly after dawn, lay a fine patina of ice and frost. Unshaven, sleepless, and hoarse from shouting orders, I had waited for the light in order to find a platform on the ice strong enough to bear the weight of the stores. Throughout the night the ice had tightened its anaconda grip on the dying ship. Rivet by rivet, plate by plate, the life was being strangled out of her. Between decks, her dying noises seemed almost animate—a line of rivets would tremble first, then bulge, and then tear with a sub-human sound as the inch-thick plating buckled and burst.

In search of the ice platform, Sailhardy and I had swung ourselves down over the ship's side at first light on to the ice. We had found it within a hundred yards of the ship. We had hammered in long ice poles with scarlet flags to delimit the safe area; to the left and right of the area, where the ice remained precarious, we had placed a double row of smaller poles carrying orange flags. The platform was slightly longer than wide, and the sun, half obscured by flying cloud, painted it sable, mink, and russet; even Sailhardy's faded, weathered anorak and Balaclava were transformed to soft champagne by the diffused light. It was typical of Sailhardy that he had planted a Norse flag at half-mast in the centre of the ice platform to honour the death of the ship.

The ship lay half over on her starboard side where the water, long since turned to solid ice, had poured through the hole in her side. The port wing of the bridge, connected to the enclosed section by an open lattice covered with a canvas dodger, leaned skywards away from the ice platform. The bright orange of the helicopter stood out on the ship's flensing platform. Helen was to fly it off to safety on the ice as soon as it was light enough. A broken davit hung like a narwhal's tusk, impotent. On the port, or sun's side, the *Antarctica*'s side was bronze-gold; to starboard, or the engine-room side, it was blue-black in her own shadow; neither shadow nor ice could mask the seared plates and mangled corpse.

Making our way back to the ship, we had marked—again by means of flags—a safe path across the ice from the platform to the ship. It was hopeless, Sailhardy and I had agreed during the night, to try to remain aboard. Apart from the noise of plates and steel beams rending, everything between decks had begun to distort at a crazy angle, making doors and bulkheads death traps, and I feared that before long the ice vice would exert its pressure fore and aft as well. Already there was an ominous bulge on the main deck below the bridge.

Throughout the previous night Helen had remained on the bridge with me. At intervals she had brought me cups of boiling cocoa. She had talked little, and before the pre-dawn cloud had begun to obscure the sky, the hard stars were blue-points in her eyes. Following the explosion, I had brought Upton, Walter and Bjerko on the bridge, but after a time, when I saw there was no immediate danger, I had Sailhardy lock them up again. Upton had been morose, unspeaking, completely withdrawn. Apart from the trouble of guarding the men, I was glad to get rid of his sullen ill temper. He and Helen had not spoken to each other. The disaster had had exactly the opposite effect on Pirow's temperament. He was tireless and brilliantly efficient, and during the long hours he had sat glued to his radio I had had an insight into his perverted genius. It seemed to make no difference to him that I had chained him up; action at his beloved instruments stimulated and engrossed him as he relayed to me reports on the catchers, their position on the troublesome radar, and the *Thorshammer*'s signals.

The night signals were, however, of little significance after the one Pirow had passed on to me immediately after the explosion. The *Thorshammer* had ordered Reidar Bull, Hanssen and Lars Brunvoll to seize myself, Upton, Pirow, and Walter. The skippers, said the message, were to rendezvous with the destroyer at Bouvet Island and hand us over.

There was nothing we could do but await their coming. We had no escape. I had told only Helen and Sailhardy what the *Thorshammer* intended to do. What I was at a loss to understand, however, was why the *Thorshammer* was not coming herself. Why order the catcher captains to arrest us? Where was the *Thorshammer* now? What was she about that was more important? From Pirow I could get no help. He had blamed sunspot interference on the radio, and fragments he had passed on to me were too garbled to be comprehensible.

Sailhardy, Helen, and I stood on the bridge while the first burdened men climbed down a hastily rigged gangplank and scrambling net and followed the path of the marker flags to the platform. The wind had not risen nearly as much as I had expected, but it was enough to

carry a series of fine snow flurries and reduce visibility in-
termittently to a few hundred yards. I did not know where
the catchers were. Nor had I any idea of the extent of the
icefield. Pirow had been trying for hours to try to pinpoint
the catchers.

Impatiently I picked up the phone to Pirow. "Any radar
contacts yet? Where the hell are those ships, Pirow. If any
man can find them, you can, either by radio or radar."

His tone never varied, and it showed no traces of a shift
of nearly fifteen hours. "No contacts, Herr Kapitän." A
slight note of irony crept into the level voice. "I appreciate
your compliment."

I wondered again how much of Kohler's success had
been due to the misdirected genius at the other end of my
line. We had respected Kohler, the humane if deadly
hunter, but we had feared the implacable Man with the
Immaculate Hand.

"Keep trying," I said. "Report the slightest sign of them
to me."

"Aye, aye, Herr Kapitän."

Helen said, "Let me go and look for them in the
helicopter, Bruce. That would give you something definite
to go on, once you knew what they were doing."

I glanced at the snow-filled sky. "The only distance you
are going to fly that machine is from here to the platform.
By this afternoon it will be a full gale. If the *Thorshammer*
wants us, let her or the catcher boys come and get us.
You're staying right here!"

"Let me do something!" she exclaimed. "Shall I fly off
now—to the platform? It's quite light enough."

"Yes," I agreed reluctantly. "For heaven's sake, be
careful though. I've ordered the men to have some full fuel
drums there ready to lash the machine to. Otherwise it
might blow away later."

She smiled. "I've been trained for just this, you know."

"Not in the Southern Ocean," I replied.

"Bruce," she went on, "when—and if—the skippers

come, what are you going to do about my father? Are you simply going to hand him over?"

I shrugged. "Our first problem is simply to survive. You forget, I'm in the same boat. The *Thorshammer* wants me as much as your father and Walter. It's only my word against theirs— I'm supposed to have shot down the seaplane."

"Bruce," broke in Sailhardy, "perhaps this sounds a little wild, but it won't be difficult. Let us take the whaleboat, you and I. We can carry her across the ice to the sea. She's light. There are plenty of supplies. We can make Bouvet, you and I. She'll stand up to any weather."

I looked deep into Helen's strange eyes. Without considering the fact that such an escape would brand me guilty anyway, she knew, and I knew, that to leave each other now was no longer possible.

I laughed it off. "You're trying to be another Shackleton or Bligh, Sailhardy. We belong in less heroic times."

"Shackleton survived seven hundred and fifty miles in an ordinary open ship's boat, and Bouvet is less than a hundred—"

I cut him short more harshly than I intended. "You are under my orders, Sailhardy. We stay. The same goes for you, Helen. Now fly off that machine. Watch yourself."

She smiled. "Aye, aye, Herr Kapitän," she mocked.

I was so intent on making sure Helen took off safely from the canted deck that I did not notice the three figures emerge from a snow flurry and make their way to the gangplank. The roar of the helicopter's rotors was over my head after a perfect take-off before I saw the crew of the *Antarctica* start to fall back round the gangplank.

Reider Bull, Hanssen, and Brunvoll strode through the men. There was no mistaking their purposefulness or the grim, bitter anger in their snow-streaked faces. Nor was there any mistaking the purpose of the Schmeisser machine pistol Bull held. A man was coming down the

gangplank shouldering a sack, and Reidar Bull thrust him
roughly to one side with an oath. Bull was big, and not
unlike Walter, but now it was his hand I noticed for the
first time. Three fingers of his left, gripping the barrel of
the Schmeisser, were gone—at some time a faulty harpoon
cable must have ripped them off. Hanssen, tall and blond,
followed Reidar Bull up the side, and Brunvoll, black,
bearded, brought up the rear. The men unloading gaped.
For the moment they forgot that every gallon of fuel and
every tin of food they humped over the side might save a
life later on.

The three skippers strode quickly up the bridge ladder
to where I was. Reidar Bull shoved over the safety catch
when he saw me. I had forgotten the Luger and long knife
stuck in my duffel-coat belt.

Reidar Bull pointed the wicked-looking weapon at me.
"Hanssen! Get those things off him! You, Brunvoll, watch
the islander." He came closer to me. "Where are the
others?"

I shrugged. "In irons. I'm trying to salvage what is left
of this ship. I would have saved the ship herself if you
three lily-livered bastards had obeyed me and brought
your catchers in to keep the lead open."

Reidar Bull's savage mood seemed to be inflamed by
my words. "Listen, Captain! You and this whole crooked
bunch are under arrest. See? I'm taking you—"

"I know," I said shortly. "You're taking me and the
others to a rendezvous at Bouvet and handing us over to
the *Thorshammer*. I heard it over the radio."

Brunvoll could not keep back his anger. "The killer
whale I have seen go and tear out a blue whale's tongue
just for the sport. You are not a killer whale, but, by God!
it made me wonder what you are when I saw you shoot
down the seaplane!"

Bull waved the Schmeisser in my face when I opened
my mouth to tell them about the Spandau-Hotchkiss.
Hanssen also swore threateningly. "Here in the Antarctic

men die hard," he said. "However desperate you are yourself, you never call in help if it will endanger their lives. That is the code. You know it, Captain. Your Captain Scott died like that, and the world still remembers. You, however, deliberately took life."

"Norwegian lives," added Reidar Bull. "Young Norwegians, who did not have your killer ways, Captain. I saw them. They flew right into your bullets. Your shooting was good—too good. Now you and your friends will pay for it." He glanced down at his shattered hand as if the seaplane crew's agony when the bullets went home were bringing alive again something in his past.

"I have put these friends of mine, as you call them, in irons because they intended to kill me," I said. "Not only myself, but Sailhardy here. Look at his face if you don't believe me."

I told them briefly about Norris's chart, Thompson Island, and what I had overheard on the Tannoy.

Reidar Bull replied with a four-letter word. The other two laughed harshly.

"I don't give a bloody damn for your fine stories—you can tell them all to the *Thorshammer*," Reidar Bull said. "My job is to take you back to the destroyer, and I shall. We've got the catchers moored against the ice edge about five miles from here. It will mean a slog across the ice, and I would advise you not to try any tricks. Now get down there!" He jerked the Schmeisser's muzzle towards the ice platform. "Hanssen! You and Lars go and bring the others there too. And get these gaping clods away"—he indicated the crew. "I want a little talk with all the prisoners before we set off."

Reidar Bull, Sailhardy, and I waited fully ten minutes on the flag-marked platform for the others. When the three of us arrived, Helen swung herself slowly down from the helicopter cockpit. She said nothing. Our eyes met. In her sea leopard coat she seemed to merge with the surroundings. The curtain of snow saved us the discomfort of being stared at by the *Antarctica*'s crew.

Upton led, followed by Walter, Bjerko, and Pirow, with Hanssen and Lars Brunvoll bringing up the rear. When Upton spotted Reidar Bull he pushed back the hood of his bright blue weatherproof jacket, the flap of which was brilliant sky-blue and hung down on his chest like the bib under a locust's chin, and hurried towards him, smiling.

"Ah, Reidar Bull!" he exclaimed. "I am glad to see you! Yes, keep that man and the islander guarded. I knew you would come to rescue me. Now get these damn manacles off me and we'll make a plan."

Reidar Bull looked nonplussed. Hanssen and Brunvoll had obviously not told Upton about the *Thorshammer*. The Norwegian's face became more sullen and angry. "You are all under arrest—no, not you, Bjerko, but you must make no attempt to help these men, do you understand?"

Upton dropped his manacled wrists slowly. His voice was full of menace. "By whose orders, Reidar Bull?"

"The *Thorshammer*'s," he replied.

Upton rounded on the three skippers. "None of you has the guts of a wingless Bouvet fly," he said. "As soon as the going became a little tough, you ran off and blabbed everything! Bah! You could have been rich men if you'd gone after the blue whales!"

Brunvoll broke in. "The hell with you and your blue whales! We've all had a bellyful of you, Sir Frederick. We don't know yet what you're up to, but it has ceased to include us, see? Your daughter sighted a big school of blue whales, but then we went off at high speed into the worst ice I have ever seen. Blast your blue whales, and your blue ice also! All we're likely to get by staying with you is a blue arse."

Hanssen had his say too. "In all our experience, none of us has ever seen ice like this. Your fine ship's finished, and it serves you damn-well right."

Upton looked contemptuously at the blond Viking.

"You're so scared you're wearing your lucky charm."

The spur of a wandering Albatross, mounted in silver at the base, was pinned in Hanssen's lapel. He started to finger it sheepishly, but Bull went on in a hard voice. "When we started out from Tristan we knew we would take some risks. We knew we would come inside Norwegian territorial waters—technically. That is nothing. A chance to make a little money, and a little risk on the side—that is fair enough. But the seaplane—we say Captain Wetherby, and his islander, Walter, Pirow, and you are bloody murderers. You're all in this together. We are turning you all in."

Upton swung on his toes. He tried his comradely charm. "Sailhardy had no part in the shooting. He was unconscious in his cabin. Let him go!"

Sailhardy's voice had an edge like the wind. "True, I was unconscious because what Captain Wetherby told you is true. They knocked me out."

Reidar Bull waved the Schmeisser. "You can go free, Sailhardy, but be careful. That is all I say. Try to help your captain and see what happens."

"If he goes, I go," retorted the islander. "If you march him to the catchers, I march too."

"Listen," I said roughly, "I am not taking the blame for what Walter did. I did not shoot down the seaplane. Ask the *Aurora*'s helmsman—"

"We did," said Brunvoll. "He saw you and Walter go up to the gun. He heard it fired."

"It is a weapon for two men, not one," Hanssen filled in. "Petersen, the helmsman, heard both the Spandau and the Hotchkiss. Two men fired that gun."

"Walter—" I started to say.

"Neither Hanssen nor Brunvoll nor I is here to pass judgment," said Reidar Bull. "We are under orders—orders from a warship of my country, and we shall carry them out."

Walter flicked a quick glance at Upton. "It is true I

went up to the gun platform with Captain Wetherby," he
said. "We crossed together from the factory ship to the
Aurora. It was Captain Wetherby's idea to shoot the
seaplane down if it shadowed the fleet. At that time I too
agreed, but my heart failed me when I saw those poor boys
come into the sights. I too am a Norwegian. Am I to kill
my own countrymen just because this English captain says
so? Just for the sake of a few blue whales? I pulled the gun
harness to one side—you saw how the first burst of tracers
went wide. But he is good on a gun, this captain. He is also
strong. He pulls the gun round and gets in a burst with the
quick-firer, the Hotchkiss. Then he tries to kill me with the
same gun. He is kill-crazy. I had to shoot him with the
Luger to stop this madness—"

"Walter, you bloody lying bastard!" I snapped. "Reidar
Bull, Brunvoll, Hanssen! These men are evil, and they are
after something which is evil too. I have come to Bouvet
to see what the Albatross' Foot is all about. I have no
other interest."

"So," said Reidar Bull, "you are so keen on this current
that you shoot down a seaplane? We are simple men, Captain Wetherby, but not as simple as that."

"It was I who pulled Walter off the gun," I protested.
Their faces were hard with disbelief. "It was I who turned
aside the first burst—"

Reidar Bull waved aside what I was saying. "You can
tell all this to the *Thorshammer*. We are not very good
men, Captain, and not very honest men, but we have seen
two of our own kind killed coldly and ruthlessly. That is
all we know. That is what made us signal the *Thorshammer*." He turned to Pirow. "Get up there in the helicopter
and signal the *Thorshammer*. No tricks." He tossed the
Luger across to Brunvoll. "Go with him, Lars, and see to
it. Pirow, tell the *Thorshammer*, I, Reidar Bull, have arrested the men who shot down the seaplane and will rendezvous with her at Bouvet, as arranged before."

When Pirow had come across the ice to the platform he

had looked utterly worn out. Now his fatigue seemed to drop like a cloak. He shot a glance at Upton and shrugged slightly. He turned to me, showing off. "The Herr Kapitän reads Morse," he said, smiling. "Perhaps he will come to the door of the cockpit and assure you that I am sending the right message."

Reidar Bull looked puzzled but agreed. I walked with Brunvoll and the Man with the Immaculate Hand to the helicopter. Helen stood back, white-faced, silent. There was a pause while Pirow, encumbered still with the manacles, went to the machine's radio.

The radio key started to clatter as he called up the destroyer.

Reidar Bull skipper catcher Crozet to Thorshammer stop I have under arrest the men who shot down and killed your seaplane crew stop I will rendezvous with you at Bouvet as arranged stop

Pirow's sending was fluent, proficient, staccato. He wasn't trying to bluff *Thorshammer* that he was anyone else. Why had he agreed so readily to send Bull's damning message? He was in the business as deep as Upton or myself.

Then came the *Thorshammer*'s reply:

Thorshammer to Reidar Bull catcher Crozet stop rendezvous at Bouvet as ordered stop part of your message not understood stop Thorshammer's seaplane ran out of fuel stop crew safe on lifecraft stop position approx 100 miles west of Bouvet stop am searching for fliers stop

I could not believe my ears: the seaplane safe on the water, out of fuel—the seaplane I had seen go to its death under a hail of bullets from the Spandau-Hotchkiss! I was so astonished that I forgot Reidar Bull and his Schmeisser and jumped up the steps into the radio compartment.

Brunvoll stood, Luger in hand, frowning, unaware of what was passing over the air.

"The seaplane!" I said incredulously to both Pirow and Brunvoll. "How can the seaplane be signalling—?"

"What are you saying?" demanded Brunvoll. "The seaplane I saw shot down—?"

Pirow grinned at me. He flicked off the transmitting key, so that the tapping which followed was for my benefit alone. Gone was the German staccato. This was the Man with the Immaculate Hand, slipping into one of his many guises. Now he projected himself into being the seaplane crew, sending emergency signals from their liferaft. The dummy signal he tapped for me was fragmentary, a little breathless, just as it would sound from a couple of fliers facing possible death on a liferaft in the wild seas. It all fell into place then—why the *Thorshammer* had not come to arrest us herself. Pirow, during his long period in the radio office, must have sent off a series of faked messages purporting to come from the seaplane crew on their liferaft. He was clever enough not to have given the *Thorshammer* time enough to get a bearing—the only man who could get a bearing on a dozen letters was Pirow himself. He must have thought up his ingenious plan while he listened to the catchers signalling the *Thorshammer*. The destroyer was at present on her way to an imaginary position given by Pirow to pick up a seaplane crew that no longer existed. He was giving Upton and himself a breathing space. He was also proving that Walter had committed no crime, for the *Thorshammer*'s radio log would show that the seaplane had been signalling long after it had, in fact, been shot down. I saw the mettle of the Man with the Immaculate Hand. The *Thorshammer* would then be arresting us for an infringement of Norwegian territorial waters and hunting the blue whale.

"Come!" I said to Brunvoll. "I want you to hear this too." I strode to the cockpit door. The circle of faces on the ice looked up at me. Helen's was troubled, anxious.

"Reidar Bull!" I called. "The *Thorshammer* has just signalled back. She says her seaplane crew is safe on the water. They were never shot down. They ran out of fuel."

"God's truth! What is this?" he roared. "Safe on the water! Am I drunk or mad?"

Brunvoll gripped my arm with a fist of iron. "I saw—every one of us saw—the seaplane fall in the water, shot to ribbons by you and Walter."

"By Walter," I said steadily. I told them what I believed Pirow had done. As I did so I saw a look of savage triumph and determination cross Upton's pewter-hued face, framed by the blue hood. Helen caught my glance and looked at her father. She half started forward, then again looked up at me. She had seen, and I had seen. I was glad of the manacles on Upton's wrists, supplemented by the Schmeisser guarding him.

Hanssen shook his head, like a boxer clearing his mind after a blow. "I see a plane fly into a gun. I see the gun fire. I see the plane crash. Now I am told it is not so."

"The three of you have been taken for the biggest ride of your careers," I said. I told them who Pirow was. Bull's face went black. "The *Thorshammer* won't listen to you now, after Pirow's signals. Heaven knows how long you'll have to hang around at Bouvet while she searches for that seaplane crew of hers."

Upton's voice was tense. "Tell them too, Wetherby, that there is no extradition for murder in the Antarctic. It's all in the Antarctic Treaty, which your bloody country signed, Reidar Bull. There is no treaty obligation to hand over anyone."

Bull clicked the Schmeisser as if to assure himself that it, at least, was real. "I don't know what extradition means," he replied. "I don't know what anything means any more, with bastards like you round me. All I know is that we march—now! You can take any small personal things." He gestured with the Schmeisser at Upton. "You first. What do you want?"

"Look in my desk drawer," he said. "There is an old chart. Bring it. There is a little leather bag next to it. There's a first-aid kit with a hypodermic too. And my guarana in the liquor cabinet. That is all I want."

"You, Captain?" asked Reidar Bull.

"My sextant," I replied. "That is all." It was the sextant with which I had plotted Thompson Island.

Sailhardy came forward, his thumb flicking in his strange way against his palm. "I march because Captain Wetherby marches, Reidar Bull. You are sailors, and you each have your ship. I also have a ship. It is everything I have in the world. To a Tristan islander, it is worth more than his life almost. I will march, but I will carry my boat."

For the first time that morning Reidar Bull's face relaxed a little. "By everything that is holy! This islander! I could almost wish he was my friend and not the Captain's!" He looked at the other two skippers. They were men who knew what it was to have one's own ship under one. There was almost no need to ask their approval. "You can load it aboard my own ship," Bull went on brusquely, as if afraid to show sentiment. "Wait! I know! Captain Wetherby can help you carry the whaleboat. It will keep him out of mischief on the march." The others grinned.

"I have a small case ready," said Helen. "I packed it ready to leave last night. It is on the bridge."

Reidar Bull's face reverted to its grimness. "You'll stay right here, miss. Captain Bjerko will remain behind and see to the unloading of the ship. When we reach the ice edge I will signal on the W/T, and you will fly the helicopter to the catchers. It may be very useful to us yet. You'll land on the ice by the catchers, and we'll manhandle it aboard my ship."

Helen started to protest, but he cut her short. "Hanssen! Go and get the things they have asked for. Be quick! I want to go before the weather gets worse." He spoke to

Bjerko. "We'll come back with the catchers after we have met the *Thorshammer* at Bouvet. She ordered all three of us to come, and the *Aurora* makes four. There'll be enough room aboard to take off the *Antarctica*'s crew. We'll be away only a couple of days. The ice won't break up before then. You'll be safe enough."

Bjerko looked dubiously at the factory ship, whose outline we could see despite the snow flurries. "I have never seen ice like this. Come back soon. I don't like it."

Nor did I. Behind the doomed ship, where the raft of ice had broken off, it had carved the likeness of a gigantic sphinx head with defined lips and a brooding forehead. Even the neck was there, in the shape of a series of striated cliffs; almost meeting a hundred and fifty feet from the surface was a double cantileverlike wing which was held at its base by three fluted columns, each one fifty feet in diameter.

I started to go over to Helen, but Bull waved me back. Upton infected us all with his tension. He appeared to be expecting something. Brunvoll seemed grateful to have something to do when Bull sent him back to guard Pirow. As Hanssen emerged from the path on his return from the ship, Upton went forward quickly and took the map from him.

It was Norris's chart of Thompson Island.

Upton knelt down and spread it open on the ice. "Come here, Reidar Bull," he said authoritatively. We all gathered round. Upton spoke quickly, and there was a tic at the corners of his mouth and eyes. His fingers were shaky as he pointed to the spidery track of the old *Sprightly* and Norris's position of Thompson Island. We were drawn inside the circle of his compelling personality.

"Have you ever heard of Thompson Island?" he demanded.

Reidar Bull glanced at the old map. He shrugged. "Yes. I have also heard of the Aurora Islands, down in the Scotia Sea. Men have searched for a hundred, maybe two hundred, years for them. These islands exist—how do you say?—in the mind only."

The faint pink flush suffused Upton's mask. I could see he was taking a big grip on himself. The twitch at the corner of his mouth got worse.

Hanssen didn't even bother to look. "I have seen a hundred things in the Southern Ocean which could have been islands—rocks streaked with guano, icebergs covered with mud. It is not surprising that we all dream a little in these waters. Many men have dreamed, but only a few islands have been found. It is the same with Thompson Island."

"Get up!" ordered Bull. "March!"

Upton squatted on his haunches still. He seemed to be losing control of his hands, they were shaking so. The manacles rattled faintly.

"Father," said Helen in an agonized voice, "come. Thompson Island can wait."

His eyes were fever-bright. "It's waited a century and more for me," he said thickly. "Reidar Bull! Hanssen! Thompson Island exists! Here is its position. Captain Wetherby has seen it, seen it, do you hear?" His voice rose. "Listen!" He turned the old chart over and quoted from Norris's own personal log, which was, with its image of blue ice, written so indelibly in my mind:

"Thompson Island is nothing but perpendicular rocks and it looks like a complete cinder, with immense veins of lava which have the appearance of black glass, but much of it is streaked with white veins."

Bull's harsh laugh sounded like floes grinding together. "Rubbish! Get up!"

Upton crouched on the ice like a wounded animal facing its hunters. His face was contorted. Helen had drawn back in horror at his break-up. He was keeping his last card—his real reason for wanting to find Thompson

Island—in reserve still. Walter licked his lips. Thompson Island had bitten into Upton's mind and eroded it in a way which was dreadful to contemplate; I waited in awe for what was to follow.

"I want Thompson Island," he said, so softly that I had to crane to hear him. He looked at the three skippers. "I'll double my original offer to you if you will take me to Thompson Island." None of them replied. Upton swung round to me. "Bruce!" he said. "Bruce, you know where it is, and so do I now. Take me there!"

Looking down on the mouthing figure on the ice and remembering what had happened to men in the past who had also wanted Thompson Island, I resolved to myself that no one would ever wring from me the secret of Thompson Island's whereabouts.

Upton fumbled with his pathetic little squash leather bag.

"Oh, God!" burst out Helen. "Bruce—"

He got it open and emptied the contents into his hand. Still crouching, he rolled the five objects across the old chart, as if he were throwing dice.

They looked like bull's-eyes.

Upton began almost to intone. "Heavenly blue, they call it. The same colour as this ice. It's really silvery white, but it takes its name from the two heavenly blue lines in its spectrum."

Reidar Bull said something in a low voice in Norwegian to the other two skippers.

"You'll come with me now, won't you, Reidar Bull, and you, Lars Brunvoll, and you, Hanssen?" he said, looking up expectantly at us. "The other money was chickenfeed next to this."

"What are you talking about?" demanded Bull roughly.

"You'll come then, Reidar Bull?" he went on. "You'll be the richest man in Norway."

"From that?" sneered Bull, indicating the bull's-eyes.

The tic tugged at the corner of Upton's mouth and eyes

as if, even now, he were reluctant to reveal his secret.

"Yes," he said. "That is caesium. It is the rarest metal in the world. It is worth two hundred pounds a pound."

Caesium! The space-age metal!

I had considered all along that it was not geographical curiosity which was driving Upton to try to find Thompson Island. Caesium had been much in the forefront when I had returned to Cambridge after the war—it is the most vital part of the fuel for space ships and space rockets. Looking down at the dicelike objects, my mind ran back to one of the young scientists at the Cavendish Laboratories who had become a bore and a butt over our after-dinner glass of port because of his endless conversations on the wonders of caesium: Upton was right in saying blue whales were nothing by comparison. Caesium, I had been told, was known to occur in minute quantities in only three places: a small place in northern Sweden, in southwest Africa, and in Kazakhstan in the Soviet Union. I wished now I could remember more of what the Cambridge bore had had to say about it. Vaguely I recalled that it had the lowest boiling point of any metal in the alkali group and was priceless not only because of its scarcity, but for the ease with which it could be made to form electrically charged fuel gas for space ships. It was, from what I could remember, the answer to the scientists' prayer for a space fuel—except that there was practically none of it to be had. There was also something about its extremely high ionization potential which made it possible to transmute its atomic heat directly into electric power without having to use an intermediate stage of steam boilers or turbines in the space ships.

I looked at Upton and I knew the answer even before I asked him. "Your face—caesium?"

Some of the wild light went from his eyes. "You know caesium? Bruce, you know it? Yes," he said, touching his face, "this is the price of my knowledge. I told you, the metal particles pass into the skin. I know more about caesium than any man living. I worked on it—more than twenty years ago now—at a little place called Ronnskar, in Sweden, on the Gulf of Bothnia. It's quite close to the port of Skelleftea—"

I cut him short. I still couldn't see how he linked Thompson with his wonder metal. "How do you know it exists on Thompson Island—where did those samples come from?"

"Norris took a hammer," he said. "You'll see from the log how he sent a ship's boat ashore, and they had to make a sudden dash back to the ship because of the weather. Three of these pieces of rock are Norris's. The other two are Pirow's. You see, Kohler used Thompson Island as a base for the *Meteor*. Pirow has been there, but he doesn't know where it is—only roughly, somewhere near Bouvet. Kohler never let on." The words came tumbling out in a flood.

Helen said gently, "Father, why did you go about it this way? Underhand, murder—all the rest of it?"

It only needed a hair-trigger to touch Upton off. "Thompson Island is mine!" he shouted. "I won't have any bloody governmental committees telling me where and what I should explore. That shameful Antarctic Treaty—"

Reidar Bull, Hanssen, and Brunvoll seemed to be at a loss. All this about caesium was going over their heads.

I asked another question to try to keep Upton on an even keel. "Where did you get Norris's samples from?"

He laughed—a strange, brittle laugh. "From Wetherby's! You see, Bruce, I bought out Wetherby's—under an assumed name, of course, Stewart and Company. You weren't to know. Don't forget I already suspected you were the only man to have seen Thompson Island. Pirow came later when I started scratching in the German Naval Archives. Those rocks there are veined with caesium—pollucite, they call the mineral salt. Do you see what Norris's log and his description of whole cliffs seamed with caesium mean to me?"

"Enough to murder a couple of innocent men?"

His laugh jarred. "Dear God, man, can't you see that nations will fight atomic wars over Thompson Island's caesium? Millions may die, not only two. They were unimportant beside this!"

I looked again at the old chart, at the five dicelike pieces of caesium rock, and at the wild eyes of the whaling tycoon. Men had suffered and died in the past to find Thompson, and now in the present the island had come back with a lure more deadly, and a threat more lethal, than anything which had gone before. As my eyes lifted they met Helen's. There was no need to reinforce my resolve never to reveal Thompson Island's whereabouts.

I turned to Reidar Bull. "The man is mad," I said harshly. "You should lock him up. Thompson Island isn't where the chart says anyway. Remember that, Sir Frederick."

The awful pink flush suffused his face, and he threw himself at me, using the manacles as a weapon. Again and again he struck at me, shouting obscenities, while Brunvoll clubbed him with the butt of the Luger. It took Brunvoll and Hanssen to drag him off me.

"Judas!" he half gasped, half screamed. "You, who know, you have betrayed me! Curse all the Wetherbys! Curse Bruce Wetherby—"

Helen stood back in anguish as he screamed. Pirow's face was grey. Reidar Bull's savage anger was stilled.

"Let us march," I said to Reidar Bull. "Sailhardy and I will fetch the whaleboat. You can send Brunvoll along too, if you like, but there isn't anywhere for us to escape to."

Hanssen held Upton now, still mouthing threats at me and the skippers.

When we returned, carrying the boat easily by upending her with the bow and stern thwarts on our heads, the party had already formed up. There was no good-bye allowed to Helen. She stood, camouflaged in her sea leopard coat, against the snow at thirty yards, next to one of the helicopter's landing wheels. Her lips moved soundlessly to me as we moved off, with Reidar Bull bringing up the rear with the Schmeisser at the ready, and Upton leading, with Brunvoll's Luger at his back. The whaleboat was no real burden; Sailhardy could have carried its weight by himself, but two of us made its bulk easier to handle, especially when the wind plucked at it. The ice was hard, and we started briskly. The *Antarctica* lay against the sick sun. The last I saw of her was when she lurched yet again, like a beaten wrestler trying to keep his shoulder off the mat.

By lunchtime, by following the markers Reidar Bull had laid at intervals across the icefield, we came to the ice edge. The four catchers—*Crozet, Kerguelen, Chimay,* and *Aurora*—were moored together. Already the ice had started to trace a needlework pattern on their rigging Unless it was cleared, they would be carrying a top-hamper that would roll them to their doom once they got outside the protection of the icefield, which damped down the great rollers of the Westerlies. Each ship had a white square on its black funnel on which was painted its name, and to the inexperienced eye all four might have been cut from the same matrix—the flared bows, the canvas-enclosed bridge, the big steam pipe running up and round the funnel, the heavy foremast with a crow's-nest, the long, low platform aft like a frigate's depth-charge platform. To a whalerman's eyes, however, they were as individual as those of us who made up the marching party. On the march Upton had given no more trouble. He had pulled his blue hood over his head, and all we could see from behind was the hunch of his shoulders.

As we paused for a breather before making the last leg to the catchers Pirow fell back alongside me. The greyness had not passed out of his face and he spoke softly and agitatedly, so that Reidar Bull behind could not hear.

"Herr Kapitän," he said, "where is the rendezvous

with the destroyer?"

I was puzzled at his tone. "Why, at Bouvet," I said. "You know that already."

"Yes," he said quickly. "But where? Off the island, or where?"

"There's only one anchorage, in the southwest, at Bollevika. That is the rendezvous."

He took my arm as if to steady himself.

"What is it, man?" I asked, he appeared so agitated.

"The *Meteor* mined the approaches to the anchorage and Bollevika itself," he said.

Pirow's words released in me a wave of depression which had been mounting ever since my unspoken farewell to Helen. Along the march, the image of that lonely figure had returned again and again. To my mind's eye rose those strange eyes which, I was able to tell myself now, had come alive and vital—she had said it herself—through me. In seeking the Albatross' Foot I, like Saul, had gone in search of asses and found instead a kingdom. Now the full reaction of that empty farewell set in. I knew, as I considered the prospect before me, that there would be little chance of meeting her again. Reidar Bull had made it quite clear that, although not a prisoner like ourselves, she would not be free to come and go. If she disobeyed Reidar Bull and stayed at the *Antarctica*, she was courting disaster; Helen could, if she could locate the *Thorshammer*, fly to the destroyer and tell her story. But would they believe her any more than Reidar Bull and the others did? The thought of my own future brought me despair: as far as the Royal Society was concerned, I was probably done for. Mere suspicion of what I was supposed to have done would be enough for that august body to finish with me—and with the Albatross' Foot. In the light of what had happened, it would appear as if the whole story of the Albatross' Foot had simply been a cover for

dubious activities in the Southern Ocean along with Upton
and his gang. What action would the *Thorshammer* take
when Reidar Bull handed us over, as he had every inten-
tion of doing? I could not see Pirow's deception about the
seaplane crew being more than a temporary red herring.
Short of Walter's confessing, I could see no way out. Their
crime was an infringement of Norwegian waters: mine was
murder, if things went the way they were going. The
thought of Helen waiting for me to become conscious, after I had fallen off the Spandau-Hotchkiss into the sea,
and the strange, deep look in her eyes when I told her what
had really happened, made my prospects more agonizing.
She believed me; Sailhardy believed me; but the events
that had enmeshed me in shooting down the seaplane were
as complex as those that had brought me to Bouvet, doorway to Thompson Island.

Automatically I felt for my sextant case, which I had
hung from my belt. Inside that sextant case lay the secret
of the whereabouts of Thompson Island. It was no more
than a notch on the vernier, the scale on which to read the
altitude of the sun and stars. It would mean nothing in
someone else's hands. I intended that Thompson Island
stay unknown.

Had I known that Kohler had mined the approaches to
Bouvet, I might have caught him months earlier. I had
sent a damaged ship to anchor temporarily at Bouvet, and
all I had heard from her was a stifled, desperate
message—*Underwater explosion*—and then no more. A
day later another merchantman had been sunk a thousand
miles away, and I had rushed off on a wild goose chase. I
had assumed from the two widely separated sinkings that
Kohler was working with a U-boat in my waters. Now I
knew that a mine had got the first ship. One might, I suppose, call Bollevika an anchorage, but often there is
scarcely any holding ground for an anchor: Lars Christensen's ship had had to steam backwards and forwards
slowly for a whole month, waiting for the shore party to

return, since she was unable to obtain anchorage at
Bollevika, which lies open to the gales and seas that sweep
in endlessly from the southwest quarter.

Pirow must have wondered from my long silence if I
disbelieved him, for he went on quickly, "Herr Kapitän
Kohler mined the South African coast as far as the hun-
dred-fathom line. The *Meteor* carried ninety-five mines.
We used eighty off South Africa. Then we came to Bouvet.
We used the other fifteen at Bouvet."

"We must tell the skippers right away," I said.

"Yes, Herr Kapitän," he said sombrely. "And you
know what the approaches will be like."

"I haven't been closer than twenty miles, but I can
guess," I said. When I had seen Bollevika the icebergs had
made a belt round the island, broken here and there by
zigzag open leads of water. Heaven help the crew of any
ship that struck a mine under those conditions, I thought.

"Reidar Bull!" I called. "Come here!" The big Norwegian, suspicious, with the Schmeisser at the ready, came
across to us. I outlined what Pirow had told me.

Reidar Bull's reaction took me unawares. "Christ!" he
exclaimed angrily. "Must I now be frightened by some
bloody fairy story which you two naval types concoct!
Hanssen! Brunvoll!" The others joined us. "Listen to this!
We mustn't keep the rendezvous at Bouvet because—so
our German friend now tells us—his ship mined the approaches to Bollevika during the war! I say—nonsense!"

"It is true," retorted Pirow angrily. "There are
several deepsea contact mines—"

Brunvoll's temper had not improved with the long hike
across the ice. "So the first person you run to tell is the
English captain, heh? Is he in command of this party?
Why must he know first, heh?"

"Because it is a scare story they have thought up between themselves," said Bull. "I don't believe a word of
it."

Hanssen grinned. "We don't need to believe or

disbelieve. We can prove it quite easily."

"What do you mean?" asked Bull.

"Let us send the *Aurora* on ahead of our own ships," he said. "If Pirow's story is a lie, which I think it is, then no harm will come of it. If it is not"—he shrugged—"it is just too bad. Good ridddance, I say."

Pirow was as white as the moment he had come onto the bridge and seen the blue icefield. "I was there! I know the place is mined!" he exclaimed. "Don't be such damned fools!"

"These men are as slippery as the Great Ice Barrier," said Brunvoll. "We may be damned fools, but we are not criminal maniacs," he went on. "Yes, send the *Aurora* in with the lot of them aboard, and we'll see what happens. If she blows up, our own ships will still be safe."

"Aye," said Reidar Bull. "But I won't send the *Aurora*'s crew. They had no hand in it."

"Easy," said Hanssen. "If we sail tonight we can be off Bouvet tomorrow morning. We'll transfer the *Aurora*'s crew at the approaches. She won't need a full crew to take her in. Walter can manage the engines for a couple of miles. Captain Wetherby will find no problems in sailing a ship."

"I don't like the idea of letting Captain Wetherby have a ship," grumbled Brunvoll. "Anything can happen: a squall, a patch of fog, and—poof!—when we look, the sea will be empty and the *Aurora* will have disappeared. If anyone needs to be guarded it is the English captain."

"We'll guard him all right," said Hanssen with a grim smile. "We'll unship that hellish gun and have it rigged forward on my harpoon platform. It'll only take a couple of hours. The *Kerguelen* can sail maybe half a mile astern of the *Aurora* as we approach the Bollevika anchorage. If any tricks are played they'll get a double stream of lead— the way the seaplane did."

It was no use arguing with men in their savage mood. I turned to Pirow. "Can you remember, even vaguely, how

Captain Kohler mined Bollevika? Did he lay a definite pattern, taking a bearing on something ashore? Was it a regular line? Have you any idea at what intervals the mines were dropped overboard?"

Pirow shuddered. "No, but I remember how the Herr Kapitän Kohler laughed after we had mined the Agulhas Bank off South Africa. We came close inshore towards a big lighthouse, which the fools had left burning—in wartime! We started mining from the hundred-fathom mark, and zigzagged shorewards. 'If anyone ever finds the plot of these mines, it is more than I could do,' Herr Kapitän Kohler said. He did the same at Bouvet. The mines were also set to float at any depth."

I was no longer so concerned as Pirow. I knew that Kohler must have used the German "Y" type of mine, which was fitted with a self-destroying device should it break loose. To lay his mines deep, as he must have done at Bouvet and off South Africa, he must have used a very light mooring wire, and the odds were that Bouvet's heavy seas had long since loosened the moorings and that the mines had destroyed themselves. My mind raced ahead: if I could get hold of the *Aurora.* . . . But I would want Sailhardy and his whaleboat.

I looked at the islander. "You hear what Pirow says, Sailhardy. I can't ask you to come, in the face of that. I'd like your boat though."

Sailhardy smiled faintly. "Were they 'Y' type mines, Bruce?"

"Yes," I answered.

The skippers looked suspicious. Mines and mining were above their heads.

"I'd come even if they weren't," he replied.

Reidar Bull shook his head. "I don't like a man going just because of his captain."

"There's no need to worry about me if the *Aurora* strikes a mine," replied Sailhardy. "The man you should have on your conscience right now is Captain Wetherby.

He did not shoot down the plane."

Brunvoll was unimpressed. "I'll follow your *Kerguelen* into Bollevika, Hanssen. We must all take bearings and check the *Aurora*'s course—we don't want to be mined ourselves through carelessness."

"We could send the helicopter in ahead as a spotter," said Reidar Bull.

"Leave Miss Upton out of this," I said roughly. "You bastards are very fond, it seems, of playing around with other people's lives while you sit safe on your arses. I know what Bouvet weather can be—fog, gales, high seas, damn-all visibility. Leave her out of it, I say! You couldn't spot a mine moored at depth from a helicopter anyway, particularly not in these seas."

"It is strange to see a man who can get behind a gun and kill become so concerned over anyone," sneered Reidar Bull. "You shouldn't keep your soft side for women only."

I had to see Helen again. Reidar Bull's remark brought home how curiously she had come to be allied in my mind with the Southern Ocean. At the moment the mines seemed unimportant beside my wish to see her.

Helen's face was before my mind's eye. "I couldn't give a seal's burp for your plan to save your skins and make us into a lot of guinea pigs," I said harshly. "I'll take the *Aurora* in—only, however, if you let me see Miss Upton again before we sail." I turned on Pirow. "Pull yourself together, man. If we strike a mine you won't know what hit you anyway."

He smiled wanly. "I wish I could detect them by radio."

Reidar Bull dropped the barrel of the Schmeisser a little. "You are a brave man, Captain Wetherby. Mikklesen said so too. War has no place in peace though. I almost wish it was Walter who shot down the seaplane."

"Am I to see Miss Upton?" I demanded.

He looked inquiringly at the other two skippers. "Very well, Captain. We have nothing to lose, and you may have something to gain by it. Tomorrow at the approaches to Bollevika—who knows?"

I remembered Bollevika, lit on a dark winter's afternoon by the fragile, strange luminosity of the solar flares that wince and bicker across the Southern Ocean from Cape Horn to the Great Ross Barrier, and my occasional sight of the ice cliffs and towering peaks while the breakneck lightning of the blue magnetic flares twitched from mountain peak to turbulent sea.

"Bollevika—who knows?" I echoed. "Will you signal Miss Upton to come now from the factory ship?"

He nodded. "March—to the catchers!"

The party trudged wearily across the remaining distance to the ice edge. Reidar Bull shouted orders to the crews to dismantle the Spandau-Hotchkiss, while he himself went aboard the *Crozet* to signal Helen. He left Brunvoll to guard us with the Schmeisser.

Upton refused to be drawn into any conversation and merely grunted when Brunvoll or Hanssen spoke to him. He and Walter were shackled. I was grateful for this since I feared another outburst on the heels of his morose fit. Walter tried to be ingratiating to our captors, and Pirow retained his terrified attitude, as if it were already certain that the *Aurora* would strike one of the mines.

Once he edged close to me. "Herr Kapitän," he said in a low voice, "Thompson Island has a safe anchorage, and there are warm springs. You know where the island is—"

"Shut up!" snapped Brunvoll. "I don't want any whispering, particularly between you two!"

I waited. I had scarcely any regard for the activity round me as lights were rigged on the decks of the *Aurora* and the *Kerguelen* and heavy tackles put in place to lift the gun into position from one to the other. We were too far away to hear the crews talking, but once or twice I saw grim glances being cast in the direction of the party. It was clear that they shared the skippers' repugnance for what I was supposed to have done. My ears were attuned to hear Helen's approach; when at last the familiar roar of the rotors hung over the ships and shore party, it took away, at least for me, some of the forlorn and desolate air of the scene: the men and the ships seemed so puny alongside the great expanse of ice; the very wind seemed to be holding back its violence in preparation for an onslaught against us. I reckoned the temperature must be somewhere around thirty degrees below freezing. We stamped and beat our arms to keep warm. The shackles on Upton and Walter, secured outside their thick gloves so that the icy metal would not burn them, clinked dismally.

The helicopter landed next to us. Helen cut the engine.

"You can have half an hour," said Brunvoll. "Then everyone goes aboard. after we've rigged the gun the men still have to get that machine lashed aboard the *Crozet*." He waved the Schmeisser. "Don't get any ideas of making a sudden break in the helicopter, although where the hell you'd go to I wouldn't know."

I swung myself up into the machine and went forward to the cabin. It was warm inside. The light from the loading lamps threw Helen's face into sharp relief. She was wrapped in the sea leopard coat. We looked at each other without saying a word. We were insulated from the world outside. I could not even hear the men working on the gun.

Helen broke the silence. "It could not have ended like that, could it, Bruce?"

I shook my head. Her face was taut and the eyes were never lovelier.

"No," I said. "But it could end another way tomorrow." I told her about the minefield. For a while she did not reply, then she reached out and took my gloved hand in a grip that revealed her feelings. "If it were not for you, Bruce, I think at this moment I would hate the Southern Ocean and all its works. It never relaxes, never gives, does it? Yet it's a part—perhaps more than half—of you, isn't it? I can't hate it because of that."

I leaned over and kissed her lips lightly. I saw the pattern of a down-horizon solar flare explosion in her eyes.

"No!" she burst out. "They shan't do it, I tell you!" She reached for the throttle switches. "They shall not, not while I can get you away!"

I knocked her hand away and pointed. Brunvoll had the Schmeisser ready aimed. "Before the rotors got going, Helen, there'd come a burst from that," I said. "Don't think that Reidar Bull, Hanssen, and Brunvoll don't mean it. They do."

"There's a ghastly pattern of things which has caught us up," she exclaimed heatedly. "Here's an ocean as big and as empty of humans as any in the world, and yet it is a human mesh which is taking you away from me."

"The mesh your father wove," I said.

"I know, I know," she went on. "But you and I realize that my father isn't the whole cause—"

"Thompson Island," I said.

"Thompson Island!" she said brokenly. "How I hate the sound of that name!"

"This moment together is borrowed time," I said gently. "It's running out."

"I'll fly patrol over the *Aurora* tomorrow," she said. "If she's mined I'll pick you up, as I did before."

"No, Helen," I said. "You know that you can't take off from a small catcher's deck pitching in the sort of sea we will run into at Bouvet."

She buried her face in her hands. "How do you think I will feel when I watch the, *Aurora* go in towards Bollevika? You, my father—Bruce, we could still get him well again with treatment!"

Brunvoll gestured from below. Helen's face was full of anguish. I kissed her, and she clung to me for a moment. Then she gook my hand and put it over the compass platform. "If Suzie Wong has a ghost, let it come and guard Bruce Wetherby's luck," she said.

I looked deep into her eyes again and then went aft and jumped down on to the ice. At the head of the *Aurora*'s gangplank, as we filed aboard, I turned and looked back. I could just make out the shadow of the sea leopard coat against the perspex window.

Upton, Walter, Pirow, Sailardy, and I were locked into one small cabin. Shortly after nightfall the catchers sailed—for Bouvet and the Bollevika approaches.

I had thought that once we were alone there would be a
fresh outburst from Upton against me. It did not come. I
spent an uneasy night, almost grateful for the guard outside the door, lest Upton's mania should return. He took
the sole bunk in the small cabin for himself and covered
his head with the blue hood. Sailhardy and I huddled on
the floor together for warmth. Pirow and Walter exchanged a few words. I cut Walter short when he tried to
speak to me. By dawn the ship was pitching heavily, and I
wondered how the transfer of the crew was to take place.
Pirow again spoke anxiously about the mines before dropping off into an exhausted sleep. It was as if I were going
into an ambush knowing it had been laid; for to me the
mine is the assassin, the thug: the torepdo, by contrast, is
the hunter, and it pits its skill against range and angle,
against water salinity, depth, and the chance of a sudden
variation of course by its quarry.

Shortly before midday the engines began to slow. It was
impossible to see outside as the porthole was frosted over.
There were several sharp alterations of course and then a
heavy thump against the side. I realized what the ice-wise
catcher captains were about. They were mooring the
Aurora alongside a small iceberg with another of the
catchers in order to transfer the men.

The cabin door opened. Brunvoll came in, carrying the
Schmeisser. His heavy clothing was streaked with ice.
With him was another burly Norwegian.

Brunvoll grinned without humour. "We're about ten
miles off Bouvet. You can now have the pleasure, Captain, of seeing whether our friend's story about the mines
is correct."

"For the last time, Brunvoll, listen!" protested Pirow.
"The place is thick with mines!"

"So you said before," he replied. He handed the other
man a key and said something. He went forward and
unclicked the manacles on Walter and Upton.

Upton's eyes were hard. "Brunvoll! The first score I have to pay is with Wetherby. The second is with you. Remember that."

Brunvoll shrugged. "Get up on deck, all of you. And remember, Captain, that the *Kerguelen* with the Spandau-Hotchkiss will be only a quarter of a mile behind you. You'll see when you get on deck, there's no sea room. There's an open water passage leading into the Bollevika anchorage, zigzag and half-frozen. There are icebergs jumbled together everywhere."

It was no use arguing. "Brunvoll," I said, "if we are mined, are the boats ready to use?"

"Yes," he replied brusquely. "I had them checked last night. The falls are all running freely. Also, the whaleboat is lashed across the winches by the foremast." He spoke to Sailhardy. "You don't have to go with this lot, you know."

"Nor does Captain Wetherby," said Sailhardy.

"On to the bridge then," replied Brunvoll.

The skippers had done what I thought. The *Aurora* was held against a small berg by a couple of ice anchors, with the *Kerguelen* immediately astern. Two men stood in the Spandau-Hotchkiss harness and pointed the wicked weapon at the *Aurora*. Moored alongside the *Kerguelen* was Brunvoll's ship *Chimay,* and half a mile astern, pitching heavily in the open water, was the *Crozet.* I half closed my eyes against the sudden onslaught of frozen spindrift carried along by the wind. It was upon the *Crozet* that my attention fixed. On her forward catwalk was lashed the helicopter. The orange stood out clearly in the wild morning. Helen would be aboard her, I told myself.

I looked about me with fear in my heart. Ahead, scarcely visible, was a mound which looked like a gigantic iceberg. It was Bouvet. We were still too far to distinguish detail clearly, except for the great soaring twin peaks capped with ice. The sea was thick with ice and icebergs. Open water, perhaps a quarter of a mile wide,

made a winding passage between the ice towards the grim
island.

Brunvoll ushered us ahead. "Walter," he said, "get
down to the engine room. The rest of you stay here."
There was a cluster of about a dozen men, the *Aurora*'s
crew, filing aboard the *Kerguelen*. Two had remained to
cast off the ice anchors.

"It's all yours, Captain," said Brunvoll. "You'll have to
steam slowly, because of this." He gestured at the ice.
"When you reach Bollevika, anchor a quarter of a mile
off-shore. I'll come aboard again."

He lifted a hand in the direction of the gun in the
Kerguelen's bows. One of the gunners raised a hand in
reply. Brunvoll and the tough Norwegian then backed
down the bridge ladder, as if still afraid we would do
something even in the face of the weapon.

I cupped my hands. "Cast off," I shouted to the men at
the ice anchors. I rang for "slow ahead." The *Aurora*
moved slowly clear, heading towards Bouvet.

Our course was dictated by the open water through the
ice. I could not have manoeuvred, even if I had wished.
The ship pitched more heavily than I would have expected, which meant that the ice was loose and the sea itself had not frozen. The *Kerguelen* followed and, in line
ahead, the *Chimay* and the *Crozet*.

When we had covered about five miles a squall swept
across the sea. It cleared, and I saw Bouvet close. The
cliffs might have been the savage black conscience of the
Southern Ocean itself. The pale sunlight inched into the
awe-provoking sky with the tenacity of the orange lichens
that stained the stark cliffs near the water's edge. The
great twin volcanic craters of the Christensen and Posa-
dowsky threw up their ice-covered heads three thousand
feet to left and right; away on the left the cliffs, instead of
being sombre basalt, were a strange sulphur colour. Running down from the twin glacier cones was a fantastic wall
of solid ice, and where the cliffs became vertical, which I

guessed was at a height of about fifteen hundred feet, the ice rose sheer out of the sea to join with the glaciers high above. The ice took its blackness from the cliffs, which it parasitized. Here and there was an eroded headland with fingerlike projections of rock, which reached out as if in supplication to the brutal face of the Westerlies; where the sea and the ice had made rocklike arches, they contorted themselves in strychnic agony. The Southern Ocean might have chosen its colours for the grim island in the same way as some old painters used to grind up Egyptian mummies for pigment when portraying scenes of death. Bouvet stood at bay, shoulder to the great winds, without a chink in its black armour, almost without light except at the edge of the flag-cloud flapping at the summit of the twin peaks, which was pale orange-white. There must have been fifty or sixty icebergs jammed on one of the outlying reefs of Bollevika, so that it was almost impossible to see the line of the coast. Bouvet stood before us—wild, evil, at war endlessly with the mighty undulations which threw themselves against the cliffs from the water below, and with the winds above which sometimes even the anemometer cannot measure.

Sailhardy was at the wheel. I glanced at the echo sounder. Twenty-five fathoms. I took a quick bearing on a headland on the port bow. That was where Christensen's party must have erected an emergency depot, or roverhullet, as they called it, stocked with provisions and fuel. I wondered if such a hut, however well built and shored up, could have survived the gales of thirty-odd years. Bollevika anchorage itself lay slightly away to starboard, but I thought I might have to do what Christensen's ship had done during the whole month his party had been ashore—steam back and forth at slow speed because the gales and rollers from the southwest would make anchoring impossible.

I opened my mouth to give Sailhardy an order when the mine exploded.

The port side was torn wide open.

Stunned and deafened, I could not for a moment believe that it had actually happened. My mind could not credit that plating, decks, beams, and rivets had been dissociated from all that they had been seconds previously. A ragged chunk of metal sang and rang in the steel wall at the back of the bridge like an Apache's arrow. It had passed clean between Sailhardy and myself. It would have taken off one of our heads had its path been a foot either side.

The *Aurora* started to roll over towards the brash sea. A gout of water rose up from her side and then smashed down, bringing chunks of ice clattering on the tilting deck. From beneath our feet came the sound of frames rending.

It was Sailhardy who saved us. I saw that he was shouting, although his voice came faint to my stunned senses. "The whaleboat! Quick! She's going so fast we'll be trapped!"

He grabbed me by the shoulder and thrust me down the bridge ladder. I stumbled over to the whaleboat and fumbled, half dazed, at the lashings. Above my head the blocks swung loose as the mast sagged. Walter came lurching from the engine-room hatchway as if he were drunk. Even in my confused state I saw he was carrying a heavy wrench and a flensing knife. He slashed at the ropes holding the whaleboat. Sailhardy reappeared, half thrusting, half carrying, Upton and Pirow. Upton appeared the least dazed of us all, except Sailhardy. He slid his little first-aid bag over his arm decisively as he too plucked at the lashings.

I snatched the last rope free of the winch, tearing my hand on a rough rowlock. I scarcely noticed. The *Aurora*'s flared bow, harpoon gun, and forward engine-room telegraph had been pushed back by the explosion to the line of the fo'c's'le ventilators. A heavy barrel from one of the starboard winches rolled past us as she prepared to plunge for the last time. Sailhardy, Walter, and I pulled the whaleboat to the side. Pirow stood like a man concussed, and Sailhardy had to thrust him into the boat, so incongruously gay in its bright Tristan colours, yellow, blue and white. Upton and Walter jumped in after us.

"Fend her off, Bruce!" called Sailhardy. "She's coming right over on us!"

I pushed the boat clear with one of the long oars. Sailhardy did the same. We pulled away as the catcher leaned over. Walter also grabbed an oar. The three of us gave a couple of strong sweeps out of range of the dying ship's last roll. Then Sailhardy took the high tiller, whose steering arm he had not had time to ship properly, leaving us at the oars.

The *Aurora* rolled over and disappeared. There was a muffled explosion as her boilers blew up, but we were well clear. She had gone down in about four minutes.

Walter stood up and looked at the fast-disappearing patch on the sea which marked the *Aurora*'s grave. "She was a fine ship—as good as they come," he said.

The other catchers had come to a stop. The *Kerguelen*'s bows started to swing away from the whaleboat in the grip of the sea.

Sailhardy glanced astern at the catchers and called to me. "Get the sail on her, Bruce! We'll beat back to the *Kerguelen* into the wind. The passage is wide enough to tack."

The islander's words goaded Upton into action. Dropping his first-aid bag, he rose quickly, snatched the knife from Walter, and in a flash was at the tiller. He held the long blade at the islander's throat.

"Beat back be damned," he said thickly. "Take her into the anchorage. We're going to land."

I looked at the great cliffs unbelievingly. "Land!" I exclaimed. "Upton, you must be crazy! You can't land on Bouvet!"

There was a sandless parody of a beach at the foot of the cliffs soaring up to the Christensen glacier. Great seas threw themselves against the rocks.

Upton's eyes were as hard and distant as our chances of
survival if we tried to make the beach. "Walter! Stop
drivelling over that bloody ship of yours! Take that
wrench and don't hesitate to use it on them if they try any
games." He thrust the knife closer against Sailhardy's
throat. "The beach!"

The islander did not speak. I could see the mania
mounting in Upton's overbright eyes.

I had to break the silence. "Can you bring the boat in,
Sailhardy?"

"The problem is not to bring her in, Bruce, but to hold
her off the rocks once we get there."

Upton jerked out his words. "Get going, do you hear?
Get the sail on her quick, before the catchers do anything!"

"You can't—" I started to say.

"I shall," he retorted. "You thought you'd make all the
running on Thompson Island, didn't you, Wetherby? Now
I'm going to tell you something. We are still going to
Thompson Island."

"What in?" I asked.

"In this whaleboat," Upton said. His words tumbled
over one another. "I've got Norris's chart here"—he
tapped his windbreaker. "Thompson is only forty-five
miles north-northeast of Bouvet. Christensen's party put
up a hut on Bouvet. We'll take stores from that. We'll slip
away before the *Thorshammer* comes."

I saw he meant it. The risks of the wild scene ahead
were nothing to him in the face of his dream. He might
force me to take him forty-five miles north-northeast of
Bouvet, but we would not find Thompson Island there. I
was inflexible in my own mind that the secret of its loca-
tion would remain mine. The roverhullet on Bouvet was
one of the chain of emergency depots that have been laid
round the palette of Antarctica, which the Norwegian
skippers had started to argue about that first night aboard
the *Antarctica* when they were drinking hard. Looking at

the ice-masked island, I hoped for the sake of the five of us that the roverhullet was still there.

"Get the foresail on her!" snarled Walter.

I tugged at the halyards, and the little rag, bright ochre-colored, stood out like a board as it picked up the Westerlies. Sailhardy stood up, cocking a foot on the tiller to steer her while he conned his way through the ice. The boat gathered way. From the *Kerguelen* came a long, ripping burst of fire. Upton jumped on a thwart and shouted obscenities at the catcher. The whaleboat was too low a target to hit, however, even for an expert marksman.

Upton's blue windbreaker hood fell back as he waved the knife at the catcher. "Come on, you cowardly bastards!" he yelled. "Come and get yourself bloody-well mined! Come on!"

Pirow seemed to have regained his morale. "The Herr Kapitän Kohler did us a favour really. The catchers won't dare come into Bollevika now."

The whaleboat picked up speed rapidly. It was impossible to see where the burst from the Spandau-Hotchkiss had gone. Sailhardy zigzagged round and through the ice, never losing his main objective, the small beach below the cliffs. The sea darkened as we neared the island. From the lowness of the boat the cliffs appeared more massive: they were scored and striated, notched and grained, by the wind and the ice. The whaleboat swept in to within a cable's length of the shore. A long swell boomed past while Sailhardy held her in check, coming round in a broad reconnoitering circle. I saw the flat table-top rock when the backwash recoiled from the cliff. I started to say no, but Sailhardy had also spotted it.

"We're going in—now!" he called. The curious modulation in his voice made it clear above the thunder of the waves against the cliffs.

He flicked a glance over his shoulder and selected his roller. He dropped to a sitting position by the tiller. He swung the stern into the comber, plumed with white ice

and blowing spindrift. Halfway to the flat rock I whipped
the sail off her. She scarcely lost way, the thrust of the
swell was so great. Sailhardy gestured to me with his left
hand: he was about to lay her broadside on her port beam.
One moment we were in deep water, the next against the
cliff. The rock lay exposed.

"Jump!" shouted Sailhardy. "Jump! Out! Out! Out!
Don't let her side touch, for God's sake!"

I was first out over the bow. Almost simultaneously
Sailhardy leaped over the stern. Our heavy boots scrab-
bled for purchase on the rock as we held her, and the other
three sprang clear. Without pausing, Sailhardy and I lifted
the boat bodily out of the water and staggered over the
broken rocks to the cliff face, out of the reach of the sea.

The beach on which we found ourselves was not much
bigger than a tennis court. It was easy to see we had come
to the one and only landing place, for where the rock
formed a natural corner, out of direct reach of the sea and
the wind, a flagstaff had been driven into the face of the
cliff so that it projected at an angle. The flag and the rope
had long since gone, and the block at the top was rusted
black. Under it was a weathered inscription in Norwegian
and English:

Captain Harald Horntvedt, master of the *Norvegia*,
formally took possession of Bouvet Island in the name
of Norway on this first day of December, 1927, and at
this spot hoisted the flag of that country in due assertion
of Norway's claim and sovereignty."

Upton read it and laughed. He seemed nearest the way I
had known him first. "The bastards!" he said without ran-
cour. "They got here first all right, and the British Government a year later waived all claims to Bouvet. But,"
he added and his voice was hard, "no one said anything
about Thompson Island."

My objective at the moment was to try to find the hut.

From the watermarks high above our heads, it was plain that the beach became submerged in a gale.

Sailhardy spotted the piece of board first. It was fastened with iron spikes to the cliff on the left, or northern edge of the beach, where a headland jutted into the sea. It said simply: "Roverhullet." A faded arrow pointed to what might have been a man-made path, running zigzag up the cliffside's confused mixture of glaciated rock and ice. I lost sight of it near a formidable projection, a veritable fortress of ice as big as the Tower of London, high above our heads.

"We've got somehow to climb the cliff," I said. "The roverhullet should be at the top—if it hasn't been blown away. It is quite likely that parts of the path have been swept away by rock falls since the Norwegians were here. Sailhardy and I will make a reconnaissance—"

"Will you, hell!" said Upton. "All you'd have to do would be to roll a few rocks down on our heads or block the path. Without the depot we'd be dead in three days—and you know it."

"Yes," I replied. "I know it. I also know how desperate our position is even if we find the hut. If you had any sense you'd get back to the catchers as quickly as the whaleboat would take us."

"There's enough rope in the boat to lash the five of us together," said Upton. "You, Wetherby, will lead. Then Sailhardy, and Pirow next. If he slips there will be two good men ahead and behind to hold him. Then myself, and Walter in the rear."

Sailhardy looked anxiously at the sky. "If it comes up a full gale the sea will sweep this beach. The boat will be lost."

Upton smiled mirthlessly. "That boat is as valuable to me now as it is to you, Sailhardy. Get it up into the corner by the flagstaff and weight her down with stones. If the path isn't too rough you and Wetherby might carry the boat up to the top later. After all the Norwegians must have transported a whole depot hut and stores to the top."

I looked up at the grim cliffs and shuddered. The Norwegians had made the climb later in the season, when there was less ice. We did not have even an ice axe to cut steps up the glacier, should it become necessary.

I had an idea. "Bring the rowlocks from the boat," I called to Sailhardy, who had already started, with great care, to weight down the boat with some of the big boulders with which the place was littered. "We may find them useful higher up as pitons. That wrench of yours may be wanted as a hammer yet, Walter."

The prospect of the climb seemed to have cowed the big Norwegian. Perhaps he too was suffering from delayed shock from the mine. He surveyed the vague pathway gloomily. "One man slips, and the rest go with him," he said. "Better we climb unroped on our own."

"No!" retorted Upton. "Get that rope round us, Sailhardy."

I took the six rough, horseshoe-shaped rowlocks. They were so cold they would have seared the flesh if my hands had not been gloved. The rope was perhaps thirty feet long. Sailhardy tied and tested each knot carefully.

When we were about to start, Pirow bowed formally and shook me by the hand. It was clear that he thought our last moments had arrived. "I wish you luck in the lead, Herr Kapitän. I wish it for myself too."

I shrugged, and we set off up the ill-defined path. After the first thirty feet it widened and, although steep, was not dangerous. We trekked up and up through the moraine. Pirow behind me started to blow heavily. I raised my hand and called a halt, lifting my eyes for the first time from the pathway. My head reeled. Fully five hundred feet below were a series of rock pools, beyond the headland which masked the beach. One slip of the boot on the narrow track would have sent us crashing to a fearsome end. Far out to sea, beyond the line of the icebergs, I could see the three catchers. My heart lifted at the orange splash on one of them—there was the helicopter aboard the *Crozet*. The thin line of ships stood blockade across the open lead of water. How Upton proposed to get past them in the whaleboat was beyond me.

We paused for five minutes, not speaking, then went on and up. The ascent became steeper and slippery. The wind on the exposed face plucked at our clothing. The weather was clearer, which was a bad sign, for it meant that the wind was coming hard off the ice. After another few hundred feet I found myself gasping the raw air, which rasped like a file in my throat. Behind me, each man had pulled his hood as close to his face as he could. On Walter's beard I could see the icicles where his breath had condensed and frozen.

We struggled on. Round a bend the pathway ran dead. Clearly defined it ended against the side of the huge fortress of rock I had noticed from below. The enormous rock overhung the cliff and the pathway. Like everything higher up, it was coated with ice. I edged closer. Then, beneath the six-inch patina of ice, I saw a steel ladder set into the rock, leading beyond an overhang twenty feet above my head.

"Walter!" I called. "Bring that wrench, or pass it up here. There's a ladder under the ice. I'll try to chip it free."

I steadied myself, and the wrench was passed cautiously from hand to hand, each man fearing he might slip. The height seemed to smooth out the rollers. I swung the heavy wrench against the ice. It bounced back. I might have been striking the rock itself. I struck again. The solid head of steel splintered into fragments. The cold had made it as brittle as glass.

I faced about precariously. "Upton! Do you want to go on with this crazy climb any farther? You're risking everyone's lives—"

The cold and the exertion had flushed his face that strange pink. "Either you go on, or you come back—into this!" he replied. He waved the knife. "Hammer the rowlocks into the ice and climb up on them. Get going!"

"Bruce," broke in Sailhardy, "let me go! I—"

But I had already started to untie the rope from my waist.

Pirow's face was pinched. "If you fall, don't fall on me, for God's sake!" he mouthed. "Don't go, Herr Kapitän!"

In reply I hammered the first crude rowlock cautiously into the ice with the shaft of the wrench a few feet above the pathway level. I swung myself up, one foot across its broad horseshoe. Nothing else stood between me and the drop to the sea a thousand feet below. Carefully, and not using much force in order not to shatter the wrench shaft or the rowlocks, I hammered in another. Using the rowlocks as pitons I reached twelve feet, where the rock overhang began. Through the ice, clear as plate-glass, I could see the rungs Christensen's men had clamped into the rock. Even with the ladder's safety assured, each load carried to the summit must have been a hair-raising experience.

I hung on a piton set below the overhang, looking for a suitable place to drive in the next. Somehow the rungs of the ladder seemed even clearer. I balanced on one leg and drove in the next rowlock.

The ice stripped off the overhang like orange peel. The rungs were clearer because here the ice was only a couple of inches thick.

My gloves clutched empty air. I started to fall. The wrench and piton clinked on the ice and shot downwards towards the rocks and sea. My foot slid off the piton. As I slipped sideways I grabbed in frantic terror. My right hand closed over one of the newly exposed rungs. Simultaneously my left fingers groped, found, and clasped. My feet swung wide, away from the rock face, over the sea below. I cast one desperate glance beneath. The four men were staring at me with as much horror as I myself felt. There was only one thing I could do: I swung myself sideways and made a desperate clutch at the rung up. My

hand closed round it. I hung for half a minute before re-
peating the manoeuvre. The muscles in my arms started to
kick. I knew they would last only another few minutes. I
edged still one rung higher and then pulled my body in
against the cliff, resting my toes on the shelf of the ice,
about six inches wide. Slowly, painfully, I pulled myself up
until my feet as well as my hands rested on the iron ladder.
The sweat froze on my face as it formed. Great gasps burst
from my lungs. I would have fallen if I had looked down.
The ladder continued at a gentler angle, once it was round
the bulge of the overhang, and brought me out to a
shallow plateau, from which the pathway continued to the
summit, now clearly visible about five hundred feet farther
up. I could not see the others because of the overhang, and
although I heard Sailhardy shouting, the wind blew the
words away. I tried shouting back, but it was futile. For
perhaps a quarter of an hour I rested and recovered my
nerve, then stumbled up the easier gradient to the summit.

I dragged myself over the top. Fifty yards from the
edge, up a gentle path, was a wooden hut, heavily shored
and stayed aganst the gales. Lars Christensen's men had
built the roverhullet well.

The hut was big enough for a dozen men, and there was
a lean-to building which I guessed must be a storeroom.
Each corner of the structure, as well as the roof, was
guyed to steel posts driven between fissures of the rock. In
front was an iron flagstaff, which had been bent double
like a sapling by the gales. Its lack of windows added to its
air of utter desolation. The backdrop of the massive
Christensen glacier made it appear puny. The front door
was held by four big sliding bolts, unlocked. I slid them
back and threw open the door. It was eerie and half dark,
and for a moment I wondered whether I would find inside
some ghastly corpse, as the famous explorer, Sir James
Clark Ross, had done in the Kerguelen Islands in the
1840s—a man with a bottle in his hand, terror in his eyes,
and gigantic footprints leading up to him.

I put such thoughts from my mind and stepped inside. It was hard to see, and there was that curious smell of frozenness which only the Antarctic can produce. The walls were lined with ice. There was a big stove in the centre of the first room, and a notice in Norwegian and English said: "This hut is for the use of distressed seamen. There are stores, provisions, fuel, and other necessaries in the storeroom beyond. Please put back whatever is not used."

I went through two more rooms and had to bend down to enter the storeroom. When I saw the piles of sleeping-bags, blankets, cases of canned food, tins of kerosene, lamps, and a host of paraphernalia so essential for survival in the Antarctic, I remembered that Christensen had originally planned to establish a weather station on Bouvet but had abandoned the thought after seeing the wildness of the place.

In a rack, heavily greased, were a number of ice axes, pitons, skis, and old-fashioned throwing harpoons, each with a length of rope attached to the shaft. There were coils of thick rope, hundreds of feet of it, but before it could be used it would have to be thawed out. I noted with approval that the boxes, and indeed the joints of the hut itself, were all dovetails and dowels. There was not a nail to be seen. These men had known their job, for in the Antarctic wood changes its nature and the cold dries it out so that nails become next to useless.

I took four ice axes and one of the harpoons, whose steel shaft must have been six feet long, and some pitons. My immediate task was to bring the party past the ice ladder to the hut. We could make the path and ladder usable later on, but for the moment they would have to cut steps in the ice as far as the exposed rungs from which I had hung.

I stood at the top of the cliff and looked out at the distant catchers before starting down the track. The *Crozet* was apart from the others. I watched in puzzlement, for I thought I could see her moving, since the orange of the helicopter stood out against the general whiteness. Whatever she was about needed Sailhardy's eyesight to discern. All I could distinguish at first was that the *Crozet* was much nearer the ice than the others, which remained in the centre of the channel.

Then I saw. Radiating like spokes from a wheel hub were a number of other open passages between the ice to the north and northeast, converging on the towering northern cliffs of the island. They would be useless for a ship to negotiate, but for the whaleboat. . . .

I craned over the cliff and looked down, ramming the harpoon's blade firmly in a crack of the rocks to hold. From my altitude the sea and the ice below gave the effect of an aerial photograph. A number of fissures in the ice belt followed the contours of the island; in other words, there were small open channels running round Bouvet which would easily take the whaleboat into one of the wider channels to the north, and so avoid the catchers, which lay to the southwest. Upton would not miss seeing them either.

I made my way slowly and cautiously down the path back to the great fortress rock and the ice ladder. I climbed over the overhang, carrying two ice axes, and shouted. Sailhardy's voice, tense with relief, came back. Crouching on the last exposed rung, I handed the axes down and felt them being seized by invisible hands. I climbed back to the top of the overhang, with its dizzy drop to the sea.

For about fifteen minutes I heard the clunk of ice steps being cut, and then Sailhardy, grinning, hauled himself alongside me.

"Bruce, boy!" he exclaimed. "I thought you were a goner that time! Is there a hut?"

I told him about the roverhullet and the supplies. "There's enough there to last us a year or more."

It was also Upton's first question when he appeared

next. He seemed in great spirits when I told him; he swung himself up and down on his toes in impatience to be off to see the hut. Pirow looked like a ghost, and Walter was sullen. All of them were blue with the cold, and it was not until we neared the top that some colour came back into Pirow's face.

Upton, Walter, and Pirow made straight for the hut, but I held back, touching Sailhardy's arm.

"I want you to take a look at the catchers," I said. "I left my glasses behind in the factory ship. The *Crozet* is easy to pick out because of the helicopter. It seems odd that she's against the ice."

Sailhardy took a long look. "It's not so strange," he said quietly. "She's doing exactly what the *Aurora* did to get a steady platform. She's tied up to an iceberg."

"You mean—"

"Why should she want a steady platform?" he asked, and then answered himself. "Because she's going to fly off the helicopter."

11 The Roverhullet

My dread that Helen would attempt the impossible with the helicopter crystallized at Sailhardy's words. The southwest quadrant of the horizon was ominously and unnaturally clear; what wild eddies would arise above Bouvet's stark cliffs when the gale hit them—the only projection in the sea for thousands of miles—I could not guess.

"We have to signal her to keep off!" I said. "There are certain to be some emergency flares in the storeroom—"

"Look!" he replied.

I too caught the flicker of light above the orange splash: the rotors were spinning.

"Quick!" I went on. "She mustn't come close. It would be suicide here." I gestured to the glacier slope behind the hut.

Sailhardy and I ran to the hut, and I led the way to the storeroom. Upton and Walter were examining the stores with satisfaction, and Pirow was busy on his knees trying to get the stove going in the outer room.

"Do you see any flares here?"

Upton's manner changed at my question, and anger started up in his eyes. "The *Thorshammer?*"

"No," I said. "Helen is flying off the helicopter. She'll kill herself. I'm going to signal her."

Although it was dim in the storeroom I could see the brightness of Upton's eyes. He moved swiftly over to the harpoon rack, whipped up one of the old-fashioned weapons, and stood with it poised above his head, pointing at Sailhardy and me. "Walter! Here! You know how to use one of these things. You'll stay just where you are, Wetherby! There will be no signalling anyone, do you understand?"

"But Helen—" I protested.

"It's probably not Helen alone, but the skippers as well," he replied. "They're coming to fetch us because they can't get into Bollevika by sea."

"For God's sake, doesn't your own daughter's life mean anything to you, except that *you* may be caught?" I exclaimed.

"She's a fine flier," he replied defensively. "She knows how to look after herself in the air."

"There's no flier born who is good enough for Bouvet's conditions," I snapped back. "Let me find some flares."

Walter balanced another long harpoon from the rack in his massive fist. I had heard it said that he was one of the finest harpoonists in the Southern Ocean. "The harpoon is like a sailing ship," he said caressingly. "There is no sailor like a sailing-ship sailor. There is no harpoon man like one trained to throw the old harpoons. There is a sense of balance—"

I turned to the stacks of cases. I never saw Walter move, but the head of the harpoon crashed into the heavy timber within a foot of my face.

Walter stood grinning, another harpoon already in his hand. Sailhardy looked unimpressed, but Upton's face was full of admiration. I was shaken by Walter's skill.

"The skippers must have seen us come up the pathway, through their glasses," said the islander. "They know we are here—right here in this hut."

"And they have the Schmeisser," I added.

Upton started to laugh. I did not like the sound of it. "There are no windows in the roverhullet, are there,

Wetherby? Are there, Sailhardy?" He didn't wait for our reply. "No one will move outside the hut—understood? Walter"—he grinned again—"how about harpooning something quite new for a change?"

"What do you mean?" asked Walter.

"The front door will stand wide open," Upton went on. "We'll hear the helicopter overhead. She'll come down low, but I guess Helen won't try to land right away before she sees the lie of the land. Reidar Bull will be in the machine for certain, with his Schmeisser. He won't expect a harpoon to be heaved at him. He'll think he's quite safe with a gun against unarmed men."

Walter held the harpoon head high and made a lightning dummy throw. "By God! I like that! I like that!" he exclaimed.

"Listen, Upton!" I said. "You've already got blood on your hands. You're making things worse. It is only a matter of time before the *Thorshammer* arrives. She can lie off the island and shell this hut into oblivion if she wishes."

Upton shook his head. "She can if she wishes," he replied. "But we won't be here. We're going to Thompson Island in the whaleboat."

"We can also go to Cape Town in the whaleboat," I said sarcastically. "It is simply sixteen hundred miles across the worst seas in the world."

There was a change in Upton's manner. He became easy and friendly, and he spoke directly to Sailhardy. "You'd sail your boat to Cape Town, wouldn't you, Sailhardy? We could stock her up. There's plenty here."

For a moment he caught Sailhardy's imagination with his curious, magnetic power of drawing a person out of himself.

"We'd have to half-deck the boat against the waves," Sailhardy said, lost in the dream Upton had conjured up. "But she'd make it. Shackleton sailed seven hundred and fifty miles to South Georgia, and his was only an ordinary ship's boat."

"Don't talk nonsense!" I said harshly. "Upton—"

We heard the roar of the rotors. "Carl!" shouted Upton. "Come here! Don't go outside! Come here, do you hear!"

Pirow came through to the storeroom, the question on his lips dying when he saw Walter with the harpoon. The hut shook as the machine came low overhead. It could not have been more than thirty feet up. The sound receded and then returned as the machine came back from the seaward side. The sound hung overhead. The note changed. The machine was coming down. Walter tensed, then ran quickly forwards. I gestured to Sailhardy. With Walter out of the way, Upton even with his harpoon, was not much of a threat, and Pirow was unarmed. Sailhardy rushed at Upton. Upton couldn't handle the harpoon. Sailhardy dodged an ineffectual thrust and grabbed the weapon from him. I snatched an ice axe from the rack and rushed after Walter.

As I darted through the doorway I saw Walter poise in his stride and lift the harpoon like a javelin thrower. The helicopter was hanging about fifteen feet above the ground in front of the hut, the nose half pointing towards the doorway. The cabin door was open, and in it stood Reidar Bull with the Schmeisser at the ready.

Walter threw. The crackle of the Schmeisser was almost simultaneous, but Walter dropped on the ground out of the line of fire and started to roll sideways. In the split second the harpoon took to reach its target, the machine dipped a few feet. It may have been Helen who did it, or an eddy of wind. The harpoon, trailing its short length of rope, arced and missed Reidar Bull.

The steel head and shaft crashed into the spinning rotors.

The rest followed at lightning speed.

I saw the bight of rope snick upwards as it became entangled in the rotors. One moment Reidar Bull was standing firing the automatic pistol; the next the harpoon rope had snatched off his head. The headless trunk stood transfixed. I never saw the head fall. The rotors gave a single flailing screech of torn metal as harpoon and blades tangled. The machine dropped like a shot partridge. The headless trunk and the Schmeisser spilled on the ground. A buckled rotor, still under power, bit into the rocky ground and cartwheeled the machine for about thirty yards past the hut into a boulder at the start of the glacier incline.

I sprinted to the wreck. Behind the perspex I could see Helen slumped over the controls. My raider's glasses, which I had left behind at the factory ship, were suspended round her neck. I hacked through the window with my ice axe. I jumped through and cut the throttle. The thumping clatter stopped. In my anxiety to get Helen clear before the machine caught fire I hacked her safety belt free. There was a mark across her forehead, and she was unconscious. I picked her up in my arms and staggered clear of the machine.

In front of the hut stood Upton, Pirow, Walter, and Sailhardy. Walter cradled the Schmeisser in his huge paws. Behind the group, blood staining the rocks, lay what remained of Reidar Bull.

I carried Helen to them. "Get the stove going," I ordered Pirow. "I don't know how badly she's hurt."

Upton was casual. "She doesn't look too bad."

"You callous bastard!" I exclaimed, but he ignored me.

"Walter," he went on, "don't hesitate to use that gun if either Wetherby or Sailhardy start anything."

"Sir Frederick!" said Pirow. "There's a radio in the helicopter. I'm going to see if it is all right."

"Wait a moment," said Upton. "The machine could still catch fire, although it doesn't seem likely now." He went over to the corpse and turned it over with his foot with a measure of cool, pleased appraisal which sickened me.

"For God's sake!" I said. "Sailhardy! Get that stove lighted, will you! And bring some blankets from the store."

Upton grinned. "Throw that thing over the cliff," he told Walter. "Here, give me the gun while you do it."

Walter hesitated.

"Throw him over the cliff!" repeated Upton. "What are you waiting for?" He balanced himself lightly on the balls of his feet.

Walter shook his head. "There should be some sort of prayer. After all, just now he was a man. Perhaps the captain will say one and then I will throw him over."

"Christ!" burst out Upton. "You, Walter! A catcher skipper!"

Walter became surly. "I'd want it that way if I was lying there, catcher skipper or no bloody catcher skipper."

"Carry on," said Upton. "There'll be no prayers while I'm around."

I did not wait to see Walter perform his grisly task. I carried Helen inside, and Sailhardy brought some blankets, in which we wrapped her. She was breathing easily, and I could not find any bones broken. Both Sailhardy and I reckoned she was merely stunned. The islander also brought from the storeroom some pieces of wood, which he chopped up. He lit a fire for our immediate warmth on a piece of metal he had found and then started the big stove in the centre of the room. The ice would take hours to melt off the walls.

In ten minutes she stirred. "Helen!" I exclaimed. "Helen!"

"I'll get a sleeping-bag for her and some more wood," said Sailhardy.

She sat up and threw her arms round me. "Bruce, my darling, my darling!" She was sobbing. I held her, but she pulled back suddenly. "Where are your glassses? I brought them from the *Antarctica*—"

"Yes," I said gently. "They were round your neck, and I have them."

"The helicopter, Bruce! Did it catch fire?"

"No," I replied. "But it will never fly again." I told her briefly about Reidar Bull.

She paled. "That means we can't ever get off this island—"

"Yes, indeed we shall," said Upton, coming in. "With bits of your helicopter, if not with the whole." He seemed scarcely concerned about her.

Walter followed, Schmeisser in hand.

"What the hell are you talking about now?" I asked.

"Get this clear, Wetherby," said Upton. "I am going to Thompson Island in Sailhardy's whaleboat. So are you—all of us, in fact. I need you to navigate. I need Sailhardy to sail it." He indicated the Schmeisser. "Beyond that, I have no use for you. Remember that."

Sailhardy came back.

"Sailhardy, you have the material now to half-deck your boat. There's all the aluminum you need. How long will it take?"

Sailhardy put down the wood and looked at me for support. "A day—maybe two—provided the weather doesn't get much worse. We'll have to carry the aluminum down to the beach though, and that will be quite a job."

Helen listened in disbelief. "Father," she said quietly, "you have caused so much misery already. Drop this idea of yours about Thompson Island. What we need most is warmth, shelter, civilization—"

He burst out laughing. Pirow returned, carrying the helicopter's radio. "Hear that, Carl! My daughter wants warmth and civilization! We've got everything we need for the moment here, and Thompson Island is forty-five miles away. Do you think I would give up now?"

Helen recoiled and sat silent. We would make the boat voyage, all right, I told myself, but when we had failed to find Thompson Island, I could then try to locate the *Thorshammer* and give ourselves up. We would be in no shape for anything else after a few days in an open boat in a Southern Ocean storm.

Pirow was jubilant. "The radio is undamaged. I'll show you. I'll fetch the batteries and aerial wire." He looked sideways at Upton. "It is a long time since the *Thorshammer* heard from that seaplane crew of hers. I'd better get on the air before the destroyer starts to

lose heart and comes to Bouvet to keep her rendezvous with the catchers."

"And us," said Walter grimly.

"And us!" echoed Upton. "Three days until we leave!
You can string the destroyer along for that length of time,
can't you, Carl? After that they can send a whole fleet to
Bouvet, but they won't find us."

"Don't you think the catchers were watching us through
their glasses?" I said. "They saw the whole business.
They'll see us leave in the whaleboat too."

"So what?" asked Upton. "They dare not risk coming
into the Bollevika anchorage because of the mines. Let
them see us go! The weather's getting worse, and that will
hide us too. Clear weather is quite exceptional here—you
know that, and I've read Kohler's reports."

"Yes," I said. "The same goes for Thompson Island."

"Don't try to fob me off before we ever get there,"
snarled Upton. "Fog or no fog, storm or no storm, we sail
in three days' time."

Pirow came back and connected the batteries and
aerial, which he looped outside over a metal stay rope.
The light was going, and the dimness added to the weird
air inside the ice-lined walls as Pirow, imitating the
seaplane crew, began his probing, tentative tapping on the
radio. We all huddled round the stove, except Walter, who
stood far enough away to prevent Sailhardy or myself
from tackling him. Helen, half propped up among her
blankets and a sleeping-bag, looked grave and troubled.

The faltering weak signal went out from the long fingers. Again I had to admire the uncanny skill of the Man
with the Immaculate Hand. He clicked over the transmitting switch, paused, listened; his fingers fiddled almost like
separate thinking entities among the dials.

"Is the *Thorshammer* answering?" Upton asked.

Pirow waved him silent. The yellow light of the
kerosene burners, hollowing his eye sockets, sketched his
remoteness from our group. Suddenly he stiffened, his left

hand reaching automatically for the switch, the right for the transmitting key. His next signal faltered more than the first.

Then he smiled. "The *Thorshammer* says, keep that key down—keep keying! She wants a fix! She must get a fix to establish the liferaft's position!"

"Are you sure you gave her enough?" Upton asked.

Pirow ignored him, but dummy-tapped with the key switched off, smiling at me: QQQ . . . QQQ . . . *I am being attacked* . . . "That is enough, is it not, Herr Kapitän? Only three letters."

I got up and strode outside. The tension in the hut, Upton's overbright eyes, the agony in Helen's, and the barbaric Walter brandishing the automatic pistol had got me down. It was bitterly cold on the plateau before the hut. Sunset saw-edged the west. I focussed my powerful glasses on the catchers' silhouettes. Yes, there they were, lights on, the *Crozet*'s reflecting from the iceberg to which she was moored. There was a frightening immensity of silence. There was a fresh breeze, gusting up to about twenty-five knots, I reckoned, but still the storm from the southwest had been far longer in coming than either Sailhardy or I had anticipated. It would accordingly be the worse when it did come. Thinking of the whaleboat's chances in the great seas, I shuddered: Upton's plan seemed more insane than ever.

I went slowly inside.

Next morning Upton woke us early. We had all slept round the stove, Upton, Pirow, and Walter taking shifts to stand guard. We had broken open cases of stores, and Sailhardy had prepared a meal, which we had eaten by the light of lanterns from the storeroom. Helen had looked tired and soon had fallen into a broken sleep. In the middle of the night there had been a sound which had seemed to me like the glacier falling on the roverhullet, but it had, in fact, been only the inner coating of ice on the walls crashing down. When Upton called next morning, the room was warm and comfortable.

"We're going to strip some big pieces of aluminum off the helicopter and take them down to the beach," he said decisively. "That should take us the best part of today. tomorrow Sailhardy and Wetherby will half-deck the boat while the rest of us get supplies down to the beach. On the third day we sail."

Some of my previous night's introversion was with me still when I thought of the puny boat and the great seas. "Weather permitting," I added.

"Weather or no weather," he replied. "You can make up your mind about that."

"And we sail down the channel into the waiting arms of the catchers," I went on.

Upton laughed. "Come, Wetherby, you're not as dumb as that."

So he had not missed the other ice leads to the north and northeast.

Helen said, "I'm helping Bruce and Sailhardy. It is my helicopter, after all."

I could not see how Sailhardy and I were to carry big sheets of aluminum down the cliffside, especially in the wind. We would be snatched off the pathway before we had gone five hundred feet. There was also the problem of negotiating the ladder section.

I started to object, but Upton stopped me. "You obviously haven't taken a close look at the stores. The Norwegians brought a winch up here with them. They must have hauled the sections of the hut up with it. There's enough rope to rig a windjammer. Here is some, already thawing."

Two big coils lay close to the fire, and the film of ice was melting.

Upton went on, "You'll also see that Christensen's men drilled some bolt holes in the rock. A few sheets of light metal won't be any worry."

He was right. After Sailhardy and I, using ice axes to

prise loose the rivets, had stripped off several large sheets from the helicopter to deck the bow and the stern of the whaleboat, it became obvious it would be simplicity itself to lower them down the cliff face by hand, without resorting to the winch, which Walter was busy rigging, while Upton kept watch with the Schmeisser. Helen was shaky when we began but seemed to pick up strength as the day progressed. By midafternoon we had ripped the metal skin from a large undamaged section to the rear of the cockpit and had stacked it ready for lowering to the beach next day. I had seen Helen smile for the first time since landing on Bouvet when Sailhardy insisted on chopping loose her seat in the cockpit and putting it in front of the fire in the roverhullet. Either Walter or Upton had kept guard from the front of the hut while we worked, and Pirow had occupied himself with the radio and preparing meals. There was not only quantity among the stores, but a wide variety, which would have kept a marooned party from boredom for months.

When Sailhardy, Helen, and I returned to the roverhullet for our midday meal, Upton had selected and stacked a pile of cases to provision the whaleboat. There were also a couple of alpine-type, light-weight stoves to heat things in the boat. To me the cases looked woefully few. Upton had asked Sailhardy how long it would take to sail the forty-five miles from Bouvet to Thompson Island. It had, the islander replied, usually taken about four hours to cover the eighteen miles from Tristan to Nightingale—perhaps a day to a day and a half's hard sailing to Thompson. The wind and the run of the sea would be behind us. Knowing there would be no Thompson Island, I finally persuaded Upton to take supplies for about ten days, which I considered would be enough when we had to beat back to Bouvet in the teeth of the gale. We would, I reminded Upton, need provisions on Thompson. We were also taking the helicopter's radio, and my hope was that after a week in the whaleboat in a blow, everyone would be only too glad to surrender to the *Thorshammer*—if we could locate her, or she us. The project seemed perilous whatever way I thought about it.

After the meal we went back to work outside. Sailhardy wrenched the last sheet of metal skin loose from the helicopter. He smiled at Helen. "Well, ma'am, I suppose it's better than using sea elephant hide to half-deck the boat with."

She mocked him gently. "So that's what you had in mind for your epic voyage from Bouvet to the Cape!"

I really think that Sailhardy was sold on the idea—if only as an idea—of making the voyage to the Cape. He was serious immediately. "You must not forget, ma'am, that on Tristan the first, and maybe some of the best, whaleboats were made of sea elephant hide stretched over wooden ribs. Three or four sea elephants would give us enough hide to do the job."

"Where do you propose to find sea elephants on Bouvet?" she asked.

He pointed at the blockhouse shape of a small island that lay at the southern entrance to Bollevika. "I'd bet you, ma'am, that you'd find some there."

"There aren't any animals on Bouvet!" she exclaimed. "Or insects. Or plants."

"You're wrong, ma'am," he replied. "If you look hard you'll see penguins on that little island. I smelled them as we came in. I'm sure there are seals round on the sheltered side of the island." He waved his hand beyond the glacier.

"If we are very lucky we might see a Ross seal—they're supposed to breed on Bouvet," I said. "It is the most beautiful creature in the Southern Ocean, and its eyes are quite wonderfully affectionate."

Helen laughed again. "How you two stick up for your Southern Ocean in every way!"

Sailhardy was carried away. "If there are Adelie penguins down there, ma'am, then I don't need Bruce for a navigator. The Adelie is the best pilot in the Antarctic.

We on Tristan know he steers by the stars and the sun, and if I were making for Cape Town, he'd be the pilot I would choose."

She shook her head, but I backed Sailhardy. "The Americans down at McMurdo Sound thought the Adelie's navigation was just one of those stories. They carried out a test. They ringed and marked five Adelies and flew them two thousand miles away. A year later the five walked back into their rookery at McMurdo. Don't laugh!"

Sailhardy touched her sea leopard coat. "That is the creature you want to be afraid of, ma'am. He's wicked through and through. He's the colour of dirty snow, and his head looks like a huge snake's—"

"I don't want to hear any more," she said, smiling. "you've convinced me. The job's done, and we can't move anything until tomorrow. I want Bruce to take me a short way up the glacier slope."

"I'll put this sheet on the pile then and get both of you some crampons and an ice axe," replied Sailhardy. He looked up the long incline, scattered here and there with boulders cemented into the ice.

"I don't want to go far," she said. "All I want to do is to get away from this feeling of being watched all the time. Will you tell that oaf with the gun?"

Sailhardy grinned and went off. Helen pulled back the hood from her hair. In the pale sun it was the colour of the khaki shale of the Orange Free State goldfields.

"Bruce," she said when the islander was out of earshot, "all this has a dreadful inevitableness about it. No one seems to be doing anything—"

I nodded towards Walter. "That automatic pistol would cut anyone in half with a burst. We must pretend to fall in with the idea of leaving here, under pressure—"

"Thompson Island—" she murmured.

"Yes," I replied. "I want to talk to you about Thompson Island. Up there, where no one can possibly hear."

Sailhardy returned with an ice axe for me and crampons for our shoes. He started to be jocular, but he too lapsed into silence when he saw our faces. Not speaking, Helen and I trekked up the slope. Above us towered the massive cone of the Christensen glacier. A rag of cloud around the peak made me uneasy about the storm which had been so tardy in coming. There was a bank of low cloud against the sun, and I wondered if the reason for the relatively light wind so far from the southwest meant a blow, not from that quarter, but from the northwest. A northwesterly cyclone meant a heavy swell from the same direction, which would throw up a tumbled sea to make our voyage all the more hazardous; worst of all, however, would be the low cloud and poor visibility which went with it.

About half a mile above the roverhullet Helen and I found our path blocked by a face of ice that rose for about two hundred feet sheer. We leaned against a big rock. I handed her my glasses. The view was stupendous. She studied the catchers for a long time, then cased the whole quadrant of sea and ice to the northwest, to the north and the northeast, until her view was obstructed by the glacier.

"Looking for Thompson Island?" I joked.

She dropped the binoculars to the length of their lanyard. She gestured to the northeast. "It's not there, is it, Bruce, despite the chart?"

"No," I said. "It's not there at all. You could not see it in its real position from here even if it were clear. The glacier is in the way."

Her eyes were a mixture of pale gold, white, and green from the sun, the sea, and the ice. "You mean Thompson Island is south of Bouvet, not north at all?"

"Yes, Helen. Not north, not north-northeast, despite what the chart says. South. Rather, south with a little east in it. Better men than your father, with better ships than a whaleboat, have searched every inch of the waters north, northeast, and northwest of Bouvet for Thompson Island.

You know with what results."

"But south! How can that be? How?"

"Sit down," I said. "It's a long story. Before I tell it to you, however, remember one thing—casium. Remember your father also. Think, too, that I could not tell you this except—"

"Except that I know it was not you who shot down the seaplane," she replied. She pulled off one glove for a moment and held my glasses with her bare hand. "I have to love inanimate, sometimes violent things, to come to the heart of Bruce Wetherby. A pair of raider's binoculars, a compass of the sea— that's the way it is. Nothing static, nothing restful, always something at war with ice or warmth or life."

"In that you can include Thompson Island," I said.

"Why are you telling me about Thompson Island?" she went on. "Why? After all, I am his daughter."

"Because," I said simply, "I believe that within a week we will all be dead in an open whaleboat."

"One week!" she echoed. "One week—of us."

I leaned forward and kissed her lips. "It will have to do for a lifetime."

Her voice was unsteady. "Sailhardy concurs in your judgment?"

"No. He secretly cherishes a hope that one day he will make a greater open boat voyage than Shackleton, or even Bligh of the *Bounty*. That blinds him. The sea is his friend, never forget, not his enemy."

She faced me. "Bruce, why, why, are you doing this thing? Why not take my father to Thompson Island? Let him have it, even if it sends him completely —completely—unstable when he finds his caesium and all the rest of it are a dream."

"It is not a dream," I said.

"It is not a dream? I heard myself what you said—that he was mad. Myself!"

"It is because I believe that there really is caesium on

Thompson Island that I am telling you this," I said slowly. "Thompson Island must never be found—never! You know what casium means to our present-day world. Your father said it himself: a full-scale atomic war could be fought over Thompson Island."

"So you are prepared to sacrifice your own life and the lives of five other people?"

"Yes," I said. "Unless I can persuade your father when we are nearing the end of our tether to give ourselves up to the *Thorshammer*—if we can find her.

"Thompson Island is actually—" I began.

She held her hand, now gloved again, over my mouth. "Bruce, my darling, are you sure you want to tell me this? Quite, quite sure?"

"It is an act of faith," I replied. "Thompson Island lies sixty-five miles to the south-southeast of Bouvet."

It was minutes before she replied, and her voice was so soft I could scarcely hear the words. "Now I can ask how you alone know this?"

"If you look on the vernier scale of my sextant—that is, the scale with which one reads the angle of the sun and the stars—you'll see there is a little notch clearly filed," I said. "That is the latitude of Thompson Island. No one has ever searched for it there."

"But why—?"

"During the war I made what I considered a major discovery about the Antarctic," I went on. "Light rays bend greatly in the Antarctic's cold air. You get refractions. You cannot take an accurate sighting."

"I don't understand. What are you trying to say?"

"The peculiar quality of light rays bending makes the positions of distant objects greatly distorted. In other words, the sextant lies. It puts the sun and the stars, on which we rely for navigation, out of position. I discovered that there is a consistent error of a hundred and ten miles—in other words, everything is a hundred and ten miles too far north. Instead of being forty-five miles to the north-northeast of Bouvet, therefore, it is sixty-five miles to the southeast."

She wrinkled up her eyes in a puzzled way which brought out all the loveliness that had lain dormant for so long. "I don't understand the mathematics of what you are saying, although I accept it, Bruce. What I can't understand, however, is why, when everyone was wrong, including Norris when he first fixed the position of Thompson Island, that error should not have remained constant—in other words, why couldn't everyone else, making the same error because of light refractions, get there all the same?"

"The same thought struck me," I said. "Your assumption is that an old-time sealer was capable of getting an accurate fix and that Bouvet's position itself was known."

"Bouvet itself?"

"I drew a map superimposing the various positions where Bouvet has been plotted," I replied. "There are at least four from reliable sources, and three from less reliable. To say that Thompson lies forty-five miles north-northeast of Bouvet doesn't mean a thing. In fact, I found on checking that the man who discovered Bouvet, the Frenchman Captain Bouvet de Lozier, first was supposed to have sighted land somewhere near where Norris said Thompson lies."

She laughed. "I'll bet you shot Bouvet's position down in flames too!"

I grinned back. "Yes, I did. You see, Bouvet based his longitude on the Cape Verde Islands, not on Greenwich—"

"I told you so!" she exclaimed delightedly. "But what about the old-time sealers you were starting to tell me about?"

I caught her mood. "Two important things: I spent months among old Wetherby's records, checking and rechecking logs and sealers' sighting reports in the Southern Ocean. Briefly, it was nothing for a sealer to be

out ten minutes in latitude under the most favourable conditions of weather, sun, and stars. Their longitude really
had them beaten though. Don't forget, even during the
Napoleonic wars the only British warships that carried
chronometers—essential for determining longitude—were
the commanders of convoys. It was only four years after
Napoleon's death that Norris found Thompson Island. After months of research I found one could more or less rely
on any old whaler being out about a degree and a half in
longitude—say, ninety miles."

And then I told her of my fruitless attempt to convince
the admiralty that Thompson Island could be found. It
had been a frustrating experience that I had never talked
about to anyone.

"I was laughed practically out of the Admiralty down
the Horse Guards Parade," I said. "I could see it in their
faces—crackpot! Prove it, they kept on saying, which was
just the opportunity I was asking for. One gentleman in
the Hydrographic Department told me pointedly that it
would throw every map ever made of the Southern Ocean
and the Antarctic into the wastepaper basket, and such
waste could not be afforded. I remember his words still:
" 'Empiricism versus absolute knowledge, Captain Wetherby. We prefer absolute knowledge.' "

"It may sound silly, but how did you arrive at the true
position of Thompson Island when your sextant lied,
along with all other sextants?"

"By taking four different sextant sightings of the
stars—not the sun—to balance the refraction errors four
ways," I said. "Norris was not—"

"Bruce!" she interrupted hastily. "Bruce! Look!"

She pointed up the incline to where the slope resumed
beyond the barrier of ice. Leaning over was the unmistakable snakelike head of a sea leopard. Unless there
was some way round and down, however, we were in no
immediate danger.

"We must get back to the roverhullet and warn them," I

said. The massive head and shoulders swayed backwards and forwards as if seeking some way down.

Suddenly, from high above towards the summit of the glacier, a white object detached itself.

I thought at first it was a chunk of ice. "Look, Helen! There's something diving down on the sea leopard!"

It was a giant bird, its neck outstretched. It plummeted down like a Stuka divebomber. It could not be making for the sea leopard, I told myself quickly. There must be some other prey we could not see on the ledge where the animal stood.

"Albatross!" exclaimed Helen.

The diving bird was upon the sea leopard. It ballooned its wings in an attempt to prevent hitting the snakelike head, but it was too late. We saw a flash of light as a claw lashed out. There was a burst of white feathers, and the white warpaint of the albatross stripped down to the red flesh underneath. I could almost see the effort of the bird's neck muscles as it tried to lift itself. It would have made it, except for a projecting saw edge of cliff. Wounded, it could not pull itself clear. It crashed into the glacier ice and came tumbling down in an untidy heap among the rocks at our feet.

Helen started to run towards the albatross, which rose up to a crouching position. It craned its fine neck and tried to rise. Across its left wing was a long tear from the sea leopard's claws.

"Bruce, we must help—" she began, but she stopped at the look in my face and the ice axe in my hand.

"No," I said gently. "No, Helen. Five minutes ago that bird was an adventurer who could have flown from here to the South Pole and back. Now it is a heap of feathers." I moved forward to administer the coup de grâce. "It'll die slowly if we leave it, but quickly and mercifully if I do it. It must die, either way."

Helen's eyes were full of pain. I raised the ice axe. As I did so, the albatross swung its neck round in the ex-

quisitely beautiful motion which is the act of courtship of
the great wanderer of the seas, a grace worthy of a Fon-
teyn. I lowered the ice axe and looked at Helen. She went
forward and examined the half-extended wing.

"It's not as bad as I thought," she said, making an effort
to control her voice. "Perhaps you and Sailhardy—"

I went closer. I expected a savage slash from the strong
beak. It did not come, but instead the albatross stood
swaying its head.

"I'll come back with Sailhardy," I said. "We'll bring
some ropes and get the bird down to the hut. At the beach
tomorrow we can catch some fish for it—there are bound
to be some left behind in the rock pools when the tide
recedes. We mustn't wait here much longer."

We hurried to the roverhullet as quickly as our crampons and the ice slope would allow. Sailhardy was
delighted at the thought of saving the albatross; rather
than ropes, he brought a fishing net which had been thawing in front of the hut on the rocks. Walter, with the gun,
did not hinder us.

At the ice cliff Sailhardy and I found the great bird still
crouching. It was a matter of minutes to put the net round
it. Together we carried it back and set it free in front of the
hut as sunset closed on our second night on Bouvet.

At first light next morning Upton began preparations
for lowering the aluminum sheets to the beach. Sailhardy,
Helen, Walter, and I set off down the cliffside track, the
Norwegian bringing up the rear with the automatic. Even
at the ladder, down which I helped Helen hand over hand,
there was no chance to jump Walter. The descent was easy
this time, with ropes secured to the upper rungs; Walter
came down them with the agility of a cat. For the last section of the descent I roped Helen to myself in front and to
Sailhardy behind.

About three hundred feet above the beach Sailhardy
stopped and called. "Look! The catchers are launching a
boat!"

Helen stood hard back against the rock face away from the fearful drop.

I trained my glasses on the ships. "The crazy idiots! What are they trying to do?"

Walter tapped the Schmeisser. "Coming to get us. I don't see Lars Brunvoll just sitting waiting."

Sailhardy pointed at the seas breaking heavily on the rocks and the beach. "No one could land from an ordinary ship's boat in that."

"The sea is the same for sailing tomorrow," I said grimly.

"We have a Tristan whaleboat," replied Sailhardy.

"My God!" exclaimed Helen, watching the white-capped rollers race across the anchorage.

The islander looked with a curious mixture of satisfaction and awe. "It will be easier when we get into the open sea, ma'am. True, the boat will pitch a lot, but she's small enough not to stretch from wave to wave. That helps quite a bit."

I focussed the glasses on the *Chimay,* Brunvoll's catcher. "Boat away!"

The tiny thing pulled hard from the ship's side with two men at the oars on either side. The man at the tiller could have been Brunvoll, but I was not sure. The boat rode clear of the catcher's lee and disappeared in a welter of spray. I saw it capsize, and the five men were flung into the water. "She's over!"

"They'd better haul them out of the water quickly!" exclaimed Sailhardy. "They won't last long in this cold."

The catcher steamed in what seemed slow motion to the struggling men, and I saw some being hauled aboard.

"Good riddance!" said Walter. "Come on, we've got work to do. Let's get down to the beach."

We scrambled down the final section to the rough shingle. The whaleboat lay where we had left her. We unroped ourselves. I looked up. From the top of the cliff the first piece of aluminum decking was starting to swing down at the end of a long rope.

Helen, Sailhardy, and I started for the boat. As our boots crunched on the shingle a tiny head rose over the side of the whaleboat. The soft, luminous brown eyes of the creature, no bigger than a full-grown dachshund, stared at us.

"It's a Ross seal!" whispered Sailhardy.

Neither he nor I had ever seen the rarest and most beautiful of Antarctic animals. Helen started forward. "Don't, ma'am," said Sailhardy, but she was already at the tiny creature. It went unhesitatingly into her arms. Its mink-grey fur was slightly darker underneath than above.

She turned to me, her eyes shining. "Bruce! Look at it! See how it trusts me!"

I laughed and stroked the lovely head of the seal pup. "That is just the trouble with the Ross seal. They trust everyone. The old sealers exterminated them by simply hitting them over the head. They trust humans completely."

Helen put the little creature on the beach. It walked from her to me and then to Sailhardy. It did not, like the common Southern fur seal, turn its flippers forward when it walked, and I was surprised that it did not slip on the wet rocks, since the underside of its flippers were covered in softest down. I had never before seen a seal's flippers with fur on them. It allowed us to stroke its head, but Helen was clearly the favorite. She picked it up again, and it nestled in the crook of her arm.

"I have never seen anything as lovely," she said, smiling. "I'm going to take it with us in the boat. We'll take fish along for it too."

It was the remembrance of Helen with the exquisite creature in her arms, half enveloped in her sea leopard coat, with the backdrop of the basalt cliffs and little beach, which was to return to my mind's eye again and again in the days to come.

"Bring it along, for sure," said Walter sullenly. "It'll

make good eating when the going gets tough."

"Walter!" I said quietly. "If you touch this pup, I'll kill you with my bare hands."

He raised the Schmeisser at my tone. "Keep back!" he said surlily. "You'll find yourself killing the bloody thing yourself when your belly cries out for fresh meat."

A sheet of aluminum clattered on its rope over our heads. Sailhardy and I seized it as it swung in the wind against the cliffs. We found that we would probably need only four sheets to half-deck the boat both fore and aft. With rope and tools we had brought down from the roverhullet, we bent, shaped, tied, and fastened the aluminum to the canvas and wooden ribs. We stopped only to unship the cases of stores Upton and Pirow lowered to stock the boat.

By the middle of the afternoon the boat was ready half-decked, but Sailhardy was not satisfied. I wanted to get away from the raw little beach to the roverhullet before the weather became worse. The sun was obscured, and great clouds drifted round the twin peaks. From time to time squalls masked the top of the cliff. Helen helped stack the cases of supplies out of reach of the sea in the corner of the cliff where Horntvedt's flagstaff was. The seal pup followed her everywhere.

Although I wished to get away, Sailhardy took a long look at the ominous weather build-up in the southwest and started in on the steering lines and the rudder. For fully an hour he flexed the supple lines through the holes, greasing and regreasing them, checking, testing again and again. He went repeatedly over the odd projection on the port side near the rudder, from which a rope ran through the stern-port into a big enclosed space below the helmsman's seat. Nothing would make him hurry his searching examination.

While he checked and Walter stamped in the growing cold, Helen and I fished in the rock pools with the seal pup, which joined in hauling up the codlike Notothenia

fish as if it had been a game. By the time Sailhardy had
finished, we had collected a pile of about twenty, which we
stacked with the other supplies. Upton had agreed the previous night to take the albatross in the boat because of
Sailhardy's insistence that the great bird would be invaluable in finding land once it could fly again—the islander reckoned it would be shortly—and so, he said, help us
locate Thompson Island. Sailhardy had reinforced his
argument by pointing out that in a small boat in bad
weather it would be virtually impossible to take an accurate sighting. I suspected, however, that Sailhardy was
more concerned with the albatross' safety than locating
Thompson Island. We had decided, too, that we could
lower the bird down the cliffside by the rope by putting the
net round it again. I was well aware of Sailhardy's methods of navigation—by the direction of a flock of petrels
flying, by feeling the temperature of the sea at hourly intervals with his hand, the colour of the water, and a host of
other esoteric sea lore. His only man-made instrument was
a kind of rough wooden backstaff by which he took angles
on the stars, but never the sun. His landfalls were as good
as mine.

While we made the climb to the roverhullet the wind
began gusting heavily and plucked at us on the exposed
rock faces. As it increased during the evening, Upton
became more uneasy and morose. Almost nothing was
said. He pored over the chart after our evening meal round
the stove and at intervals opened the door and looked out.
On one occasion I caught a glimpse of the catchers' lights
rising and falling. The night had a resonant, ominous
background of sound from the waves thundering on the
cliffs below and the wind tearing at the glacier above. I
went with Upton to the door and found the albatross huddled against the front wall. I called Sailhardy, and we carried it, unprotesting, through to the storeroom. We did
not need to tell each other how little we thought of
our chances of leaving Bouvet the next day.

In the middle of the night my sailor's instinct suddenly brought me broad awake. I raised myself up in my sleeping-bag—we had each selected our own for the boat—and looked round. The dim light of the stove etched Walter's brutish unshaven face with sockets of shadows for eyes, evil, as he sat cross-legged with the Schmeisser across his knees. Helen lay with her back towards me, and the yellow light made even softer the colour of her hair lying loosely on the flap of the sleeping-bag. Pirow turned uneasily, as if his mind were on the faked messages he had sent earlier in the evening, but it was Upton's face which brought me fear and revulsion: the pewter hue was tinged with blue, including the eyelids, as if the caesium were justifying the blue in its spectrum. Perhaps the light added to the grotesqueness, for there was no sign of age, not a wrinkle anywhere: everything was taut; it was the face of a dead man, mummified with his dreams on his face.

Sailhardy had heard too and was awake. It had sounded to me like a double bass string being plucked. Both of us guessed what had happened—one of the steel cables holding the hut had parted. The wind shook the walls, and a peckle of hail rattled against them. We kicked ourselves out of our sleeping-bags and crawled across to Walter.

I spoke softly, so as not to wake the others. "That was one of the guy ropes, wasn't it?"

Walter was on edge. "Aye, it was. I'll tell you straight, Captain, although we're on the wrong sides, I don't like this bloody wind. It'll be blowing a full gale by morning. Christ! What will it be like at sea?"

"Try to persuade your boss about that," I replied roughly. The wind carried a burst of low thunder from the breaking waves. "We won't last more than a couple of days."

"Bruce! We must rig a new rope—now! If anything else gives, the roverhullet will go over the cliff," whispered Sailhardy. "I reckon we would be better at sea than here," he added defensively.

"Jesus!" said Walter. "Okay. See what you can do."

In the storeroom we cut off a length of the thick rope which had been used for lowering the aluminum and supplies. We opened the door. The icy wind took our breath away. We drew our windbreaker hoods round our heads. The air was laden with flying spicules. We could not see but felt our way to the corners of the hut to locate the broken stay. It was one of two in front. With expert hands, although in gloves, Sailhardy knotted one end of the rope round the iron pole in the rock and the other to the trailing end from the roof.

Upton was waiting by the stove when we returned. Helen and Pirow were also awake.

I turned back my hood and pulled off my gloves. "Are you still going ahead with this insane idea of yours?" I asked Upton.

"If I have to drive every one of you down to the beach at the point of the automatic—yes," he replied.

I glanced at Helen. "You can do that, but you won't be able to drive a fully laden boat into the breakers at the point of a gun," I retorted. "If we ever get the boat into the water, I'll tell you what will happen—she'll be smashed against the rocks by the next roller."

"Don't try to stop me, Wetherby!" he shouted. "We sail tomorrow, sea or no sea, gale or no gale!"

"Listen—"

"I won't listen to a Wetherby!" he yelled, completely out of control. The contorted face bore no relation to the sleeping mask. "Thompson Island is mine, I tell you!"

There was no point in arguing, but on the rough little beach next morning, following a nightmare descent after slinging the albatross down in the net, he saw what I meant. We had loaded the boat while she lay behind the corner of the cliff. Great seas crashed onto the rocks. Under favorable conditions, lifting the boat as she was—the helicopter's radio under the stern decking added to the weight—was a job for six men. Upton and Pirow would not hear of leaving the radio, and we had used it as ballast in the net with the albatross. The tiny seal pup, which had shared Helen's sleeping-bag in the roverhullet, had come down the pathway buttoned inside her coat. Upton raised no objection: I think he was trying to make a gesture to her.

"It is hopeless!" I said. "There's no future in going on with this nonsense, Upton. Let's get back up to the hut while we still can."

"Shut up, damn you!" he snapped. "I am going to Thompson Island today! Get that clear."

The day was still dim even though it was mid-morning. The sun was shut out by thick driving cloud which seemed to have a ceiling lower than the cliffs. New icebergs had piled up with the gale, but there were open passages between huge rafts of ice. The roar of the surf was matched by the ice crashing and grinding.

I knew Sailhardy too admitted the futility of the scheme, although he did not say so.

"There would be only one way to launch a boat in this," said Walter. "Proper davits and a ship's side."

Upton swung roung on him so suddenly that the blue bib of his windbreaker, stained now with salt, flapped in his face. "Davits! My God! Walter, you've got it!"

"I don't see any davits," answered Walter heavily.

"Look!" Upton went on excitedly. "Up there!"

We all looked up the cliffside track, as if half expecting to see some davits materialize.

"The rock! The rock and the overhang!" went on Upton. "Get up there, Walter, and secure two ropes on either side of the overhang—from the rungs of the ladder. They'll serve the same purpose as falls from a davit. All we have to do is run the ends round the thwarts of the whaleboat, lift and fend her clear of the cliff, and we'll get a clean launch above the waves."

The scheme seemed impossible to me. "Upton, we'll be thrown against the cliffs as soon as we touch the water!"

He snatched the Schmeisser from Walter and pointed it at me. "Take your choice," he said, his voice deadly with menace. "You assist, or else you can stay here—with a dozen bullets in you." I looked helplessly at Helen, who stood white-faced, silent, cuddling the seal pup. I shrugged. There was nothing I could do.

Walter scrambled up the pathway, and more quickly than I expected the two ropes snaked down. Sailhardy and I ran them round the thwarts and, when Walter returned, the three of us, with Pirow helping, lifted the boat shoulder high and secured them. The boat was suspended head high against the cliff and, when we let her go, would swing forward about fifty feet round the second cliff, which enclosed the beach from the north, until she was directly below the overhang. One false move and the canvas side would be torn open. The albatross was under the forward decking. I helped Helen in by lifting her up on my shoulders. Pirow and Upton followed, using Walter's shoulders. The two of them hauled Walter up, then Sailhardy, and, last, myself. We fended her off the cliffside with the oars and inched forward until we hung free above the waves.

Sailhardy and I eased the ropes loose round the stern and forward thwarts respectively. I waited his signal. The smallest lack of synchronization between us when we cast off would pitch us all into the sea, now rising and falling under the keel.

Sailhardy tensed, watching sea and wind. "Let go!" he shouted.

The boat dropped heavily into the water. Sailhardy moved quickly to the tiller, and I whipped up the ochre-coloured mainsail. The boat gathered way swfitly towards an ice lead running to the gaunt, sulphur-coloured northwesterly shoulder of Bouvet, which is known as Cape Circumcision. Sailhardy then stood up on the stern decking, steering with his right foot on the tiller head while he conned a passage through the ice.

I turned from securing the mainsail halyard to say

something to the islander. I looked aghast at the horizon, so that he too swung round to see. The bank of ragged cloud, drifting on a level with the glacier, gave the impression of a line squall, but I recognized it as the spearhead of the storm I had anticipated. There was a flurry of icy rain. Cloud segments started to writhe up and down in contorted whorls a mile wide. Deliberately a cloud shape started to reach down towards the sea's surface. To the northwest, two other vast and perfectly drawn rulers of cloud slanted seawards. Suddenly all gathered into an immense funnel, spinning on an axis a mile wide and held upright by its own gyroscopic motion, then pitched forward and lunged into the sea. A great gout of spray and ice rose. Swaying like a Bali dancer, the wedded mass of sea and cloud moved towards us. We cleared the stark cape as the waterspout crashed against the cliffs, a quarter of a mile astern of the frail boat.

Bouvet vanished in the turmoil.

To hide his agitation Sailhardy became formal. "Course for Thompson Island?"

"Steer northeast by a half east," I ordered.

12 Under Parry's Arc

For three days Sailhardy scarcely left the tiller. Our estimate of the time we would take to reach the locality of Thompson Island as marked on Norris's chart had been hopelessly astray. We had reckoned about a day and a half at the outside for the forty-five miles from Bouvet to Thompson. The storm decreed otherwise. From the time Bouvet had disappeared, sea and wind had made our lives a freezing wet hell. How many times Sailhardy's skill had saved the boat during the night I do not know, but I had witnessed it at least half a dozen times during the daylight hours. Several times the islander had had to drag the boat's bows round to face the gale in order to ride it out without being swamped, before putting her back on course—as best he could—for Thompson Island.

By dead reckoning, I considered that the whaleboat must have reached the approximate vicinity of Thompson Island on the chart. My noon sight was almost due—for what it was worth in the bucking boat. There was a vast drift of storm cloud, through which there was an occasional glimpse of sun. This was the position sight which would, I hoped, persuade Upton that there was no Thompson Island where the chart said. Upton, Sailhardy, Walter, and I were in good shape, but I was worried about Helen. The wild gyrations of the boat had exhausted her, and she was very silent. Pirow had sent off more faked liferaft signals to the *Thorshammer* and, on the first day after leaving Bouvet, had told us with a grin that the catchers had signalled the *Thorshammer*, telling of our escape, adding that we stood no chance in the wild weather. The *Thorshammer* had replied, Pirow said, that her chief concern was to find the liferaft: the destroyer refused to accept the catchers' repeated assertions that the signals were faked.

I crawled along the rough gratings on the bottom of the boat to Pirow's cubbyhole, where my sextant was stored away from the prevailing wetness. I gave the thumb's-up sign to Sailhardy, sitting steering. His right shoulder and arm were caked with congealed ice, and the accumulated spicules round his hood seemed to carve deeper the lines of his strong face. He grinned back.

Upton jumped to a sitting position on the forward thwart. He shot a glance round the empty sea. Visibility was about a mile. "Is it time, Wetherby? Are you going to shoot the sun now?"

I paused and showed him the time. "In a quarter of an hour."

At our voices, Walter, who was still in his sleeping-bag, pulled himself out and looked round. "You could pass by bloody Thompson Island and never see it in this."

"Shut up!" snapped Upton. "We're close, and if we have to beat round in circles for a week I'll find it. What about that bird—is it showing any signs of wanting to fly?"

The albatross was clinging like a figurehead to the decking in the bows. It was picking up strength daily. We had fed both the seal pup and the bird on the fish we had caught, which the albatross accepted docilely.

Walter shook his head glumly. "If land were close it'd be wanting to be off—and there's not a sign of it."

Upton became more agitated. "We're looking after the damned thing too well. It's no wonder that bird doesn't want to leave when every home comfort is laid on for it."

I took my sextant from its case and wiped the fogged eyepieces. A flurry of fine sleet and snow blocked out the sun. I stood, trying to keep my balance. The horizon swung wildly.

I took the instrument from my eyes. "It's hopeless, Upton."

He grabbed the Schmeisser from Walter. "Get on with it! Get on with it!"

I looked at Helen. Up to that moment, I think, she still thought there was some remote hope for her father. Now she saw him as a madman trying to force the sun to shine at pistol point. Her head sank forward so that her chin rested on the seal pup's head.

I shrugged. "What do you expect me to do, manufacture a sun and a horizon?"

"You're stalling, Wetherby! You know the answers, and, by God, I'm going to get them out of you!"

"Bruce!" called Sailhardy. "There's a break coming —quick!"

The islander's keen eyes had detected a gap in the flying wrack. I rammed the eyepiece to my eye, one finger on the vernier scale. For a brief moment a sallow light appeared while I battled to keep the horizon glass steady. My fingers twiddled the micromenter screw. Then the flying cloud obscured the sun.

"Blast! Blast! Blast!" burst out Upton. "Did you—?"

"Yes," I replied, "I got a fix. Not too bad under these appalling conditions."

"Where is Thompson Island—which way?" he demanded, without a thought for the intricacies of a navigator's calculations. It showed the state of his mind. I did not reply but put down the sextant on the thwart and started to work out our position.

"Give me the chart," I said to Upton.

He pulled the parchment from his windbreaker and handed it to me. I made a little cross on it. I felt I had to

go through with the useless charade. It was idle trying to
explain to Upton the errors and difficulties of using an
outdated chart.

"There," I said. "We are now one mile to the north of
Thompson Island."

I looked at Helen as her father swung round and
scanned the sea to starboard. She was sobbing gently.

"Bring her about!" he ordered Sailhardy. Despite the
danger of the sea catching us beam-on, the islander
manoeuvred the boat. The whaleboat was now trying to
work across the run of the sea and the wind. One could
only guess speed, but I let half an hour pass.

We reached the position where Thompson Island was
supposed to be.

The sea was empty.

As far as the eye could see, the sea was a turmoil of
blowing spindrift under a blanket of cloud.

"According to my calculations, we're sailing over the
solid land of Thompson Island at this moment," I said.

The irony in my voice brought him to me. "It's another
filthy Wetherby trick!" he screamed. "It's a trick, I tell
you! You bastard!" He thrust the Schmeisser against my
chest.

"Father! Don't!" Helen stumbled over, but he thrust her
aside roughly.

"What have you done with Thompson Island?" he
shouted. "Thompson Island! Thompson Island!"

He was so beside himself that I do not think he consciously grabbed the sextant, but, despite the fact that he
was unaware of its workings, he picked it up and tried to
read the fix I had made.

He stiffened. When he spoke the hysteria was gone, and
in its place was a coldness which was more deadly.
"Why," he asked, "would a man make a notch on his sextant, Wetherby? Why, I ask you as a navigator of sorts
too, Walter, why would a man file a little notch?"

"Let me see," said Walter. Upton handed him the sextant; his eyes never left my face.

"What does it mean, Walter? Read it! Would the position of the notch be anywhere near here?"

"I'm not the bloody Captain, and I need time for a thing like this," said Walter sullenly. "This is a fancy instrument too."

Upton was frighteningly quiet. "You've got a minute to tell me whether the notch indicates Thompson Island, Wetherby."

I pretended to acquiesce. "Yes," I said. "That is the position of Thompson Island." Helen gazed at me, wide-eyed. "Here, let me show you."

I was barely a jump ahead of Upton. Walter, unthinkingly, handed me the instrument.

"Walter! Don't—" Upton was too late.

I took the sextant and tossed it overboard.

It was fully two minutes before Upton spoke in a strangled voice. "In God's name, what did the notch in the sextant say, Walter? What is the real position of Thompson? *Where* is Thompson Island?"

"I don't know. I hadn't a chance to see. I don't know my way round a fancy thing like that sextant. The island can't be so far from here though, because the notch lay close to his reading today."

Upton's hands were shaking so that I thought he would fire the Schmeisser involuntarily. "Where did your notch show Thompson Island to be, Wetherby? Where, man, where?"

I laughed harshly. "Look around you, Upton! It's not here, is it? And while I live you won't find out either."

He levelled the Schmeisser at me. "You'll take me there! I say, you'll take—"

I cut him short. "We're in the middle of damn-all in as bad a storm as I've seen. It may get worse. If you've any sense left you'll tell Pirow to signal the *Thorshammer* now—now, do you hear?—and try to have her pick us up while there is still time."

"Never!" he exclaimed. "In the space of a few minutes you have become the most valuable person in the world to me. You, and you alone, know where Thompson Island really is."

Heaven help us if he should find out that Helen knew, I thought.

His voice was unsteady. "You would not have thrown away the sextant if you had not believed in the caesium, would you, Bruce?" He became almost imploring. "Bruce, I know about caesium and you know about Thompson Island. We could be a great team—" He saw the look in my face and his eyes became hard. "Very well then. We search. We'll search the sea for Thompson Island."

I saw that he meant it, despite the weather. I knew too, that many expeditions with specially equipped ships had searched thousands of square miles of these selfsame waters for Thompson Island, all without success. A search in the tiny whaleboat would result in one thing only—death within a few days. If I set course—I would now have to rely on Sailhardy's methods of navigation—to pass near Bouvet, we might be able to regain the roverhullet. I felt sure that in the exhausted state we would find ourselves then, Upton would be forced to lie up, and I could try to get a signal off to the *Thorshammer*. I was gravely concerned at Helen's weak state, and a search, which I knew in advance to be futile, would bring tragedy.

"No," I said, "we do not search. It would be suicide. Sailhardy will have to navigate—his own way."

"You mean—?" breathed Upton.

I turned away from his overwrought face to the islander. "Steer south with a little east in it."

Sailhardy looked keenly at me and then, without a word, brought the whaleboat round to the course. The gale seemed to be mounting in fury, and we were driven forward by a tiny storm staysail, no bigger than a man's shirt, which I rigged.

The whaleboat tore to the south and east—towards Thompson Island.

By afternoon it was a full fifty-knot blow, near the top of the Beaufort wind scale. If we could have hove to, we would have, but there was nothing to be be done but try to keep afloat. For three days the whaleboat raced like a frightened animal before the gale. There was no stopping, guiding, or holding it. Sailhardy and I shared the tiller watches. As we sat huddled over almost double in the high stern, the wind threw against our backs a volley of ice, snow, and frozen spray. At times I found myself sobbing at the remorseless beat, and the long bursts of the fusilade, until I thought I could endure no longer; then would come a merciful lull, only to be followed by a further savage volley, scything everything before it. I was barely conscious of bits of ice, growlers, and small bergs storming past in the uncertain light, which changed from pale green by day to almost complete blackness by night. Wherever the spray settled it froze, until our faces, the mast, thwarts, gratings, and canvas sides were coated. The motion of the boat prevented any heating, and the meals were sorry affairs scooped with fingers out of cans. Walter and Upton shared the forward decked-in section with the albatross, and Pirow was in the stern section with the radio. It was dark inside his cubbyhole, and he might have been dead except for the occasional flicker of sound as he continued to fox the *Thorshammer*. The irregular ribs and rough gratings made sleeping a hell, and the wicked chill penetrated the waterproofing and fleece of our sleeping-bags. I had stretched the ochre-coloured mainsail from the stern decking to a thwart, and under it Helen, Sailhardy, and I huddled, either he or I being on tiller watch. The seal pup shared Helen's sleeping-bag and brought a tiny patch of warmth in the pervading cold. When I had called Sailhardy during the previous night and crept into my sleeping-bag, I had been desperately worried to hear her talking deliriously.

Now, in the middle of the morning, seeing her lying semicomatose, I made up my mind to carry out the plan I

had formulated when I had thrown my sextant overboard—to overpower Pirow and signal the *Thorshammer*.
If she could find us—and it was a big "if" in the gale—the
secret of Thompson Island would still be safe, for no one
would listen to Upton's ravings. I knew, too, that I must
act speedily. The strength was running out of me; and
when taking over the tiller from Sailhardy for the dawn
watch, I saw what a toll the Southern Ocean had taken of
his great strength: his eyes were sunken after the cruel
watches of the past week, and he had been slow in speaking, wiping his lips with the back of his gloves to clear
away the frozen saliva and mucus on the stubble of his
upper lip. Upton and Walter had given up their gun watch
over Sailhardy and me—it was hardly possible in the
storm—but they still watched me carefully whenever I
moved from my sleeping-bag.

I looked at my watch: ten-thirty. Sailhardy had been at
the tiller since eight o'clock. I had heard Pirow give a brief
signal when the islander had taken over, and, being mid-
morning, Upton and Walter would not be suspicious on
hearing another after a break of several hours. I would
have to muster all my strength to overpower Pirow
speedily and get off a meassage before they missed me. I
looked down at Helen. The ice had rimmed her closed eyes,
making them strangely ethereal. She broke into an in-
coherent mutter. I caught nothing except my name. The
exquisite little seal pup peeped out from the mouth of her
sleeping-bag. Up forward there was no sign from Upton or
Walter.

I inched out of my sleeping-bag and dragged myself
along the gratings to Pirow's cubbyhole. It was so dim that
it took me a minute to make out the Man with the Immaculate Hand. He was sitting in front of the radio. I
heard him move and I jammed myself hard down on the
gratings. The snap of a switch followed. He became
silhouetted as a weak dial light came alive. I could not see
his face, but from the stoop of his shoulders it was clear

that he, like the rest of us, was nearing the end of his tether. Let him start sending, I thought, let him get the preliminaries done. Then I'll jump him when the *Thorshammer* is listening.

The weak signal started: *Thorshammer Thorshammer*.

It scarcely needed Pirow's skill to bluff the destroyer now. The signal was genuinely weak and faltering.

Pirow threw over the receiving switch. I was surprised to hear the strength of the *Thorshammer*'s reply. She must be very close to come through as clearly as that.

Thorshammer to liferaft stop personal Captain Olstad to Lieutenant Mosby stop keep your key down stop let your batteries run out stop we are close stop we will find you stop keep your key down stop

Pirow started to exclaim in German. I slithered forward along the gratings. My left arm went hard round his windpipe He gave a strangled gasp. With my free right hand I locked down the transmitting key. My instinct told me something was wrong. I wrenched round. Walter was coming on hands and knees from the bow, a flensing knife in his fist. Behind him Upton was standing, the Schmeisser pointed.

I threw myself out of the cubbyhole, but I was still full length. Walter leaped to his feet at the entrance as I shot out. He paused momentarily. Perhaps even he would not kill a man lying at his feet. I jerked sideways and, jackknifing my body, kicked his legs from under him. He was adroit. He fell heavily, twisting like a cat, and took the fall on his shoulder, but it kept his right hand under him for a moment. I grabbed for his thick beard and swung astride his powerful body. The knife thrust would come before Sailhardy could help me. My hands clamped on his beard, and I jerked his head a couple of inches sideways. The crude skill of the Tristan boatmen had not succeeded in smoothing one of the gnarled knots in the ribs. It would

serve as a garotte as efficient as anything in South
America. I felt Walter's knife hand go up for the plunge. I
rammed the top of his spine, where it joins the head, hard
against the knot. His mouth was wrenched wide open.
Fear burst into his eyes.

"Drop that knife!"

I heard the weapon clunk against the bottom-boards.
We were within three feet of Helen. I saw that her eyes
were open and she was staring, terrified, at what was going
on. Now is the time, I told myself savagely with the feel of
the thick beard in my hands and kill-lust in my heart, to
get the record straight about the shooting down of the
seaplane—from Walter's own lips.

"Walter! Say it, and say it quickly. Who shot down the
seaplane? Who ordered it?"

Helen's eyes dilated with horror and fixed on her father.
I heard three clicks. I jerked round without releasing Walter. Upton was tugging at the Schmeisser's trigger. It was
pointed into my back. My fear and the explanation of the
misfire were almost simultaneous. The firing mechanism
was locked by oil which had frozen solid.

I scarcely recognized my own voice. "Upton! You can
go on clicking that blasted thing as long as you like in this
weather, but it won't fire." I shoved Walter's head farther
back. His spine would snap in a moment. "Tell her! Tell
who it was!"

"I shot it down. Sir Frederick ordered me to."

I took the knife and dragged myself upright uncertainly.
I lost my footing as the whaleboat rolled, and I crashed
heavily on the thwart. The knife spun across to Upton's
feet. He picked it up. Walter pulled himself forwards and
crouched on his hands and knees near Upton, unable to
rise, his face livid.

Upton's eyes were bright. He seemed in better shape
than any of us. "I should say thank you to this frozen
gun," he said slowly as I gasped for breath. "I forgot for a
moment that I need you to find Thompson Island. Don't

be a bloody fool again and waste your strength. I want it all for Thompson Island."

"Thompson Island! For God's sake, Upton! Your daughter's not going to last—"

"But you are," he said. "You are the one person who matters to me. We will find Thompson Island—together."

My weary brain made a hurried calculation. Assuming that we had travelled directly due southeast from the Norris chart position of Thompson Island, we might well have covered in the past three days the hundred and ten miles that separated the true and false positions of the island. In my weak state, and for Helen's sake, I was almost tempted to try to find the warmth and the good anchorage Pirow had spoken of—how many days ago now? Though how I could locate the island without my sextant I did not know. Sailhardy might be able to, with his strange methods of natural navigation. Bouvet, with its well-stocked roverhullet, was a better proposition than an unknown anchorage, if we could find it again, but at that moment I would have welcomed any shelter away from the storm. I did not, however, intend Upton to know how near I was to agreeing to find Thompson Island.

"You were mad to leave Bouvet," I said. "Listen, had Thompson Island been where Norris charted it, what could come of finding it? There might be all the caesium in the world, but you couldn't take it away in this little boat. You might find it, but you would have to give its position away in order to be rescued."

Upton's answer underlined the state of his mind. "You're wrong, Bruce. There's a whole fleet of ships waiting at Thompson. We wouldn't need to be rescued." He laughed to himself. "You can take your pick when we get there—you can have a liner, or a freighter, or a tanker, just what you wish.

There was no point in going on with talk of that kind. I crawled into my sleeping-bag to try to get some rest before taking the afternoon watch from Sailhardy. Upton stood grinning down at me, and then he too stumbled forward out of reach of the ice-sharpened file of wind. I fell into a broken, uneasy state, half sleep and half semi-consciousness; towards midday I drew Helen's head into the crook of my arm. She did not wake but mumbled something which I could not follow. I feared the coming night.

Sailhardy too must have passed out at the tiller, for half the afternoon was gone when I heard him slither down the decking and shake me. His articulation was thick, and the long vowels seemed to have difficulty in getting past his cracked lips. He tried to say something but gave it up and instead gave a curious, stiff, and unnatural wave of his arm at the sea and the wind. It was a gesture of surrender. I was aware of a life-sapping lethargy in my limbs and arms. Why not, I argued, leave the whaleboat to its own devices with the rudder lashed rather than forsake the warmth and shelter of my sleeping-bag for the raw hell of the tiller seat? Better to let the boat broach to and sink, for none of us, I felt sure, would see the next day out. I chafed Helen's hands, which were as cold as a corpse's; the seal pup provided a tiny patch of warmth. I watched Sailhardy, his eyes shut, drag himself half into his sleeping-bag and then fall full length on the gratings. I sat upright. It took me about five minutes to kick myself clear of my own bag. Forward, Upton and Walter lay like dead men. There was silence from Pirow's cubbyhole. The only sign of life was the albatross near the two men in the bows, which was moving its wing as if exercising it.

I slipped across the ice-covered metal decking to the tiller and undid the lashing, which Sailhardy had secured before leaving his last watch. I crouched as the gale stabbed thin lances of frozen spray at my back. For what seemed an endless time I tried to keep my seared, burning eyes on the waves and steer the boat away from the worst. Vaguely I noticed that the quality of the light began to change. My soggy mind told me night was at hand, but I had no will or strength left to call Sailhardy or unclamp my gloved hand from the steering arm. The whaleboat drove on, racing down each long roller, heaving laboriously up the next, while all the time the gale ice-blasted my back, hood, and arms with flying granules.

It was my sailor's instinct alone, and nothing to do with my will, which jerked me to full consciousness.

The whaleboat lay in a calm sea of diaphanous white light.

The fury of the Westerlies was dead.

The silence was more unnerving than the storm.

My hand, clamped on the tiller, no longer swung, corrected, swung, to keep her stern to the waves. The wind was gone, I told myself, because I had died at my post. It was a dead light too: a diffused, whitish light tinged with blue. I glanced at my watch. Almost six hours had passed and it was after midnight. I saw where the light was coming from. Except for some loose patches of cloud the sky was clear. Then a series of immense flares laced the sky in green, flame, blue, and violet—the Southern Lights! One wing rose up like a scarlet and violet scimitar from the direction of the South Pole and brandished its wild glory across the unreal sky. The flares outlined the dome of the heavens, one moment rising in bursting splendour along sky paths like the spokes of a wheel, the next receding towards the Pole in a petulant bicker of light. Never, however, did they lose their colours, and the broken cloud which passed across the face of the Aurora enhanced rather than diminished the grandeur. I looked round me unbelievingly, for there was no ice on the water, and even in the absence of the Southern lights there was a whiteness being reflected from something I could not see. The albatross stood like a figurehead on the bow decking, flexing and reflexing its damaged wing and gazing ahead.

My first thought was for Helen. With the boat lying still, I could get one of the alpine stoves going and give her something hot. I prised my numb hand from the tiller and straightened my cramped limbs. It took me ten minutes of rubbing and banging my arms and legs before I could leave my position.

"Helen!" I said, shaking her. She lay without moving. She was breathing shallowly, and the drawn face, with the Antarctic's beauty mask of white light over it, sent a tremor of fear through me. "Helen!" I tried to kiss her, but all I felt was the crackle of ice and the skin tearing from my lips.

I found one of the stoves and a can of soup. I lit it, and its tiny circle of warmth was more comforting to me than the great blazes that danced across the sky.

Sailhardy lay still. He was still alive, but only just. There was a stir from forward, and Upton sat up in his sleeping-bag. He looked at me, at the sky and the sea, in disbelief. He crawled over to me. "Why isn't there ice on the water, Bruce?" His use of my Christian name was an indication of his own distress. His sunken eyes came alive. "Thompson Island! You've brought me to Thompson Island!"

I tried to laugh, but the cold held my jaw. "I have not the remotest idea where we are. I couldn't give a damn for Thompson or any other mystery at the moment. All I want is some hot food."

I propped Helen's head against me and gave her a spoonful of hot soup. She took it uncertainly; her eyes remained closed. The seal pup stared inquisitively. I filled the spoon again, then drank from the can myself and passed it over to Upton. I felt the warmth of it flood inside me. He passed the can back, three-quarters empty. "Get another couple of cans—in there," I said, indicating the stern cubbyhole. He was back quickly and heated them. I tried to get Helen to take some more.

"Try and get some down Sailhardy's throat," I told him. "He's pretty near finished."

Helen opened her eyes. The glazed look of delirium was gone. "What is it, Bruce? Did you find Thompson

Island?" The way she said it made the name sound like a curse.

"I don't know where we are," I said. "I don't see land. All I know is that it is calm and the sea is free of ice. I can't even account for the light."

I gave her more hot soup and did the same for Sailhardy. It must have been an hour before he was fully conscious, and he seemed very weak and lethargic. Upton roused both Walter and Pirow, who looked like a ghost. We brought out the second alpine stove and cooked our first hot meal in a week. It was nearly dawn by the time we had finished.

The light began to change almost imperceptibly. The hemisphere-reaching flares of the Southern Lights drew back into their icy matrix. The whole upper lobe of the sky became one great sweep of light in a huge arch that stretched, not north and south like the Southern Lights, but east and west. The gigantic tracery was faint and white, although there seemed to be a background of rising colour. It was something I had scarcely ever hoped to see—the rare Parry's Arc. It seemed a fitting glory for our deliverance, if indeed deliverance it were.

I told Helen what it was, and she sat up. The faint white began to be laced with brilliant reds, scarlets, greens, violets, and blues; then the arc itself became double in a breathtaking display of ethereal pyrotechnics. Spreading itself across the whole sky, the arc elongated itself into an ellipse that seemed to stretch from the Weddell Sea to Australia.

"My God!" called Upton from the bows.

The light was bright enough to reveal an awesome spectacle: as far as the eye could see, the whole horizon to windward was a gigantic mass of icebergs, between a thousand and fifteen hundred feet high. Behind them reached still higher—higher than the cliffs of the great Ross Barrier itself—a wall of ice. We lay in a bay, probably fifty miles across, of ice. Perhaps five miles astern, on our starboard quarter, the northwestern cliff of the floating ice continent—it was scarcely less than that—thrust a squared buttress into the Southern Ocean. Under the uncertain light it was impossible to tell where it began and ended, and out to port there seemed to be a patch of heavy fog.

I realized then that we were in the presence of the phenomenon that had first enabled Norris to see Thompson Island, and seventy years later, Captain Fuller, and for the third recorded time, myself. In irregular cycles a great continent of ice builds up along the shores of the Antarctic mainland, detaches itself, and drifts northwards—towards Thompson and Bouvet Islands. Any big icefield will clear visibility, but it takes a continent of ice to clear the fog-shrouded shores of Thompson Island, which lies in the heart of the Southern Ocean's weather machine.

I remembered that when the Japanese had conducted aerial surveys of the Antarctic coastline directly to the south of Bouvet, they were surprised to find that theirs bore little resemblance to Lars Christensen's air photographs of three decades previously. It also struck me that in the same year that Captain Fuller saw Thompson Island, three famous clippers, including the *Cutty Sark*, had reported passing clean through a continent of ice— she had used those words in her log to describe it—and all three had barely escaped destruction.

I rose to my knees and looked round the horizon. The great flare of Parry's Arc which had lit the distant ice barrier had faded, however, and it was impossible to see much. We were all too weak and too overcome to do anything but stare.

"Look at the albatross, boy!" croaked Sailhardy.

The bird was balancing itself above the cutwater with its wings wide. The last scarlets, reds, golds, blues, and violets of Parry's Arc made a tracery across their whiteness. For a moment it hung on, uncertain, flapping its wings. Then the bird launched itself, dipped for a moment towards the water, picked up, wheeled round the whaleboat twice, and struck off towards a point beyond the port bow.

There was a commotion at my feet, and I looked at Helen's sleeping-bag. The seal pup was fighting to kick itself free. The little animal shot out of the mouth of the bag. It leaped on to the thwart next to me and stood with its head cocked, every muscle tense.

Someone waas knocking on the bottom of the boat.

13 Thompson Island

For a moment I thought Sailhardy or Helen was striking the bottom-boards in some final convulsion of weakness.

Knock! Knock! Knock! Someone might have been rapping a knuckle on the underside of the boat.

Sailhardy's eyes opened and he put his ear to the gratings. I knelt down and did the same.

The islander exclaimed faintly, "It's the Tristan Knocker!"

"The Tristan Knocker?"

I could see his excitement, but he was so weak that he had to speak deliberately to get the words out. "It's got a scientific name in South Georgia, but on Tristan we call it the Knocker. It's a big fish, like a cod. That is the noise they make when they are courting! Look at the seal!"

The little animal had slithered across the thwart and was gazing excitedly at the sea. At any moment it would go over the side.

Upton stood over us, gaunt, wild-eyed. "What is it? What is it, you two?"

Sailhardy sat up. "It's land! The Tristan Knocker spawns in shallow water. There's land close!"

The seal pup dived over the side. It was just light enough to see in the dawn. The albatross made a point of white against the dark patch out to port which I thought to be fog.

Upton's face was alive. "Land! Thompson Island!"

Helen turned her face away.

"If it is the *Meteor*'s base I will know it," said Pirow. "You can't mistake the entrance and the headland."

Walter screwed up his eyes, but the albatross was now out of sight. "That would be the way to go, sure, but how? There is no wind, and we are too weak to row."

"Get up to the tiller, Wetherby," Upton said.

"There is no way on her—" I began.

"There will be," he replied. "I'm going to row!"

He went forward and returned with the bag he had salvaged from the factory ship. He pulled out the guarana bottle and the hypodermic. He filled the syringe carefully. We watched, fascinated. With Walter helping, he heaved one of the big oars into position in the thole. Gripping the oar with his right hand, he took the hypodermic in his left and thrust the point into the muscles of his right. Quickly he changed hands and repeated the strange performance.

"What the—?" I asked.

"Caffeine," he said shortly. "Now get up to the tiller."

"This is not the time to start giving yourself fancy drugs—"

He did not take his eyes off my face but sat at the oar, clamping and unclamping his fingers. Then he did not seem to be able to open them any more.

He grinned. "I am going to row this boat to Thompson Island. Caffeine paralyzes the muscles. I can't take my hands off the oars. They're going to stay there until we reach Thompson Island. Steer!"

"Over there—where the albatross went?"

"Yes!"

I clambered stiffly up to the tiller seat. The boat felt lopsided with one oar, but I brought her head round towards the dark patch. The sun came up and turned the vast amphitheatre of ice into a breathtaking panorama.

The sea was blue-green and calm, and my eyes could scarcely tolerate the whiteness of the barrier. We were heading away from the nearest cliffs, which rose to full view, in the direction of a belt of fog that completely blanked off the eastern and southern shores of the barrier. The seal pup sported about the boat with a Tristan Knocker in its mouth.

Pirow and Walter cooked more food, and Walter took a short trick at another oar but soon gave it up. Helen brought me some hot food and had some herself, but she looked deadly pale. Upton's stroke became progressively weaker. Suddenly I felt a strong thrust underneath the boat. It took us so quickly that we were into the belt of fog before I realized that the boat was in the grip of a powerful current. I felt the warmth first, and then the wetness, of the fog. Upton, dragging the oar which he could not unclench, was hidden from view; the fog was so thick that Helen, only a few feet away, became a murky outline. The current swept the boat on and on. Once Helen called to me in a frightened, disembodied voice to ask where we were going. The warmth was as unexpected as the darkness. I reached down cautiously and tested the water with an ungloved hand; it too was warm by comparison with the normal icy seas of the Southern Ocean.

We broke out of the fog.

Thompson Island lay before our eyes.

I identified it immediately: the low, level east point like a blue whale's snout was unmistakable. I had seen it with my own eyes, and I had studied Captain Norris's sketches of it. The entrance sloped away abruptly, and to the west was the point Norris had called Dalrymple Head. It was upon neither of these, however, that our eyes fixed in wonder and awe. It was upon the giant glacier that capped—to use Norris's own words—the island like a nightmare caul. It was the strange colour that made one automatically think of it as evil. It rose up two thousand feet sheer, its foot in the inner anchorage, which was still out of sight. It had none of the opaque whiteness and soft undertones of blue and green of the floating ice continent that encircled the island and had aroused our wonder earlier: the caul was bottle-green and translucent to such a degree that one could see huge trapped boulders deep inside its heart; there was a tracery of white in a group about halfway up, which looked as if it might have been the entombed skeletons of half a dozen blue whales. The baleful green gave an inherent quality of malice, heightened by my realization that the anchorage entrance of ragged basalt and pumice cliffs resembled the open jaws of a serpent. There was no sign of ice or snow on them. By contrast, the caul towered in archangelic glory and stretched away out of sight to the south.

Upton, hampered by the oar, gazed speechlessly. His voice was thick when he gestured at the cliffs flanking the entrance. "Caesium! Caesium!"

Striated and grooved with white, like the stripes on a ze-bra's flank, were the veins of priceless ore.

I had never seen Upton so moved. The gaunt face was radiant under its patina of stubble, argyria, and fatigue. "Mine!" he exclaimed. "All mine!"

The strong current swept us in towards the point like driftwood.

Pirow was smiling. The sight of Thompson Island had restored his morale. "The fleet is waiting for you, Herr Kapitän!"

I turned to look at him as the boat was swept round the headland into a long fjord.

"See!" he said.

Canted against the northern bank of the anchorage was a liner. I did not need to see her name. That Clyde-built silhouette was as familiar to me as London Bridge. For months I had studied it—the streamlined funnel set far-ther aft than was usual during the war, and the peculiar derricks forward. The liner's picture had hung in the chartroom of H.M.S. *Scott*. The liner's last agonized signal, outward bound to Melbourne in 1942, came to my mind:

QQQ . . . QQQ . . . QQQ . . . 45 degrees south 10 degrees west stop liner Kyle of Lochalsh stop am being attacked by unknown ship . . .

Before my eyes, in Thompson Island's harbour, lay the *Kyle of Lochalsh*.

A little farther down the fjord, half beached, was the tanker *Gronland*. Rommel never knew that Kohler had won one of the Afrika Korps' battles in the frozen fastness of the Southern Ocean. The loss of the fifteen thousand tons of aviation spirit and diesel oil she was carrying to the Middle East had reduced still further Britain's hold there. The *Gronland* had vanished while under my charge. The tanker's heavy feeder hoses were still over the side. I saw now the source of Kohler's apparently unlimited supply of fuel.

Another of Kohler's victims was tied up alongside the *Gronland*, a Liberty ship whose deck cargo of tanks and lorries looked absurdly new in the bright light inside the fjord. She too had disappeared without trace far to the south of the Cape of Good Hope.

They were *my* ships and Kohler's ships in the fjord.

I shared neither Upton's elation nor Pirow's satisfaction, and my thoughts were reflected by the pain in Helen's eyes. The natural harbour could, I saw, be a perfect staging post for aircraft travelling from Cape Town to Sydney via the South Pole, and a strategic base of the first order for flying patrol over the vital sea route round the Cape. But I felt a surge of despair at the sight of the caesium veins. Upton's personal battle had ended in triumph, but the world's struggle over this hidden island of incalculable wealth would end in chaos. Yet, I told myself

we were drawn farther into the fjord, Helen and I alone
were still the only ones who knew the secret of the island's
position.

I eyed Upton. If I could get hold of the Schmeisser . . .

There were a score of other ships scattered about the
anchorage. Some of the names I could read, others not.
The beautiful Danish training sailing ship *Kobenhavn* was
there: her disappearance in the Southern Ocean without
trace before the war, with a crew of sixty cadets, had been
a sea mystery as deep as the loss of the *Marie Celeste*.
Near the *Kobenhavn* was the *Berwick*, one of the great
teak fliers that had broken all records from Calcutta to
London in the 1860s. A big iron-sided windjammer was
broken in half across a reef. In addition, stacked like fragments of corpses in a mortuary, were ships' masts, teak
and oaken timbers, figureheads, stanchions, cabin doors,
big old-fashioned teak binnacles with Kelvin compasses
and oil sidelights; broken oars, harness casks, whole
deckhouses; a long mainyard pointed skywards as if it had
been dropped from a plane, the foot ropes and gaskets still
in position.

Overwhelmed by the sight, I steered automatically for
the far end of the fjord, where I could see jets of steam in
the rocks, spurting from some underground volcanic
source. The glacier was more impressive close up: where
the tongue of ice entered the water it was sharp, not
smooth and rounded as one would expect from the wash
and weathering of the current. It would be warm where the
steam jets were, I told myself, and all of us needed
warmth. Upton did not speak but stared like a man in a
dream at the caesium seams as we slid along with the current.

Pirow waved as we passed the *Gronland*. "Look, Herr
Kapitän, it was you in H.M.S. *Scott* that made us slip
those hoses and get away to sea so quickly."

The fine ships were as much his victims as Kohler's—
the Man with the Immaculate Hand.

I brought the whaleboat into the shallows, sliding to a standstill against a rough beach of basalt and pumice. A jet of steam blew from a fissure in the rock twenty feet above our heads. It seemed to be choking with warmth, and I pulled off my gloves. I jumped uncertainly over the side to secure the boat. As I felt land under my seaboots, a wave of emotion and weakness almost overcame me. I threw a bight of rope round a rock to moor the boat. A tiny springtail—the wingless fly of Antarctica—settled on my hand. I had thought I would never see a land creature again.

I picked Helen up and carried her ashore, bringing the sleeping-bag for her to lie on. I had to assist Sailhardy.

"Walter," said Upton, "bring me some hot water and see if we can get my hands loose." The palms must have been raw from the rowing, but he seemed oblivious of pain. "Take the Schmeisser, you bloody fool! I don't want Wetherby to get hold of it at this stage." His eyes were hard. "You won't be so lucky this time, Wetherby. The oil in the gun will have unfrozen by now."

Pirow clambered out too and stood next to me. He looked down the fjord. "*Liebe Gott!*" he said huskily. "It is good to be back!" There were pride, arrogance, and a touch of triumph in his ashen face.

The undamaged state of the ships—Kohler's victims—puzzled me. There had never been any hint from Kohler's signals in the German war records that he had used Thompson Island as his base. It was clear that Kohler had kept Pirow in the dark as to the position of this Southern Ocean base. The German sea fox had done the same to his own Oberkommando der Marine. In two years he had sent the High Command only half a dozen short messages, listing his amazing successes. He, like Pirow, believed that as long as you kept off the air while raiding, you lived.

"Did you send boarding parties and bring the ships in afterwards?" I asked Pirow.

He shook his head. "The Herr Kapitän Kohler was a sailor like yourself. He used what the Southern Ocean gave him. Why risk the *Meteor* in action when ships would come to him here in the fjord?"

"What do you mean?"

"The current," replied the Man with the Immaculate Hand. "It is deep and powerful. You want to see what happens to a ship in its grip. It is no ordinary current, Herr Kapitän—you see the vessels it has brought in from the ocean to this graveyard."

"A current is not that powerful."

"No, Herr Kapitän, it is not. Farther out it is a strong current, which will bring a derelict in and all the sort of stuff you see here. Near Thompson Island, however, it becomes a killer. It sweeps in past the entrance on the side of the fjord where we are now, and then—look!" He pointed at the foot of the glacier. There was a great swirling eddy. "It seems to nosedive there. We lost a boat's crew trying to investigate it closely. On the other side of the fjord the counter-current is weak by comparison. The Herr Kapitän Kohler had his anchorage there, and he always entered the fjord on the counter-current side."

"You mean, you just sat here and—"

He held out his hands. "The ships came because I signalled them. Sometimes it was a fake distress call, sometimes"—he grinned—"an order from the officer commanding the South Shetlands Naval Force—you, in other words, Herr Kapitän Wetherby. It was merely necessary to bring them into the fog belt, where the current becomes so powerful, and it did the rest. It brought them in like lambs to the slaughter."

"The *Kyle of Lochalsh* was armed with six-inch guns," I replied.

He nodded across the fjord. "You have not noticed the *Meteor*'s gun emplacement over there. We unshipped one of our 5.9-inch guns and mounted it—on that side so that we could cover the enemy as he was swept along this side of the fjord. We had every inch of the fjord taped for ranges. Resistance would have been suicide."

I was filled with foreboding. Pirow's boasting seemed meaningless now. The weapons and victims of our war were insignificant beside the potential in the rock seams above our heads.

Walter was massaging Upton's hands with warm water. I carried Helen a short distance up the stream of warm, sulphur-smelling water to where it cut through the pumice on its way to the fjord. I shifted some lumps of pumice to make a support for her back.

"What is my father going to do now?" she asked. My own anxiety was reflected in her voice.

"He talked about ships, and here they are," I replied. "But you can't sail away without a crew in any of them, even assuming that they are in any shape after all these years."

"Listen!" she said.

Pirow was talking animatedly. "The Herr Kapitän Kohler thought the 5.9-inch gun in the emplacement was better technically than those Harwood had at the Battle of the River Plate," he enthused. "But Kohler always marvelled at the English rate of fire. That gun is automatic on the ranges—every inch of the fjord is tabulated. You simply can't miss."

Upton got his hands free. He gave them a quick glance and then turned to Walter. "Could you load a gun like that?"

Pirow said, "There is no need to pick up the shells. There is a hoist which brings them right to the breach."

"Christ!" said Walter. "All this sounds as if you are planning a war."

"I've got my island and I've got the means to defend it," went on Upton, stretching himself.

"There is a big magazine under the gun," went on Pirow. "When the *Meteor* put to sea, a gun crew was left behind—except the last time, in order to engage H.M.S. *Scott*. There are probably some small arms too."

"Bruce," whispered Helen, "it gets worse, not better. You must get to the radio and signal the *Thorshammer*. I am desperately afraid of what he is up to!"

Sailhardy came slowly over to us. "Did you hear, Bruce?"

"Yes."

"Will that gun be of any use after all this time?"

Hope started into Helen's face. Sailhardy did not wait for my reply. "It must have a film of rust inside the barrel," he said. "If Upton tries to fire it he'll blow himself to pieces."

I shook my head. "If the gun had been on this side of the fjord, the warm side, I might have been hopeful. There aren't any warm springs over there. The temperature is polar near the glacier. Things don't rust in the dry Antarctic cold. Just after the war the Americans found a shotgun at least fifty years old in a camp by the Ross Sea. The barrel was still burnished bright."

Upton, Walter, and Pirow left the boat and walked stiffly along the beach, Upton flexing his fingers.

"Bruce," said Helen eagerly, "here is your moment! Look, they're all three wrapped up in what they're saying. The radio is in the boat. Signal now!"

"Be quick, boy!" Sailhardy exclaimed. "Watch that gun, for God's sake! I'll shout if they turn!"

I raced, stumbling on the rough pumice, to the whaleboat. I threw myself under the decking to get at the radio. I clicked over the switch. There was still some power left in the batteries. I fiddled for a moment with the tuning dials and took the first frequency which dropped into my mind—twenty-four metres—raider's frequency.

Dot-dot-dot . . . dash-dash-dash . . . dot-dot-dot . . . *sos sos*

I flicked over the receiving switch, holding one earpiece against my head and listening for the telltale crunch of boots on the shingle with my other ear.

No reply.

I cast round desperately. I wasn't a skilled operator like Pirow and probably the signal was weak. I must get through to the *Thorshammer*, give our position, and warn her about the current and the gun.

In my anxiety my wartime code signal came to me. It was all I could think of.

GBXZ, I tapped.

No reply. I switched frantically to the eighteen-metre band.

GBXZ . . . to all British warships . . .

I clicked over. The reply was loud and clear: *DR . . . DR . . . am coming to your aid. Keep transmitting for DF bearing. VKYI . . .*

VKYI—what the hell was that?

Thorshammer . . . beware . . . liferaft . . .

Sailhardy shouted but the warning was not in time. It was Walter who tore at me, sending the headphones spinning. Pirow was there too, clutching at me as if I had outraged his precious radio. Walter pulled me half out of the cubbyhole on to the gratings. I thrust him aside. He wasn't that strong yet.

"He got off a message and the key is locked!" exclaimed Pirow. "God alone knows what he's said!"

Upton stood by the boat. "Have you switched it off?"

Pirow nodded.

Upton turned to me. "What did you say to the destroyer?"

"The hell with you," I retorted. "Anyway, the *Thorshammer* is coming for you. She's got the bearing now she's been asking for so often."

"Get in there," Upton told Pirow. "See what the *Thorshammer* is saying. Call it out while we watch Wetherby."

In a moment Pirow called. "I can't understand. She's saying *GBXZ*. That is the British wartime code—*to all British warships*. And now, *DR*—*coming to your assistance*."

"Are you sure it's the *Thorshammer* signalling?"

"Yes," called Pirow. "She's telling us to keep transmitting." There was a short pause. "Now she's calling, *Liferaft! Liferaft! Keep transmitting! Keep your key down! Can you hear me? Can you hear me?*"

"Carl," said Upton. "Come out of there!" Pirow was badly shaken. "I want you to send a message, do you hear? Just the same weak sort of message you have been faking up as coming from the liferaft. You are to give our exact position."

"Don't be crazy!" said Walter. "You're telling the *Thorshammer* to come and get us—just what this bastard has been doing!"

I did not like Upton's look. "I'm telling her to come —not necessarily to come and get us. What is our position, Wetherby?"

"Go to hell," I replied. "Find out the position of Thompson Island yourself."

"No matter," said Upton. "Put the key down, as the destroyer wants, Carl. Let her get a good bearing. Find out how far away she is and how soon she will be here. That is very important."

Pirow's mouth was taut. "Can I elaborate a little bit—technically, I mean?"

"Do what you bloody-well like, but bring that warship here to Thompson."

"I don't understand—" began Walter.

"You don't have to," replied Upton. "I want you strong. Feed yourself up—right now. Carl will give us an idea how soon the destroyer can be here. You have to load 5.9-inch shells into the hoist of that gun over there."

The big Norwegian looked astonished. "You're—you're going to fight it out with the *Thorshammer?*"

"No," he said. He waved at the graveyard. "None of these fought it out with the *Meteor*. I'll play Kohler's game. The fjord is ranged to the yard. All we have to do is to get on the gun and point it. Let the *Thorshammer* come in on the current—Carl will see to that. You're a harpoon gunner, Walter. It will be easy. The destroyer will be a sitting duck."

"By God!" exclaimed Walter.

I was incredulous. It seemed to me the final insanity. I could see that Helen thought so too. "You can't sink a warship, Upton! You can't—"

"I would sink a whole fleet for those," he replied, pointing at the veins of caesium. "I am going to blow her out of the water. The surprise will be complete. The crew certainly won't be at action stations when she comes in on the current."

"Don't be ridiculous," I said.

He waved again at the caesium veins. "They said Thompson Island was ridiculous. You know, they laughed at you too, just the same way they laughed about your Albatross' Foot. I believed in Thompson Island, and now I have it. Britain, Norway, Germany, America—they have spent millions searching for Thompson. No, they sneered, it did no exist. You *knew* it existed; I had only my faith. I also believed in caesium—here it is."

Pirow came out. "The batteries are very low, so I've switched off. There's enough power for only a few more signals. The *Thorshammer* is happy though. She's got her bearing and she's on the way."

"When will she be here? When, man?"

Pirow was very certain of himself. "Not before evening, if she had our exact position. The bearing wasn't all that good. She'll still have to search around—say, in a radius of ten miles. She's certain to locate Thompson Island by radar during the night, but I guess her surprise will be so big that she won't risk coming in until daylight."

"Food! What we want is hot food!" exclaimed Upton. "This afternoon we will cross the fjord to the gun. No rowing for you, Walter—Wetherby and Sailhardy will do that. I want you fit to work that gun by tomorrow morning."

We gathered driftwood and made a big fire on the rough shingle close to the boat. Without the fire, it was warm enough to shed our heavy clothing, and by afternoon we were all feeling fitter, and I was relieved to see some colour in Helen's pale cheeks. She was very silent, however, and apart from the preparation of the food did and said little.

After another substantial meal at midday, we set off across the fjord to the gun emplacement. Sailhardy had taken more of a beating than I thought, and he seemed to flag at his oar very much at the end of the pull. Although the current was so powerful, it had not the grip on the shallow draught of the light whaleboat it would have had on a big ship. It was relatively easy to steer at a shallow angle across the current towards the glacier head and then use the counter-current on the emplacement side to coast down to the gun itself.

The sight of the gun filled me with dismay. It was a magnificent 5.9-incher, mounted in a concrete emplacement about twenty feet above the level of the fjord on a shelf of rock. Concrete had also been poured over the rock at water level to provide a landing stage, in which were sunk several metal mooring rings. Helen bit her lips when she saw the gun and cast me a glance of apprehension; Sailhardy looked strained and reserved, but Upton and Walter were jubilant. We tied up, and Walter and Upton jumped ashore. Walter guarded us with the Schmeisser while Upton investigated. It was clear to me that a destroyer, even ready for action, would fight a one-sided battle against the gun. Upton ran back to us down the concrete steps from the gun itself, carrying a Czech pistol which he must have found in the arsenal.

"Come on, Wetherby! Come and have a look! The *Thorshammer*'s in for the surprise of her life!"

There was no doubt about that. On the firing platform I realized again what a genius of a gunnery officer Kohler must have had. For a moment, as I stared along the sights of the weapon, I remembered what Kohler's guns had done to H.M.S. *Scott* before I could get close to sink him with torpedoes: one of the 5.9-inch shells had gone through the starboard boiler while her whole 30,000 horsepower was thrusting her in for the kill, and she had gone over to starboard with a list that drew the awe and admiration of the Simonstown Dockyard when eventually I made my stricken way through the Roaring Forties to Cape Town. One boiler room and the after mess deck had been full of water and dead men,.and at times the starboard gunwale had been awash. I remembered, too, how when Kohler's superb salvo had crashed home into the vitals of my ship I had automatically ordered Sailhardy, on the torpedo tubes, to fire all torpedoes into the sea "set to sink" before we ourselves were blown up by them. His voice had been steady over the phone back to the bridge: he had asked me to lay H.M.S. *Scott* broadside to her target and to let him fire them at the enemy rather than into the sea. Water Water pouring in, H.M.S. *Scott* had swung beam-on to the wild sea. Sailhardy, like Nelson's gunners at Trafalgar, had fired over open sights on the roll of the sea. Two of his salvo of four torpedoes had sent the *Meteor* reeling to the bottom of the sea.

I dragged myself back into the present. Kohler's gunnery genius had rigged an effective hand hoist for the heavy shells, which meant that firing them was easy. There was a complete set of calibrated ranges according to the speed of the current and the physical features of the fjord. The headland was sketched next to its range—oddly enough in yards and not meters—9300. Where the cliff started to ascend from the entrance there was a patch of pumice like a brick kiln: it was marked as such on the range chart—8000 yards.

I did not want to see any more. The *Thorshammer*'s fate was sealed once she came round the headland into the fjord. I went back to the boat without speaking. Walter inspected the gun while Upton guarded us, and then Pirow removed the radio from the cubbyhole and spent the best part of an hour rigging it at the rear of the gun.

The journey back to the warm side of the fjord was easy: we drifted down the slack counter-current on the glacier side towards the entrance and then rowed into the strong current, which carried us down past the ships' graveyard to our original landing beach with its steam jets.

We collected more driftwood and lit a big fire. The sun's last light made the glacier caul more evilly green than before. Darkness fell. The stars themselves looked baleful, reflecting off the glacier. We ate another huge meal, then lay in our sleeping-bags. Upton had told us to be ready to leave for the gun before dawn. Walter, who seemed to have regained much of his strength, sat by the blaze with the Schmeisser. I lay awake, turning endless, futile schemes over in my mind. I fell into an uneasy sleep.

The air of unreality of the fjord, the gun and the destroyer coming to her doom was heightened when Upton woke us: the Southern Lights lit the fjord in blue and violet and glittered off the glacier-caul, dominating everything. Sailhardy and I rowed like sleepwalkers. Helen drew her hood over her face when the chill of the glacier struck us. I could not see her eyes, but I felt inwardly that they too must have taken on the unreal light of our surroundings. Pirow was talkative, tense, back in his wartime role of the Man with the Immaculate Hand. Upton and Walter eagerly discussed ranges and speed of loading. The afternoon before, they had slid one of the long naval shells into the breach and swung the muzzle of the weapon from one range to the next, according to the calibrations. Then they had set it on the headland target. All that was left to do now was to pull the firing lanyard when the destroyer appeared.

The whaleboat eased alongside the landing stage.

"Come on, Walter! Come on, Carl!" said Upton. He turned to me. "You three stay right here in the boat, see? We're going to be busy as soon as it is light, but don't try anything, do you hear?"

"Do you expect me to sit here with my hands folded if the *Thorshammer* returns your fire?" I asked.

"She won't," he said confidently. "You're quite safe."

Helen dropped back the hood of her coat. "Father, for the sake of—"

He turned his back and said harshly to Pirow, "Call out the *Thorshammer*'s signals and yours to her."

In the silence the boots of the three men clumped up the concrete steps to the gun. I heard the radio come alive. Pirow repeated the *Thorshammer*'s signals in a low chant:

" '*DR—I am coming to your aid . . .*' Shall I reply, Sir Frederick?" he asked in his normal voice.

In the silence Upton's voice was clear. "How soon will it be light, Walter?"

"Half an hour maybe."

"Light enough to fire?"

"Aye, I can see the outline of the headland already."

Across the fjord the tracery of old masts and the silhouettes of the dead ships were starting to show against the first light, which was unobstructed by the low entrance to the anchorage, unlike the glacier end where we were, which was still in blackness.

Upton's voice was exultant. "Bring her in, Carl! Bring her in!"

"*Liferaft*," stumbled the Man with the Immaculate Hand. "*Mosby to Thorshammer. Cannot send much longer.*"

The transmission rose, fell, ebbed—weakness, a surge of strength, then exhaustion.

"*Hold on, hold on!*"

Pirow was calling out the *Thorshammer*'s signals.

"*Taking bearings on this transmission.*"

I could almost see Pirow grinning at his cat-and-mouse game.

"*Can't last much longer . . .*" he trailed off; then, like an exhausted man taking a grip of himself. "*Are you close, Thorshammer?*"

"*Thick fog. Radar shows land or big iceberg. Keep sending. Keep sending.*"

Upton broke in. "Say it is ice, not land, Pirow. She

mustn't be warned. She must not know anything until she comes round the point on the current."

Pirow resumed his chant while he transmitted.

"Ice. No land. Clear visibility here."

"Strong current," came back the *Thorshammer. "Are you experiencing same?"*

Upton's voice came back, jubilant. "We've got her, Carl! We've got her, Walter! She's in the fog belt, caught by the current!"

I stood up and shouted. "Upton! Stop this madness! Stop—"

His face was livid as he leaned over the edge of the firing platform. "Shutup, do you hear! Shut up!" He pointed the pistol at me. "You've outlived your usefulness!"

"Sir Frederick!" called Pirow. "She's saying, *Put your key down, put your key down!* Do I?"

The interruption diverted Upton's attention and saved my life. "For God's sake, how long will she take to get here in the grip of the current?" he asked, disappearing from view.

"About twenty minutes, I guess," replied Pirow.

"Lock the key down!" said Upton. The chatter of the key turned to a continuous failing note as the power ran out.

He continued to forget me in the intensity of waiting.

Ten minutes passed.

Suddenly Sailhardy raised his head. "Bruce! There's a wind! Feel!"

The dawn wind began to steal off the cold glacier side of the fjord towards the warm current side.

"I'll cast her off—you get that sail up damn quick," he whispered. To Helen, who was white and drawn, he went on, "You must take the tiller, ma'am, while Bruce and I get her clear with the oars. Right?"

She nodded and glanced apprehensively at the gun. The three men were out of sight.

"Bruce!" whispered Sailhardy. "My God! Look!"

The *Thorshammer* burst round the point, crabwise, half out of control. Her turbines were fighting the relentless current. She was not being much more successful against it than Kohler's vcitims. As a gunnery target, the elongated profile could not have been better.

"Cast off! Cast off!" In my anxiety I raised my voice. Sailhardy freed the painter, but he too knew that they must have heard me up above. He thrust the tiller into Helen's hands while I grabbed one oar and he another. "Steer towards the *Thorshammer,* ma'am! Zigzag, Bruce! You first, me second!"

I threw all my strength against the long oar. I straightened from the first punishing stroke and froze. Walter stood on the emplacement, the Schmeisser raised chest high. Sailhardy had seen too, and he tugged at his oar to make the whaleboat yaw. It was a powerful stroke, but it was not enough. Helen rose in agonized slow motion. The front of her right shoulder was polka-dotted as the heavy bullets tore through flesh and the sea-leopard coat. She slumped back. Then she reached underneath the useless right arm to grip the tiller with her left hand. Another burst tore the water round the boat. I tugged desperately at my oar to get out of range and, at the end of the stroke, whipped up the mainsail. Its faded ochre inched us out of range of the Schmeisser.

As I straightened I heard a noise which I thought was the blood racing past my eardrums because of my effort at the oar. I paused, uncertain. It sounded like distant gunfire. Then the guns sounded as if it had been fired right under our stern. The shell screamed across the fjord.

"Pull!" yelled Sailhardy. "Pull! Help the sail!"

"Helen—" I began.

"Leave her for a moment! Pull! Oh, my God!"

The director tower behind the *Thorshammer*'s bridge mushroomed with a direct hit. It was a curious nodule-shaped projection, and it seemed to hold still for a moment before becoming a wild tangle of steel masts and tracery of the search radar.

I jumped on to the thwart and screamed helplessly at the gun emplacement. "Walter! Upton! You bloody, bloody fools! Stop it, you crazy bastards! Stop!"

I looked square into the muzzle of the gun. I drew back, waiting for the ear-splitting crash, then the blast threw me full length on the bottom gratings. I lifted myself to see the heavy armour-piercing shell shear through the *Thorshammer*'s modern, enclosed bridge. In the silence following the burst I heard the clang as the *Thorshammer*'s gongs sounded "action stations." It was too late. The destroyer yawed, sagged, and yawed again as she swung out of control. With a grinding crash she cannoned into the side of the *Kyle of Lochalsh*. Simultaneously her twin 4.5-inch guns opened up. The shells bounced off the armour plate of the glacier a thousand feet above Upton's head. The destroyer canted farther, biting against the old liner's side. Her next pair of shells screamed high over the glacier. They were so wide that it was clear to me what was going on—the director tower and bridge was a holocaust of stinking cordite fumes and roasting flesh; the guns in the forward turret were firing aimlessly by local control.

We were almost halfway across the fjord when the wind gripped the whaleboat's mainsail: she was sailing fast.

"Lay the boat alongside the *Thorshammer*," I ordered. "Get farther down the fjord, and then swing into the strong current. She'll sweep down on the *Thorshammer* by herself."

We shipped the oars. I was first at Helen's side, but the islander's hands as he prised hers from the tiller were gentle. Blood dripped down her sleeve on to the steering arm.

"Stop my father!" she whispered. "Go back! Do anything, but stop this senseless killing!"

I eased her onto the gratings, but I seemed to be choking with the heat. The wind filling the sail seemed hot too.

"Listen!" said Sailhardy incredulously. "Gunfire!"

From the southern side of the island came the sound of heavy guns. The concussion swelled, boomed, reverberated down the fjord.

"Oh, God!" whimpered Helen as another savage scream from the emplacement ended in a burst of flaring metal and tinctured smoke from *Thorshammer*. Helen fainted against me, her blood staining my hands and jacket.

Then I saw. The sea by the entrance started to boil. I pointed to the water. "Sailhardy! Tunny!"

Before he could reply there was another rumble of heavy gunfire from the southern side of the island.

"The Albatross' Foot!" he cried out. "The other prong of the Albatross' Foot!"

So here was proof of that other's prong—finally established in these bizarre and horrible circumstances. I saw how the Albatross' Foot joined forces with the Thompson Island millrace and swept in to the head of the glacier where it must plunge into some gigantic, subterranean fissure. I dipped my hand overside. It was warm.

Sailhardy shook his head, as if to clear it. "That isn't gunfire we're hearing from beyond there—the ice is breaking up!"

To produce sound like that, I told myself, vast fields of ice must be shattering under the impact of the warm Albatross' Foot. Any moment the glacier would start to disintegrate. But would that solid caul break up quickly enough to put a stop to Upton's madness?

I made a lightning decision. "Lay the whaleboat alongside, Sailhardy! Come with me!"

Another shell screamed across the fjord from Upton's gun and burst on the old liner's superstructure. The *Thorshammer*'s twin Bofors, situated aft the steel-latticed emergency conning position, chattered ineffectually. They couldn't bear on Upton's gun, and it showed what a sorry

state her fire control was in. Sailhardy laid the boat
alongside the landward side of the destroyer. I scrambled
over the low bulwarks. She had taken a frightful beating.
There seemed to be bodies everywhere. The bridge was a
shambles. Sailhardy passed me Helen's limp body. I
guessed right that the wardroom had been turned into an
emergency casualty station. I pushed past the orderlies
and wounded men and put Helen down on the wardroom
table, which was serving as an operating table. To the doctor there, I pointed out silently the row of bullet holes in
her shoulder. He began to swear angrily, but I turned and
raced back to Sailhardy on deck.

An officer was standing behind the forward turret,
shouting. Half his uniform jacket seemed to have been
burned off his shoulders and his cap was gone. Dazed men
dragged themselves towards what seemed to be the only
orderly mustering point on the ship, while others helped
and half supported the wounded towards the wardroom
companionway from which I had emerged. The *Thorshammer* was afire aft, but the worst damage was above
our heads on the bridge and fire control.

No one took any notice of Sailhardy and myself except
a young sub-lieutenant who stood on the steel wing of the
emergency conning position towards the stern and
shouted at us as we squeezed through a narrow opening
between it and a deck boiler-room ventilator.

"Torpedoes—" I started to say to Sailhardy, but he
pulled me forcibly to the deck as another shell came
towards the stricken destroyer. It was, however, a trifle
high and plunged through the twisted wreckage of the
radar scanner, bursting prematurely above the old liner.
Her steel sides rang like a bell.

We sprinted for the quadruple torpedo tubes on the port
side facing across the fjord. Together we swung round the
sawn-off snouts. The islander sighted them on the gun
emplacement.

"Belay there!" I ordered.

He looked at me, astonished.

"Bring them to bear ten degrees astern—on the glacier," I added.

"Bruce—"

The thunder of the great barrage of ice drowned the noise of the next 5.9-inch shell. The glacier caul had started to split. The translucent bottle-green suddenly became pocked with white, like a car's windscreen shattering. Thousands of tons of ice started to move. But would they move quickly or far enough to stop Upton's murderous fire? I asked myself.

The answer lay under Sailhardy's hand.

"Bearing ten degrees astern," he said. "Target bears. Glacier head bears—steady!"

"Fire one!" I ordered.

Sailhardy threw over the tripping lever. The sharp slap of the firing charge was lost in the thunder of the ice barrage. The sibilant cylinder of death slipped into the water.

"Fire two!"

No need to tell Sailhardy to spread them to case the entire head of the glacier.

"Fire three!"

"Fire four!"

No concussion reached us as the warheads burst against the glacier head; the thunder of the ice swamped all sound. Four columns of water rose like spouts from a blue whale in tribute to the islander's marksmanship. The glacier, now disintegrating, had clamped itself between two separate land masses, although Norris's sketches had showed only one. Fissures ran up the ice cliffs like a boarding party, frosted white leaping to the summit of the green glacier. The ice wavered, hung, wavered, and then thousands of tons crashed down onto the gun emplacement.

I left Sailhardy looking at the debacle. I skirted the forward gun turret, from which the crew had emerged and were gazing in awestruck silence at the opposite shore.

The officer in charge seized me by the hand and started to exclaim in Norwegian, gesturing towards the glacier head and the torpedo tubes. I shook myself free of his congratulations and made my way to the crowded wardroom.

Helen was lying on the table, her eyes closed. The surgeon was putting the finishing touches to the bandages round her shoulder and armpit.

"Is she—?"

She smiled and opened her eyes at the sound of my voice.

The doctor smiled. "Not too serious—nothing vital has been touched," he said in English. "She has been very lucky indeed. It's a new one on me to have to attend a woman who has been shot up."

As the doctor was speaking a man in uniform came over from a bunk. His head was in bandages and his left arm in a sling. "Why have the 4.5's stopped firing? Did that sonofabitch knock out the forward turret too? Why has everything stopped?"

I saw his rings of rank. "Captain Olstad?"

"Yes!" he snapped. "Who the hell are you? What is happening on deck?"

The doctor taped down the last of Helen's bandages. I picked her up to carry her to a bunk.

"It's quite a story, which I think you should hear," I said. "Don't worry, there won't be any more shells from the gun across the fjord."

The young sub-lieutenant I had seen on the emergency conning position clattered down the companionway, saluted, and spoke rapidly in Norwegian to Olstad, indicating me.

I put Helen down gently, but she clung to me. Olstad came and sat at the foot of the bunk. Helen propped herself against my shoulder.

"Who are you?" he demanded. "How do you and another civilian understand about firing torpedoes?"

I told him who I was. "The other civilian, as you call him, was once the finest torpedo man afloat."

"Bruce," said Helen. "My father—" She looked round the crowded wardroom, overheated now by the steam tubes which ran round it and the crowd of men who lay, sat, or stood waiting their turn with the doctor. A boy minus a hand sobbed hysterically, and a seaman, hideously burned about the eyes, screamed through the morphia which had been hastily administered.

"Oh, God!" she exclaimed. "These are the living, but how many are dead? Bruce, darling, why is the gun silent? What—?"

"The glacier started to topple on to the emplacement," I said. "To stop the slaughter here I hastened it with four torpedoes."

She hid her face.

Olstad said savagely, "Who were the murderers who crippled my ship and killed my men without provocation? In God's name, why was it done? It is not war!"

"Have you ever heard of Thompson Island?" I asked.

Olstad's face reflected his incredulity. "Thompson Island! You mean—?"

"Exactly," I said. "This is Thompson Island. The man who opened fire on you had an obsession about it." I told him how Upton had come to Tristan and had implicated me in his schemes when he found out I had Norris's chart. Olstad's face went hard when I told him how Walter had shot down the seaplane and how the Man with the Immaculate Hand had strung him along with the faked signals. While I spoke the doctor and his orderlies dressed, bandaged, and drugged the wounded, who were laid on mattresses on the floor. Olstad nodded in silent wonder when I explained the mystery of the Albatross' Foot and how it had caused the break-up of the glacier across the fjord. He looked keenly at me when I said I had sighted Thompson Island during the war and shook his head over the rejection by the Admiralty and the Royal Society of my discovery of light refraction and its bearing on the true position of Thompson Island.

Sailhardy came in and his face lighted to see Helen sitting up.

Olstad looked from Sailhardy to me in unconcealed admiration. "We Norwegians have always loved a voyage into the unknown. We have preserved the Kon-Tiki raft in a museum. If ever another boat deserves to be kept, it is your whaleboat. I find it hard to believe that anyone could have made a trip like that in an open boat, in such a storm, and survived. With your permission, I would like to take the whaleboat back to Norway with me. Tomorrow we must have a ceremony in honour of Thompson Island. We will hoist flags and fire guns."

I made my decision. "Captain Olstad, there is a function which you as captain are empowered to perform. I ask that it should have priority over any ceremonial."

The Norwegian looked surprised at my tone. "The safety of my ship and the welfare of my crew are my first consideration, I am afraid, Captain Wetherby. Any request must be subsidiary to that. The *Thorshammer* is a job for a dockyard. It will take months to make her seaworthy. Here I am, stuck in an unknown harbour, thousands of miles from anywhere—"

"You have overlooked the four catchers," I broke in. "Signal them to come here. Warn them to approach from the southeast, as Kohler used to do; otherwise they'll be in trouble at the entrance to the fjord. You can leave a skeleton crew to look after the *Thorshammer* while the catchers take us to Cape Town. You can arrange assistance from there."

"That is excellent," he said. He grinned suddenly. "It is going to take a hell of a lot of explaining though. What is your request, Captain Wetherby?"

I took Helen's hand in mine. "You are entitled to perform a marriage service, are you not?"

Olstad's face broke into a boyish grin. "By heavens, Captain! You and this lady?"

Helen's eyes were as luminous as Parry's Arc. At my words she sat upright.

Olstad shook us both by the hand. "This will be good for Thompson Island! A wedding to mark its rediscovery! It will be good for the morale of my crew too. There is still some sad work to be done burying those poor lads lying on deck."

A massive peal of thunder, more distant now, shook the ship as the ice barrage continued to the south of the island.

Olstad's face went tense, but relaxed when he realized it was not gunfire. "I would like to hear about your trip in your own words," he said to Sailhardy.

"What he really wanted was to sail from Bouvet to Cape Town," I put in.

"The hardship, the storm—" Olstad started to say. Then he shrugged. "Upton must have been mad rather than obsessed to have done all this merely in order to discover one useless little island."

A cold stab went through me. Something of what I was thinking must have been in the minds of Helen and Sailhardy too. They both watched me as I stayed silent. Who, I asked myself, except Upton with his highly specialized knowledge, shared by perhaps four other scientists in Sweden and Cambridge, could identify the veins for what they were—the bearers of the world's most priceless metal? Who among ordinary scientists was capable of placing pollucite and caesium? If we kept silent, who would know? I myself had seen a score of islands in the Southern Ocean streaked white from other causes. The savage current and perpetual fog belt made access itself to Thompson Island hazardous into the bargain. Once the first flush of its rediscovery had passed, would Thompson Island not sink back into oblivion again—provided the secret of the caesium were kept?

"Useless?" I echoed.

Olstad shrugged again. "Perhaps it has some value as a harbour for whalers, but what else, with the risks? Bouvet is close, but few catchers use its anchorage."

I was about to say something about global strategy, the importance of the Cape of Good Hope sea route, and flights over the South Pole, but I saw the look in Helen's eyes.

"Yes," I said slowly. "Thompson Island seems to have only a certain limited value as a whalers' harbour."

Sailhardy inclined his head as if listening to the distant ice.

Helen reached up and touched my arm. "Old John Wetherby would have liked it that way," she said.